THE QUEEN AT LEISURE

To

Wishes X

Keep swinging. X X

Derek Ansell

Derek Ansell

20-7-16

CSP

Canaan-Star Publishing

First published by Canaan-Star Publishing, United Kingdom.

www.canaan-star.co.uk

A Catalogue record for this book is available from the British Library.

ISBN: 978-1-909484-27-6

Book cover designed by Eugene Rijn R. Saratorio.
Author photo by Nadia Ansell.
Printed and bound in United Kingdom by Lightning Source, (UK) Ltd.

Historical Fiction

For Sarah. With love.

About The Author

Derek Ansell was born in Highbury, North London which makes him a lifelong Arsenal supporter, with all the ups and downs that entails!

He has worked as a Commercial Artist, Van Driver, Publisher's book sorter, Sales Rep, Area Manager and Survey collector. He currently writes music and drama criticism and record reviews for a jazz magazine and a weekly newspaper and has done for many years.

His first book, *The Whitechapel Murders,* was published by Citron Press in 1998. He has published two biographies of jazz musicians, Hank Mobley and Jackie McLean, both by Northway Publications, London, the Mobley in 2008 and reprinted in 2015. A novel, *My Brother's Keeper,* was published by Chiado Publications, Portugal in 2013 and all books are currently in print. Main love, when not writing is music, specifically modern jazz, baroque and classical music generally.

Derek Ansell is married to Sarah and has three daughters, three granddaughters and two grandsons. He lives in Newbury, Berkshire, and visits the local pub regularly!

ONE

19th May 1536

There is just six minutes remaining before the great cannon roars on Tower Green and the Queen of England will be dead. I sit here in my chamber, rubbing my hands together fretfully, in trepidation but knowing that nobody can do anything to halt or change the destiny of that unfortunate woman. Five minutes to nine remain and beads of perspiration actually break out on my forehead. I wish verily that I could remain serene and calm for I am in no way to blame for her misfortune although her imminent death will be to my great advantage whether I wish it or not. I place my hands on my lap but I am not at ease and I then pick up my cloak that I have been embroidering this last few days but I am unable, or unwilling, to concentrate my mind upon my labours. I lay the garment down.

It is not the thought of death itself; that happens frequently enough in all conscience; thieves and vagabonds of all persuasion die on the gallows, at the stake or are beheaded. It is the thought of a queen, next to the king the highest in the land, dying in that manner.

I rise and walk steadily over to the window and open it. A cool and seemingly ominous breeze blows in from the River Thames opposite although it is a warm day withal even though the bursts of sunshine are intermittent and infrequent. Down below my window the Chelsea street is rough- hewn and pitted, mud churned up from a rainstorm two days ago, still piled in little drifts or harsh tracks where carts and coaches have left their markings. A solitary woman passes by slowly, carrying a bowl of food of some kind and then a rough looking man emerges from the inn further along the road and walks steadily in this direction. Hooves are heard suddenly and a rider comes past on his horse and disappears out of sight as swiftly as he emerged. On the river three boats are moving infinitely slowly across the water.

I turn and walk back to the fireplace where the remnants of several logs burn slowly, their sulphuric odours rising from the bright red embers. It is too warm a May morning for the fire although the servants lit it before I awoke and later I instructed that they should add no more logs this morn. I walk slowly back to my seat but before I gain access to it the great cannon booms out from Tower Green and stops me dead in my tracks; the reverberations seem palpable in this room and I am surprised and shocked that the sound is so loud, at this distance from the tower. I find that I am visibly shaking for a few seconds but I take a moment to pause before retracing my steps back to the now open window.

Down below the house is a-stir with movement; servants, pages, cooks, all sent to care for me but I crave solitude.

As I look down again at the street below I see a man in a white smock standing motionless, his head bowed. Another stares out across the river as if momentarily frozen into absolute stillness. There is an ominous silence all around, enveloping us; a tenseness in the very air following that deep, resounding boom that carried along the water and seemed to shake the very foundations of the buildings along the way. I look out across the river and see three boatmen, silent, unmoving, resting on their oars. Everybody in London is aware of the grim significance of that shattering boom and if, as has been widely reported and commented on, Queen Anne was most unpopular with the people of this country, her dreadful demise is still a harrowing shock and an event to strike fear and sorrow into the lowliest citizen.

I sit in silence, not moving, not doing anything for some considerable time. I almost drift into troubled sleep but sounds stir me. There is some movement down below in the street now and a few hushed voices can be heard filtering through the still slightly misty air but I turn away and return to pick up my embroidery. I find I can begin again now, slowly, laboriously and with little enthusiasm for the task in hand but I will carry on for a while. I cannot erase thoughts of that woman from my mind, try as I might. I did not like her, I found her arrogant and rude, imperious and even, often insulting but I kept calm throughout all her assaults on my character and my person. I can swear, in all honesty, that I, Jane Seymour, as her Lady in Waiting, did nothing, at any time, to disturb her equilibrium. If the king flirted with me, and he is notorious for flirting with all the women of the Royal household and indeed with many outside it, I did not reciprocate or encourage him in any way or at any time.

I am restless though; I put down my embroidery, which has changed very little since I picked it up, walk out of my chamber and down to the ground floor level. There is a bigger fire burning in the kitchen and a pot of beef stew over it, simmering quietly. I stand still in the kitchen for a while, taking in the stillness, the silence, the ominous silence. Madge appears suddenly, silently, at my side as she often does, I never hear her approach until I turn and see her almost next to me. She curtsies.

'May I get you anything, Mistress?'

'No, thank you,' I reply. 'All is well.'

'Yes Mistress. Will you dine at the usual time?'

'Yes,' I say, absently; I am not thinking clearly at this moment...

'And will you be dining here tomorrow Mistress?'

No, that will not be possible for my Gracious Lord, His Majesty the King has promised that he will send for me today to escort me from Chelsea to White Hall but I do not know at what hour. I shake my head to indicate that I will not be dining on the morrow and turn to walk out of the kitchen area.

Then I turn and face her again.

'Oh, perhaps a small tumbler of mead Madge?'

'Yes Mistress, I'll bring it right away.'

I return to my embroidery with little more enthusiasm. The King found this house for me and installed me in it throughout the weeks of investigation and trials and, finally, the execution of the five men accused of adultery with the queen and, this very morning, Queen Anne herself. The mansion is packed with servants and attendants but I see little of any of them, by choice; I wish to be alone. I reflect that Anne and I were not always at loggerheads. Soon after I first entered her service she fell into the habit of talking quite intimately to me at the quiet hour after dinner when we would retire to a corner and relax. She told me how ruthlessly the King had pursued her while married to Catherine and how she had resisted all his advances on the grounds that he was married and she could not succumb. She gradually brought him round to the point where he was courting her, asking her to marry him and seeming to ignore the fact that he was already married and could not do so. But he resolutely determined to annul the union with Catherine. Anne told me that she kept her honour intact until she was married to Henry and obviously regarded it as a supreme achievement.

I continue with my embroidery, musing on how well I absorbed that intelligence from Anne and how well I, in turn, utilised it when, finally and very recently, he indicated his desire to marry me. To say I was shocked would be to grossly underestimate my state of mind. Of course he had flirted with me on several occasions and I, in truth, had entered into the spirit of his playfulness but always being careful not to cross the line of propriety.

Madge brings the drink and sets it down on my occasional table. I thank her and ask if the servant Elizabeth has returned yet. She has and I ask Madge to send her to me. Looking toward the window I note a flash of sunlight but it manages to fade almost as soon as it appears. The day is still ominously quiet and foreboding, as well as grey and dull for the most part on a spring morning. As I reflect on the truly monumental events of the past year, I can say with complete candour and utmost honesty that the idea that I should become Queen of England, never, for one solitary moment, entered my mind. I can also assert that I did nothing to encourage my Lord, the King and nothing to compromise Anne's relationship with her husband. That I would never do.

Elizabeth enters the chamber after knocking and stands before me. She is a chubby girl, bright eyed and cheerful enough and has looked after me well these past few weeks, as indeed have all the servants and attendants even though most are scattered around the house; this is a time I must be alone.

'Was it quiet in the square this morning Elizabeth?'

'It was Madam, a strange atmosphere everywhere.'

'Yes,' I say, calmly and reflectively.

'The women did stand in small groups whispering softly and urgently Mistress.'

'Did you get good onions?'

'There wasn't much choice Madam but I picked the very best I could find. And bread with fine flour.'

I bid her to ask the cook to ensure bread with fine white flour is served with the beef at dinner and she nods swiftly. She tells me that she overheard a merchant saying that he had just come hence from Tower Green and that the Queen was subdued, looked pale and terrified, as well she might but had offered no speech other than her prayers and a bid to all in attendance to pray for the King, a fine and worthy monarch. I nod and dismiss her.

I sit down again and sip my mead slowly. I wish I could think about something other than the events of the past few months but I cannot. It is impossible. I recall, painfully, entering the King's private chamber and returning some books he had loaned to me. He had looked up on that occasion and smiled at me, indicated a table to place the books on and requested me to wait awhile. He had some papers in his hands which he swiftly put aside and looked up at me, staring at me intently as I stood before him, frozen into stillness and awaiting his pleasure. It became disconcerting but I had dared not move a muscle.

'Well, Jane, you are a demure little thing, are you not?'

'Am I Sir?'

'Indeed you are. Come over here and sit with me.'

I moved forward tentatively and made for a nearby chair but he put out his arm to detain me and bid me sit down on his lap. I hesitated but he pulled me towards him roughly and I found myself indeed, seated on his lap with his arms circling my waist. We remained like that for some time as he occasionally spoke about some light court matter concerning the maids of honour and then he suddenly and without warning, turned my face towards his and planted a kiss on my lips. I must have let out a little gasp for he laughed a loud, throaty sound and then he put his face to my cheek as his hand went up under my gown and began rustling through my many petticoats with a rare dexterity. I gripped his hand with all my strength and stopped the progress of his before it reached his desired destination and blurted out the words, 'no sir, no, you must not.' It was just after this that the queen burst in and seeing me on her husband's lap screamed at me and demanded to know, in loud raucous tones what the hell I thought I was doing. I arose and departed the chamber with rare haste although she followed me right down the long corridor screaming abuse at me the entire time.

What though, does the future hold in store for us all, now? My feuding with the queen pales into insignificance considering the monumental events occurring daily throughout the civilized world. Henry, in his determination to end his marriage to Katherine and equally obstinate desire to make Anne Boleyn his queen had defied the Roman Catholic Church and set up a new Church of England with himself as undisputed head. Unprecedented, in the civilised world, the repercussions of his actions have been rumbling on for years with daily fears that the Emperor of Rome will instigate an invasion of our Island to restore the Holy Roman church. The king will have none of it and grows more belligerently determined to exercise his full authority over the church daily.

As this day of tragedy and gloom continues, I grow ever more restless. Will the king indeed send for me to transport me to White hall and if so, at what hour? I can hear music faintly but not any sounds that are familiar and expected. It grows louder as I rise and walk over to the window once again. Outside the inn a man in heavy brown cloth and cap is playing the hurdy-gurdy but it is not the usual bright airs and dance tunes everybody is familiar with; this music is dark and sombre, a deep melancholy dirge played slowly and with the strings resonating morbidly. Two grim faced agricultural workers in their white smocks stand motionless, except when they lift their tankards of ale to their lips. The musician has certainly captured the sadness and foreboding of this terrible day.

At dinner I eat slowly, picking delicately at my food in half- hearted fashion, turning over a ripe piece of beef endlessly with my spoon before finally committing it to my mouth. The beef is juicy and tender, the stew tasty with the pleasant tang of onion and artichoke adding flavour. On any other day I would enjoy it and eat heartily but my mood at present will not allow me. In the end I push my plate away, stew unfinished and take a swig of mead from my tankard. Elizabeth appears suddenly as soon as I push the plate away and asks if she can get me anything else.

'A small portion of dried fruit Elizabeth please,' I reply desolately.

She brings me a plate piled with fruits and embellished with small white marzipan balls but it is far more than I can eat. I smile, thank her and dismiss her and continue eating slowly, picking out the choicest morsels and leaving the rest on my plate. My thoughts are still inescapably with the woman I served long as maid of honour, who became so jealous and abusive towards me. Much as I disliked her I would have wished any end to her life on her other than the cruel demise that befell her. I recall the day that I wore a jewel about my neck which the king had given to me. I do confess that I had intended her to see it and hoped it would arouse curiosity and perhaps even suspicion in her for she had vexed me considerably on many occasions; I was not, however, prepared for the violence of her reaction. She looked at it, stared hard at it and then at me and asked to see it and examine it in harsh tones. I hesitated, fearful of her red faced anger and stepped back away from her but she advanced and violently wrenched it from my neck, causing pain to me and to her own hand. She opened it and saw within a miniature portrait of the king and let out a little squeal of anger and asked me to explain the meaning of it. I replied that it was a kind gift from his majesty and who was to tell him who he should and should not lavish gifts upon? She threw the jewel to the ground angrily and retorted that she would take this matter up with the king and I would pay for my unscrupulous behaviour by being banned from the court and dismissed me from her presence. I did not worry unduly however because I knew Henry was unhappy with her and he had hinted to me that divorce was on his mind. It was only a very short time later that I received the following letter from his majesty.

MY DEAR FRIEND AND MISTRESS

The bearer of these few lines from thy entirely devoted servant will
Deliver into thy fair hands a token of my true affection for thee, hoping you will
Keep it forever in your sincere love for me.
Advertising you that there is at present
A ballad made lately of great derision made against us, which if it go abroad and Is seen by you;
I pray you to pay no manner of regard to it. I am not at present Informed who is the setter forth of this malignant

writing; but if he is found out He will be straitly punished for it.
For the things ye lacked, I have minded my lord to supply them to you as soon as He could buy them. Thus hoping, shortly to receive you in these arms, I end for the present.

Your own loving servant and sovereign

HR.

The king has made his feelings clear and, I must confess, a malignant ballad penned about his majesty and myself is the least of my worries even if it were to be sung and laughed over in every inn and alehouse in the country. The king has made it clear enough in all conscience that he intends to make me his wife and queen and the manner of his disposing of his wife Anne, with dreadful finality and avoidance of the perils of seeking another divorce, behoves me to look to my own conduct and behaviour to attempt to make my future safe and beyond ultimate peril and to make him as goodly a wife and lover as any man ever attained. This I must and will do.

TWO

May 20th 1536.

The day seems interminable, as I await the summons to the King's presence that seems never to come. Has he forgotten or forsaken me? I know only that he has lavished gifts upon me these past two months and clandestinely declared his love for me and his desire to make me his wife. It occurs to me suddenly that I have never actually agreed to marry him, in so many words. Until the momentous happening of a few hours ago, it did not seem right and proper to do so. I sit in the still of the evening contemplating my thoughts of His Majesty and my own personal feelings.

Madge and Elizabeth together knock and I bid them enter. They want to know if I should like more candles lighted and I nod and ask them to proceed. Soon the chamber is ablaze with light. Candles, and there are abundant quantities in this chamber, are all aglow; bright, gleaming flames spurting upwards with wisps of smoke curling around and collecting together in the air above. Outside the window all is pitch black night excepting only the occasional twinkling lights from the river indicating the movement of late night barges. It is well past the midnight hour.

With nothing else to contemplate and being too restless to attempt reading, sewing or embroidery again, I begin to reflect on His Majesty the King. He has told me oft of his love for me and I must confess I am in awe and full of excitement thinking about my possible future, filled with trepidation though I surely am. When I last stood before him I was impressed as always by his manly bulk, the sheer size and girth of him and his neat, masculine beard and twinkling eyes. His powerful frame and strong arms have impressed many a maiden although, in truth, the last few months have seen his bulk increase and he looks set to become even more bulky and heavy in the extreme. I do find his physical appearance attractive and, at times, almost overwhelming but I intend, if I am indeed to become his queen, to serve and love and obey him, in such activity that I may never vex or displease him.

At last, I am startled by a heavy knocking at the door outside. I hear voices and Elizabeth approaches, knocks and enters and announces that the Duke of Norfolk is here to see me. Thomas Howard is a large, heavily built man with craggy features and a long, prominent nose; he does not wait to be invited in but, rather, pushes past the servant girl, putting her momentarily off balance and strides into the room to face me. Elizabeth retreats as she notes my wave of the hand.

'My Lord,' I say, quietly.

'I regret the lateness of the hour Lady Jane, he begins smoothly, 'but the King's pleasure was that I should escort you to the palace after dark.'

'It is certainly that,' I observe softly.

'Are you ready?'

'I am,' I say. 'Elizabeth packed my travel bag a full eight hours ago.'

'Then we must go instantly,' he says abruptly. 'Come Jane, we must not tarry further.'

In less than five minutes I find that he has bustled me across the road to the landing stage and settled me in an unmarked, plain black barge and we are surging out to mid river sending up sudden spurts of white spray. He sits across facing me, his craggy face pock marked and ugly; I dislike this man very much. He is Lord High Steward and presided over the trial, sentence and execution of Queen Anne, his own niece. How can any man even consider such an assignment? We glide along silently through the dark night and in my reverie I do not hear Howard speak until, irritated, he repeats his words, louder.

'I said, we will soon be there at this rate, the tide favours our progress.'

'Yes, My Lord,' I respond, in bleak tones.

'Cheer up Jane,' he says, grinning. 'Your life is about to change dramatically, and much for the better.'

I incline my head to him but cannot manage to smile.

I am wondering how he knows so much about how my life is about to change but the answer is obvious when I ponder on it; he is a close associate of the king and doubtless Henry has discussed his plans in detail with him. He is, in fact, one of the king's most loyal toadies and as such occupies an important and dangerous position. I must not cross him, much as he disgusts me.

'The king commands that you enter into the ante-chamber and join him using the adjoining passage to his rooms.'

'Yes, My Lord.'

'It is unlikely that anyone will be abroad at this hour but his Grace requires secrecy in view of, um, recent events.'

'Of course,' I say, almost silently.

He grins broadly at me and turns his face away to look up river.

* * * *

In the king's chamber, His Grace stands firm, feet apart, dressed in colourful finery, a broad grin on his face as he receives me. His eyes twinkle and he appears in very good humour as I enter and stand in front of him.

'Well, Jane, my love, we are together at last.'

'Yes sir.'

He regards me carefully and in great detail, seeming to take in every inch of my body as though I stood here naked. His gaze is intense, intimidating and I feel quite uncomfortable for some time. I am aware though, of his proximity, his breathing and most potent of all, his masculinity. He frowns suddenly.

'Well do not look so glum and despondent, what ails you?'

I shake my head and say that nothing ails me and he moves forward and plants a kiss on my forehead. He questions my furrowed brow and I say, gently, that grim events have left a sour taste in my mouth. He shakes his head vigorously and replies, 'nonsense Jane, the whore is dead and all is well, at last, and you need fret no longer.' He lets out a loud guffaw which frightens me momentarily by the ferocity of his outburst. He bustles about energetically, animated suddenly and in high good humour which cannot be ignored; he says we must have a drink and bids me be seated as he pours two goblets of fine French wine.

He returns with the goblets and hands one to me and sits by me on the couch. He takes my drink and puts it down on the table and takes hold of my shoulders and turns me to face him squarely. I look questioningly towards him.

'You look like a frightened deer, with those big blue eyes Jane,' he tells me, grinning almost menacingly. 'Don't be alarmed, I only want to look at you.'

'To look at me sir?'

'Yes,' he breathes softly, mood changing instantly, as if by magic. 'I've loved that smooth, white porcelain skin and fair hair since I first saw you at Wulf Hall last year.'

I smile and look down at my legs and remain silent.

He hands me my goblet and I take a sip as he takes a large draft from his full sized globe. The wine is sweet and refreshing to taste and I feel a slight feeling of rejuvenation as I take a second and then a third sip. His Majesty is reminding me of my constant refusals, over the past four months, to accept gifts from him, returning them and reiterating that I prize my honour highly and would rather die a thousand times than tarnish that honour. I tell him that this is so and the reason that I refused to lie with him when he requested me to do so was because he was married to another and I could not, in all conscience, agree to his requests. He smiles broadly.

'All that is changed now Jane.'

'Indeed sir.'

'So what ails you now?'

'I worry Your Grace that it is so soon after the death of Queen Anne.

He is suddenly furious and his red face, corrugated brow and harsh expression startles me. He leaps up and begins pacing the room and I begin to wish I had kept my own counsel and said nothing. He roars out a catalogue of grudges against the late queen, accusing her of witchcraft, adultery, incest with her own brother and complaining that she was seduced by the devil and mesmerised him into marrying her. She was, according to him, an evil, calculating whore who had to die and will not be mourned. He approaches me as he calms down, slowly, finally; sits and faces me squarely and reiterates that he will not tolerate hearing the name of that accursed whore in his presence forthwith and do I fully understand. I nod and assure him that I do, indeed understand. He is silent for a minute as I listen to his heavy, laboured breathing after his outburst and then, he says 'I do believe, Jane that she did lie with more than a hundred men over the years.'

In the stunned silence that follows, I realise that he believes, or has persuaded himself, that every charge levelled against the queen was true. Even if he himself instigated those charges he appears to have persuaded himself that they were true. I myself can have no such knowledge or surety but I do doubt that Anne was so foolish as to conduct such adulterous liaisons and allow herself to be discovered. I do believe she was too wise for such indiscretions on a grand scale. I must, however, keep such intelligence and speculation to myself for I do not wish to instigate another outburst.

'Well Jane,' he says, leaping up and circling the room once again, 'am I to make you my wife? Am I to make you my queen?'

'Is that what you desire my lord?' I ask quietly.

He returns slowly to the couch, sits and glares at me, his expression ponderous. He tells me that it is, exactly what he desires for his love for me knows no bounds. He takes my hand and asks if I will marry him. I say yes, I will and I smile and confess love for him but modify it by saying that until I heard his words of love I had never thought for one moment that he would consider me as his wife and lover.

'You are too modest by far Jane,' he intones gruffly. 'My little white lamb.'

I begin to feel more confident and easeful, sipping again from my wine goblet and suggest, quietly but pleasantly that it has been a long day, the lateness of the hour is taking its toll and I should, now, think about returning to a bedchamber and getting some sleep. He laughs, a sudden rapturous sound and says that now that we are to be married, my place is to lie with him in his bed.

'But sir, should we not wait a while?' I ask expectantly.

'Tomorrow morning Jane, nay this morning as ever is, at nine-o-clock, we shall be betrothed you and me, in a small closet, with just a few witnesses.'

'So soon?' I ask my surprise evident in my expression no doubt.

'Yes, Jane and we will be married within the week.

I am surprised and shocked that he has been so confident of my response that he has set up these arrangements, for plans must surely have been made for some little time. I raise my eyebrows slowly but he merely smiles and pulls my face towards his and kisses me. I resign myself to the inevitable, telling myself that I really must have known, given his advances and intimations over the past four weeks.

The King's bed is warm and comfortable, prepared with hot bedpans which attendants have been preparing as we sat and conversed earlier. The feather coverlets are soft and easy on my flesh. His caresses are swift and clumsy though and he is heavy on me and lumbering in his anxiety to complete the lovemaking. Having drunk much and probably eaten wolfishly earlier, he is not in the best state physically and I am very glad when it is over and I can lie back and let sleep take me. Before I drift off, tears run down my face unbidden and I turn away but His Majesty is already snoring.

THREE

We are betrothed. A short ceremony in a small chamber with two Ladies-in-waiting, the ever present Duke of Norfolk, as witnesses and it is over. The king has given me a beautiful pearl necklace and a ring as tokens of our betrothal. I move slowly over to the window and look out upon the parklands of White Hall palace, as my Lord, the king, is in earnest conversation with Thomas Cromwell, who has just entered the room. The two ladies-in-waiting hover close to me; I do not know either of them as yet and cannot say whether or not I will retain them when I become queen.

The king looks magnificent in his brightly coloured finery. He has dressed up for this occasion and although we had to arise early after a very late night, he looks relatively fresh and bright. I wish I could say the same for myself for, although I have tried hard to make myself look attractive and presentable, I fear I have scarcely succeeded. The king approaches and takes my arm and leads me over to Cromwell, a bleak and cheerless looking individual, dressed in black from head to toe and with a hat of the same colour.

'You know Cromwell, Jane,' His Grace says by way of opening a three way conversation. Cromwell stares at me and his dark, bleak eyes cause me to feel uncomfortable just looking at him. He inclines his head, a brief gesture and I return the movement.

'The dawn of a bright new era,' Cromwell says in flat, heavy tones.

I nod.

'One which, by the grace of God, will be blessed with a son and heir.'

‘It is to be hoped sir,’ I say quietly, ‘that such will come to pass.’

The hard, cruel eyes bore into mine and he makes his observation sound like a threat rather than a wish for the near future. Henry appears to be enjoying this exchange, looking from me to Cromwell and then letting out a loud guffaw. Cromwell asks if he can have the ear of the king for a few brief minutes but Henry dismisses him irritably, telling him that the business of parliament must wait another day. Cromwell leaves looking dispirited and the king leads me to a small anti-room and bids me sit down. He sits with me and calls for wine which is brought swiftly to us.

‘Now Jane,’ he says, between draughts of wine,’ the die is cast, we shall be married in ten days.’

‘Will Cromwell be present my Lord?’ I ask, frowning.

‘Why, do you want him kept away?’

‘I don’t like that man,’ I say, wearily. ‘He looks evil and cruel.’

He laughs heartily and says, ‘oh Jane, he is my first minister and works tirelessly in my interest. I need his faithful services and you must accustom yourself to him, get to know him well.’

‘I would rather not,’ I say softly. ‘His eyes are hard and he stares at me as though he would hurt me just for the amusement of so doing.’

‘My little white lamb,’ he replies, smiling and gazing at me with love. ‘You really must not think such thoughts.’

‘That man,’ I say, taking courage suddenly, perhaps because of the wine I am supping, ‘will come to a bad end and finish up with his head on the block.’

'I think not Jane,' he replies soberly. 'I trust no man completely, for I cannot afford to do so in these difficult times but he is the least likely, I think, to let me down'

The king gazes at me for a few seconds before speaking. Then he begins, slowly at first, telling me that I am his one true love and he is happy that now we are together and about to become man and wife. He reiterates that he has been badly served by two false marriages, both annulled as they were not recognised by God but now, at last, he is with the woman who will be his one true queen in a matter of days and his sole companion for the rest of his days on earth. I smile and tell him I will be happy to love and serve him and I will never be false to him. My motto shall be to obey and serve and I shall honour it for the rest of my life. He is pleased. He tells me that he has much to do, preparations for our wedding must go ahead and there is a lot still to be arranged. It is vital that secrecy is observed for the next several days and he has arranged for a brand new coach to pick me up after we have feasted and convey me to Wulfhall at Savernake, to spend some days in the country, with my family. Messengers have been dispatched so I will be expected and I am to rest now, then eat and then commence my journey. I begin to question the wisdom of this action but he will accept no discussion or argument; it is for the best for state reasons as much as any other and I must trust him implicitly in this endeavour.

* * * *

What a journey. I am thrust from side to side, up and down, bruised and battered as though I have been put upon the rack! The road out of London, through Buckinghamshire and Berkshire, then onwards into Wiltshire is rutted and pitted virtually all the way with deep furrows and track marks, mud caked and piled up when it is dry; slushy and running when it be wet. We stop briefly at an Inn near Wycombe to water the horses and for me to take refreshment and visit the privy. I eat pork cake with boiled onions and drink mead and then we are off again; the further into the depths of the countryside we get, the worse the roads become. I am feeling tired and weary, long before a half of the journey is completed.

We have travelled for hours now and without a break. I can hold back no more and I bid the coachman stop the coach and, cautioning both of them to avert their eyes, I crouch down behind a straggly bush to relieve myself. It is not easy with my petticoats and generally heavy garments, moved and pulled hither and thither, to pass water without wetting any fabric but I manage somehow and clamber back into the car; I arrange all of my several cushions that a thoughtful Henry has had provided for me but it does little to alleviate the battering and bruising I receive from the constantly rising and falling coach body. Darkness descends and we rattle on and on, the noise from the wheels on the hard ground and the groans and creeks of my conveyance disturbing my equilibrium constantly.

It is with great relief that we finally reach Savernake forest and then pull up in the courtyard in front of my old home, Wulfhall, where father and mother are awaiting my arrival. Servants rush forward to take my travel case and assist me out of the vehicle, as soon as we come to a complete standstill. The awful journey aside, it is good to be home; I stand and sniff the fresh country air with a trace of wood-smoke and remember it all so well. It is all so refreshing after the acrid smoke and mist that pervades London all the year round and stretches into the country, to Chelsea where I have been most recently domiciled, and beyond.

My mother awaits me in the long room, her brightly coloured gown gleaming and a big smile on her pale features. I do believe she looked very much as I do now when she was very young, her pale skin and fair hair, her best features if a portrait I have seen is a faithful reproduction. She moves forward as I enter and takes me and hugs me and then plants a kiss on my cheek. Then she holds me at arm's length to look me up and down.

'Jane, Jane,' she exclaims happily. 'Daughter you look so well and vibrant.'

'I am well, mother,' I say, smiling. 'Although I'm none too sure about vibrant.'

'Well, you look fine indeed,' she assures me, leading me gently but firmly to comfortable chairs under a large and colourful tapestry. She settles me and presses me to take something to drink and I settle for cider as it is fresh and ripe in these parts and quite refreshing. My mother is still beaming at me as the liquid is brought to our table and I take a long drink from the goblet. I am just beginning to breathe easily and feel comfortable again after the privations of the journey from London.

'And what is all this I hear,' she says, smiling again and throwing up her arms in mock horror. 'That my little girl is to be queen of England?'

'Where did you hear that mother?' I ask, frowning slightly.

'It is all over the village, my dear girl,' she says softly.

'Is it?'

'Your father heard it from the warden of Savernake forest.'

'And where is my father?' I ask.

'As it happens,' she tells me gravely, 'with the warden of Savernake. They are discussing patrols because there has been so much poaching going on. They were meeting at the tavern so a great deal of ale will be consumed no doubt.'

How does news travel so very fast, I wonder, as I look at my mother sitting there with the smile still hovering on her lips? She seems to have aged so much since I have been at court, I think, with a little grip of pain to my intestine; with her wrinkles and the grey in her previously straw coloured hair. She isn't that old, my mother but I am upset that she has been sorely used by my father's adultery, the worst case being when he bedded my brother's wife. I could wish to spend more time with my gentle mother and look after her in her declining years but it is not to be now. I feel suddenly quite sad.

'So is it true daughter?' my mother asks, eyes gleaming expectantly.

'Yes, mother it is true, his grace proposed to me last evening and it was made official this morning,' I say, happily. 'We are betrothed.'

'Oh Jane, Jane,' is all she can manage in response but she looks at me with tears filling her eyes and an expression of complete contentment. She takes hold of both my hands in hers and squeezes them and grips so hard, for so long, that I have to disengage her hand gently but forcibly. She cannot believe it, she tells me, dabbing her eyes but smiling withal the entire time; she can scarcely believe that her little girl is to become the queen of England. The die is cast, I tell her but I must rest up here for a few days until my lord sends for me.

'I'm surprised though, that the rumours are abroad already.'

'Oh Jane, word has been out this past few weeks, you cannot prevent the people finding out what is happening at court,' she tells me, speaking softly but smiling still.

'No, I suppose not.'

'Do you reside at Hampton Court or White Hall dear?'

My face clouds over and I tell her that I have been in a mansion in Chelsea that the king had settled me in, for some weeks now. My thoughts drift back to yesterday and the long hours spent alone and I tell her how wretched I had been feeling and conclude that it was the unhappiest day of my life. My mother becomes concerned and bids me to shush as she lays both her hands back on mine, more gently this time. I find I am speaking my innermost thoughts out loud as I talk of the barbaric end of that poor woman and how she did not deserve such treatment, whatever she had done. My mother tells me ever so gently that there was nothing I could do and it was in no way my fault. I know it but can't escape the knowledge that people will hold me to account, in their minds if not in open accusation. We both fall silent then, alone with our own misgivings over the situation.

'You know, don't you Jane, that she was distantly related to you?' mother asks, the pain showing in her eyes as she looks into mine.

'Anne's parents were half cousins of my mother,' she continues sadly. 'Which makes you half second cousins.'

'Yes, I knew,' I say quietly. 'I do believe you told me just before I went to court to serve Queen Katherine.'

We snap out of our gloomy reverie as mother announces that we have boiled hen with leeks for late dinner, which she has waited for, not prepared to eat herself until my arrival. My father dined earlier prior to his trip to Savernake. Mother rings a bell at her side table and as Mary appears and curtsies, she asks if the food is ready to be served.

'It is, my lady, just now.'

'Very well, we'll go in to the great hall in two minutes,' she says and the servant lowers her knee, nods her young head and departs. I eat heartily, for I have not tasted a morsel for over five hours, perhaps more and the soft, succulent hen is delicious. My mother picks in desultory fashion at her food and I wish I could stimulate her appetite and blow away her fears for my future, unspoken by her as yet but I know they are uppermost in her mind as they are, indeed, in mine. After the meal, which restores me somewhat, we linger at table as I gradually consume a fair sized tankard of fine, golden ale. My mother sips sweet white wine. I am content, for the moment, at peace and at leisure although sad in the knowledge that it will be a long time before I am able to visit my childhood home again after this sojourn.

FOUR

May 1536.

I sleep exceptionally well after the rigours of my journey from London and do not wake until one of the servants pulls back the curtains of my bed and the sunlight streaks in through the window. I wash with the jug of water, hot from the fire downstairs and dress and go down to find that a goodly breakfast has been laid out. There are boiled eggs, just this minute placed in front of me, brawn, fruit, pork slices and fine white flour bread. I pick up the tankard of beer first and take a drink before slowly tackling an egg with some bread. I will not be able to do justice to this spread for I am not as ravenous as I was last night and I also fear for my slim maidenly shape, should I decide to indulge too blatantly.

My father enters the hall and I rise immediately to greet him, throwing my arms round him and hugging him and apologising for not staying up late last night due to my tiredness after a gruelling journey. He stands regarding me as I in turn look at him. Sir John Seymour has been a fine soldier in his day, fighting in the field, decorated there by the king and always, in his youth, a tall well-built and fine looking man. As with my mother yesterday, I find myself looking at his slightly bent frame, white hair and long, straggly beard and realise that he is an old man, now in his fifty ninth year.

He indicates to me that I should sit down and resume my breakfast. I cut myself another wedge of bread and pour out a tankard of beer for my father.

'So,' he booms, in a gruff voice that is so familiar to me, 'things have come to quite a pass at court these past two weeks.'

'Indeed they have father,' I reply quietly.

'And you, daughter,' he says after a short pause. 'Are to be the Queen of England.'

'I am sir.'

'Hmmm,' he growls, frowns at me and then says: 'have you made a whore of yourself for the king?'

'No father, I have not, 'I respond angrily. 'I would not and I'm surprised you can even ask such a thing.'

'I know the king Jane,' he says, rough voice unmodulated. 'And he will stop at nothing to bed the women he has his eyes on. I've seen it happen too many times.'

'I told the king I could not be courted by him as he had a wife.'

My father chuckles rather cruelly and makes jest about that restriction causing him to hurry along his plan to rid Queen Anne of her head. I protest that it had nothing to do with me and I had no idea of his intentions; I thought, in my naivety, that he merely wanted to flirt and banter with me to amuse himself. My father cautions me to be careful and never, ever, under any circumstances, underestimate the king's moods or intentions. I am now, he tells me, in a very fortunate but a definitely vulnerable situation. I must be cautioned to keep counsel only with family members that I trust implicitly and never say anything to anybody that might cause the king offence. I must be very careful, from hereon in, to be careful of my speech, to take care what I say and who I say it to, at all times. I smile.

'The king loves me father,' I say quietly. 'And I will do all in my power to cultivate that love, expand it and please him at all times. I know what I am doing.'

My father looks at me and his dark eyes bore into mine disconcertingly. 'I wonder if you do?' he says, still glaring at me inquisitively. I smile and reach out to put my hand over his on the table.

'I sincerely hope you do.'

'Don't worry father,' I say brightly. 'It will all turn out well.'

He shakes his head, smiles and then says that he can see that I am fairly sensible, my nature is gentle and passive, warm and loving and I am a complete contrast to the loud, imperious, self-seeking Anne who, by her aggressive and selfish nature practically invited the king to have her head chopped into a bucket.

'Oh, don't say that please father. That poor woman, do you not feel sadness for her fate?'

'That woman asked for all she got and would not say a word in your favour if the roles were reversed.'

He cautions me once more to think hard upon his words and not take them lightly. I assure him that I don't and won't and finish breakfasting with thoughts intruding into my reverie, but I resolutely push them down in my mind. It is a bright, warm day, the sun is shining and I intend to make the most of my leisurely few days in the country.

As my father, accompanied by my mother, returns from the kitchen area, I express a desire to go out riding. My mother smiles and says it is a good day for it but my father wears a frown. He says he would accompany me but has some business to attend and papers to peruse. I assure him I will be fine on my own and will not venture far. After deliberating for a few seconds he says 'come Jane,' and takes my hand to lead me out to the stables.

'I have a fine white mare, docile; she should be just right for you,' he tells me. He instructs the stable boys to ready the horse and tells one of them that he must ride by my side throughout.

'Oh no, father, I would wish to ride alone, 'I say, pouting at him.

'The terrain is rough and pitted from rain,' he says.

'I'll be fine,' I assure him. 'I'm an experienced rider, as you well know.'

After a very brief hesitation he says that will be all right but he instructs the boy to ride twenty five paces behind me and keep me in his sights until I return.

'It isn't necessary,' I say, as I mount,' but if it pleases you.'

The pure country air is exhilarating as I ride off, fresh breezes blowing into my face and reminding me how pleasant country riding is after the foul air and bad odours in London and environs. I try to ignore the boy, riding behind me and even whip the horse up into a faster gallop. The horse is nimble and responsive; she is easy to control and I am content and at ease as I ride into the forest area, where I slow down to a trot to take in the trees and shrubs, foliage and bushes surrounding me. It is a long time since I have enjoyed the relaxation and pleasures of home and the Wiltshire countryside of my youth. I feel a momentary pang of regret as I realise that this pleasant and rejuvenating interlude will be over far too quickly and I must return to a challenging life at court.

*   *   *   *

May 1536.

I walk in leisurely fashion round the grounds with my mother pointing out the changes that have been made since I was last home. Fresh topiary shapes abound in symmetrical fashion for my mother has always had a good eye for pretty layouts and instructs our gardeners well. The many varied trees too, are well shaped and in good health as far as it is possible to judge. We move around in ever increasing circles as my mother tells me how proud she and father are, that now my brothers are at court and I am to be the next Queen of England. She recalls the time last year when the King's progress stopped to include a visit to Wulfhall, the time that I first saw him and he saw me! They felt so honoured and now, things have moved on apace to the present situation but she cautions me to be a good wife, to be kind and obedient to the king and never to vex or defy him under any circumstances.

'Mother believe me I never would, it is not my place.'

'I believe you are a sensible girl,' she replies but looking concerned and doubtful notwithstanding, 'but there are many perils ahead.'

We reach a stone seat and I suggest sitting for a while. I begin to explain to her that I made sure that my relationship with the king was right and proper from the very beginning. I tell her that when he first showed signs of flirting with me I was flattered but kept a strong sense of propriety. I explain about his gifts to me and, in particular, the time he sent a purse containing a letter and a large amount of gold coin. I returned it, instructing the messenger to thank his majesty and beseech him to consider that I am a gentlewoman of good and honourable stock, without reproach and that I had no greater wealth than my honour and that for a thousand deaths I would not wish to impair it. I also tell mother that I had told the king that if he wished to make me a present of money, I prayed that it would be when God would send me a good offer of marriage. What I do not tell my mother is that when I received the purse my heart leapt, that I thought about the king and his great physical presence, his strength, the glint in his eyes, his overpowering masculinity and the way he had looked at me the day previously and before returning it, I kissed the letter. This she does not need to know.

I look up and see my father approaching, slowly now, for he walks with much less pace than I recall. He reaches us and I look up to observe that he seems agitated somewhat. Alert and with a look in his eyes that I have never seen before; I believe it is fear and it causes me to shudder.

'A messenger has called,' he says gravely. 'From the king.'

'What does he say John,' my mother asks quietly.

My father looks down at me and says that I am to return to Chelsea tomorrow. A carriage will be sent at ten in the morning. I must be ready to depart and wait to hear further from my lord after that. I nod and say that all is well and they must not worry or fret for me. My mother tells me sorrowfully that she had hoped I would stay much longer than a few brief days but I assure her that I will be well and affairs of state cannot be halted or delayed. If I am indeed to be married on the thirtieth there is little time to complete all the necessary arrangements. My mother rises.

'Very well, my dear,' she says. 'Let us go in to dinner.'

* * * *

24th May 1536

The carriage that arrives in the courtyard is large and imposing and drawn by four fine horses. There are four coachmen and four courtiers and a smaller carriage brings up the rear of the procession. It is all very grand and different from the conveyance I arrived in. The king's coat of arms has been blocked out so secrecy is still very much on his majesty's mind. My baggage and travel bag are loaded on to the conveyance and I prepare to bid farewell to my parents. I can see from their expressions that they are in a state of confusion; happy and proud that I am to become queen but fearful for my future. I do not share their misgivings for I am convinced of the king's love for me and confident that I can overcome all obstacles to make him a good wife and myself a satisfactory marriage.

'Goodbye mother,' I say as I embrace her and kiss her cheek.

'Safe journey, my dear,' she responds.

I embrace my father and he says, 'goodbye Jane, may God be with you and deliver you safely.'

I board the coach.

FIVE

25TH May 1536.

How different today, to the last time I gazed down from this window. The sun is bright, the sky is blue and people are abroad in the streets of Chelsea. A shepherd with a herd of pigs, moving them slowly across the rough terrain, a woman with a basket, straining somewhat under the weight of carrying it I think. Two merchants standing outside the inn with tankards in hand, laughing and talking gaily. Boats on the river moving stealthily along, the oarsmen pulling with strength and purpose.

My equilibrium is restored and I face a future with some degree of hope and confidence. The king visited me incognito last night, late and under cover of his strange attire, wearing a large black cape and hood, smuggled in by his courtiers at dead of night and staying but two hours but he left in fine good humour and happy and contented. I wore a simple gown of pure white satin which pleased him much. He remarked how well it blended with my pale complexion, fair hair and pale blue eyes, little realising, I venture to suggest, that I had selected it just for the purpose it served. When his messenger advised me that he was coming, in disguise and quietly as a mouse at play, late at night, I prepared myself well. He reiterated his love for me, which I returned heartily and told me that he has always desired a pretty wife, an English rose, pure and gentle of disposition and a complete contrast to the dark haired, olive skinned Anne and the similarly constituted Katherine. They were never wives to him, he advised me and their fiery natures and dark forbidding looks always set him on edge when all he ever desired, domestically, was a quiet, peaceful, loving companion who would soothe his brow after the rigours of the day's affairs of state.

I can provide what his heart desires, I know I can. It is all I desire myself in a love match. And when I wish to ask a favour of him, when the time is right, I know how to approach him and how to quietly, peacefully persuade him. I am not so foolish as to think that I am the first to bring domestic harmony to the king; I am well aware that both Katherine and Anne have had their moments of bliss and satisfied his demands. I know too that he has loved them both in the past; however he wishes to persuade himself to the contrary. That intelligence however, is for my private knowledge and will never be whispered abroad.

Elizabeth knocks and when I bid her enter she tells me there is a merchant at the door with samples for me and he expresses a desire to see me by Royal command. I ask her to take him to the kitchen and give him a tankard of mead and I will be down directly. She goes and I set aside my embroidery and walk into my bedchamber to tidy myself and brush my hair before putting on my cap.

When I am down in the dining hall, I summon him and he comes in and introduces himself as Master Thomas Redbarn. He is a short, balding man of some forty years of age, wearing a brown smock and carrying a large, flat, deep carton. He speaks with an odd, nasal gruffness and the accent peculiar to the merchant classes of London.

'I am commanded,' he begins, 'Mistress Seymour, to request that you look through these cloth samples and, if one pleases you, select for your marriage dress.'

'Are you to make it for me Master Redbarn?' I ask, smiling and indicating that he should place the carton on the long table.

'Indeed I am Mistress,' he replies. 'If it so pleases you.'

'All alone?' I ask, smiling still and teasing him rather unkindly for I see that he is nervous and ill at ease.

'No Mistress, I have fifteen seamstresses' at my disposal.'

'I'm pleased to hear it,' I tell him, in truth. 'For there is little time if it is to be made up and ready to wear in five days' time.'

He assures me that it will be done, with time to spare, even if it occasions him and his women working long hours into the night and it is his duty, pleasure and privilege to serve the king and my good self. I thank him graciously and invite him to return to the kitchen and tell Elizabeth that I desire her to pour him some more mead and I will peruse the samples directly.

They are exquisite. I pore contentedly over rich satins, silks and brocade and realise immediately that these are not the products of Master Redbarn's workshop but have been purloined from the very best cloth houses in London. The king has seen that only the very finest has been sent for my perusal and Master Redbarn has been chosen to execute the work, presumably on reputation of dedication to his craft. I do not take more than thirty minutes or so; discarding a particularly appealing taffeta, I choose a sumptuous and beautiful milk white brocade and recall the craft man.

'This is the one, the only one,' I tell him. 'And I will want it heavily embroidered with gold brocade.'

'My pleasure, my lady,' he says, gaily. 'I will get to work this very afternoon.

Dinner is a slow and solitary hour. I manage to eat heartily enough but only small portions, beginning with a little wild boar followed by slow roasted rabbit and bread. I drink ale at this hour although it is not a favourite. But time weighs heavily for this and the next four days and I feel in limbo. To eat and linger over the consumption of my dinner is one of the few pleasures I receive.

I have been informed by a messenger that a visitor will arrive after midnight, quietly, and unobtrusively and unrecognised by any abroad in the streets and thoroughfares. I ensure that I am wearing a soft pink gown of rich satin that will complement my fair skin and hair and please my 'visitor.' I spend some time sewing after eating but my heart is not really in it.

The hours drag by and I am growing impatient for company; too much solitary dallying is not good for me but I can bear it. The midnight hour arrives, announced by the solemn tolling of a church clock somewhere nearby. Barely a minute passes and he arrives, shown in by Elizabeth and not removing his heavy black cloak and hood until she has left the chamber. When he strips off his outer garments I see that he wears a colourful combination of silk shirt and bright blue breeches. He smiles at me and moves forward to take hold of my shoulders and plant a kiss upon my lips.

Good evening Your Grace,' I say, softly

'Some wine Mistress Seymour?' he asks, dismissing formalities instantly.

'I will get it and pour it myself,' I say softly.

'Why so Jane, are your servants paralysed?'

'No, My Lord, 'I say quickly, 'although I instructed Elizabeth to go to bed after your arrival.'

'Rouse her,' he commands roughly, moving to a seat and spreading himself out in it.

I walk slowly to the seat and sit down next to him. I say that I would like to pour his wine myself, if he will allow because Elizabeth has to be up before six in the morning and he and I do not. I tell him that I will enjoy pouring out his wine. He stares hard at me for some seconds and then, quite suddenly and spontaneously, roars with laughter. I wait for his laughter to subside, framing a question with my raised eyebrows but then taking care to compose my features into a soft, demure expression as he does not speak.

'Oh Jane, Jane, you are a soft and silly creature, my little white lamb. I cannot bring myself to upbraid you and the idea of wine poured from your own sweet hands appeals to me very much.'

I fetch and pour it without due ceremony and he empties his goblet in one gulp.

'You are thirsty after your boat trip sir,' I say, instantly filling his goblet.

He begins to calm down somewhat after his second drink and complains briefly about stupid, ignorant courtiers and what he has to endure from them. I listen sympathetically and his frown turns gradually to a smile as he admires my gown and what is contained within it. My gown is to his taste he says, even though it covers up most of my clear, porcelain flesh. He expresses the opinion that he would find it more conducive to calmness and peace at this hour if we were to retire to my bedchamber and I would allow him to contemplate the rest of my fine, pale white skin. We enter the chamber and he makes himself comfortable on my bed as I slowly disrobe, ensuring that my movements are slow and deliberate. Finally, I stand naked before him and I'm unable to prevent a blush suffusing my cheeks.

What follows surprises and delights me. He is aware of my shyness and he proceeds to demonstrate that he is more than capable of being gentle and a considerate, competent lover. The thought occurs to me that he has had enough practice, God knows and enough women to fill a regiment but I do not allow it to spoil the moment.

As he leaves and I hear the heavy fall of many pairs of boots upon the ground outside, I sigh and drift into peaceful sleep.

* * * *

26th May 1536.

The same messenger has called, delivered the same message and departed. I am now dressed in a pale yellow gown, my hair brushed out and down past my shoulders, waiting for the midnight visit. On arrival I hear the heavy boot sounds upon the stairs and he enters, ushered in by Madge, clothed in the usual black, heavy cape and with the hood obscuring most of his face. Something about his appearance jars with me however and I am uncomfortable momentarily.

'Greetings sir,' I say, recovering swiftly but aware that his body shape seems awkward somehow and unfamiliar.

'Greetings to you Mistress Seymour,' says Thomas Cromwell, removing his hood to reveal an unpleasant grin on his rather pale, insipid face. I make a sharp intake of breath but will myself to recover my equilibrium swiftly, anxious not to let this man observe me flustered.

'Well sir,' I say, aware that my tone of voice has hardened. 'You are an unexpected late night visitor, to be sure.'

'Yes, I ask your indulgence for the lateness of the hour,' he says in his usual flat tones, 'but His Highness commanded me to check that all was well with you and you do not want for any item.'

'I have everything I need,' I tell him, coldly, aware of the severity of my speech.

'That is well,' he says, nodding. 'My visit will be brief.'

For the sake of politeness and good manners I invite him to be seated and offer him a drink. He says that white wine would be very gratefully accepted and I call for Madge who brings it and pours. I join him in consuming the liquid. He hands me a written sheet with the order of the marriage ceremony and tells me that he can go through it with me, if I wish and elaborate any points that I am unsure about. I inform him that I am well versed in the order of service and not in need of further instruction. He sighs, clears his throat then speaks.

'Might I suggest, respectfully,' he says, looking self- assured, 'your familiarity lies with the order in the Catholic church, as defined by the Bishop of Rome.'

'No sir,' I respond starkly. 'I have familiarised myself with all things appertaining to our new church.'

He sighs once again and looks at me as if despairing of my ability to understand his position. As he is sure I am well aware, he continues in slow, measured tones, the King is rightly insistent that everybody, from the lowest to the highest in the land, show full respect and allegiance to our new Church of England, of which he is the undisputed and sole head.

'Of course.'

'It is merely that he is extremely touchy on this matter.'

'Of which I am well aware and need no further guidance on the subject.'

He shakes his head from side to side, slowly and in negative manner and remains silent for some time. I maintain a frosty countenance but resolve not to speak again until he does.

'You know Mistress Seymour,' he begins, speaking clearly and in a somewhat clipped accent, 'I am not your enemy. In reality indeed, I could be said to have aided your being chosen as the king's suitor.'

'I venture to suggest sir,' I reply, 'that you only aided my cause by ensuring that Queen Anne's head was removed from her body.'

He is shocked and put out as I see instantly from the change of his expression. He is obviously not used to being spoken to in such a blunt manner and, by a woman! I will not attempt to repair any damage I may have done; this odious man of low birth has the king's ear and will advise and attempt to manipulate him, as he has done for the past several years since ensuring his elevation from nobody to Henry's chief minister. But I flatter myself that I know a toady when I see one and this man is just that. He is useful to the king only in the extent to which he will carry out every last wish he makes and agree with everything that His Majesty says. He is a social and political climber and manipulator and will not hinder me. Am I not about to become even closer to the king than even Cromwell is? Can I not use my own wiles and gentle, reasoned persuasion to change that which I consider unjust? I believe, sincerely, that the king's love for me and mine for him will make for harmonious union and although I shall take great care to avoid the subjects that infuriate him most, I know I can persuade and suggest and try to ensure that he always feels that changes were his idea in the first place. Cromwell looks restless and I am already wishing that this 'short visit' would be concluded.

'I repeat,' he says gravely, 'I am not your enemy Mistress Seymour. The road ahead is long and hard and we may need to succour each other in the coming months and years, you and me.'

'I will not hinder you, if you do not hinder me sir,' I say in a soft voice.

'Why talk of hindering? Why should we not speak of working together?'

I tell him that I have no desire to work together with any one or, indeed, to conspire with anyone behind the king's back. My marriage to the king will be an honest and loving union where trust between us must and will be, paramount. Cromwell's face wears an expression of dark anger. I see him struggling to compose and control his feelings and, when he speaks he appears calmer than I know him to really be.

'Your ambition does you credit Mistress Seymour,' he snaps out rapidly. 'Although I wonder if you realise the extent of the task you set yourself. The king's one great desire, nay I should say overwhelming obsession, is to produce a son and heir to his throne.'

'Indeed, 'I say calmly. 'And I hope and pray that God will bless our union with a child-----'

I stop, pause and look straight at Cromwell.

'-----of the right sex.'

'And if God doesn't?'

'Then you and I must look to a way to keep our heads Master Cromwell,' I say, smiling and he stares at me, blandly.

At last he rises, inclines his head very slightly towards me and says,' I bid you good evening Mistress Seymour,' and he walks out of the chamber and, collecting his henchmen from the kitchen, leaves the house.

I pick up my goblet and drink the remains of my wine. That man, I tell myself, will go to any lengths to give the king exactly what he wants. Whether it be right or wrong, good or evil, if the king desires it, that man will move heaven and earth to acquire it for him. He would, I believe, make a pact with the devil if he saw progress for himself by it. I will not align myself with him as either friend or foe.

SIX

30TH MAY 1536.

To Whitehall Palace, York Place for my marriage to the king of England. If I had an idea of a large Royal Wedding with every pomp and full regalia, crowds thronging outside the palace, a triumphant return to Hampton Court and music and dancing into the small hours, I could not have been more mistaken. It is to be a small, private ceremony in the Queen's Closet. My Lord, the king has decreed that he desires to marry me at a quiet place, in private except for close friends and associates and thereafter, to introduce me slowly to the people, who may, he fears, feel resentment towards him after the death of Anne. Our marriage is, in truth, very soon after the death of the unfortunate Anne, a mere eleven days but, he tells me, he will not wait, he cannot wait. I am the love of his life, he assures me and he wants the deed done. His words!

For my own part I cannot but agree that initial secrecy is most probably a good idea. I would not wish to be unpopular with the good people of England before my life as their queen begins. If, as My Lord commands, I am to be introduced slowly and somewhat surreptitiously, then so be it; I shall prepare myself carefully over the next few days and weeks to be worthy and acceptable to the populace. They shall not find me wanting in any respect, of that I am resolutely determined.

It is a fine, warm day, with sunshine over the city and only the lightest, most refreshing of breezes. I am very happy with my gown of brilliant white brocade with intertwining gold embroidery encased in the cloth. I hope that I look regal and assured as I certainly feel so.

As I enter the Queen's Closet, with The Duke of Suffolk a hush descends on the chamber. Suffolk nods in my direction and I smile; he is the only one of the king's close friends that I am fairly happy to have at my side. He is courtly and a true gentleman, tall, upright and almost always cheery of disposition. I see the king with Sir Anthony Denny by his side, his best man. He has been close to Henry for many years and is a true friend to him.

The king is resplendent in his fine robes; he has an orange coloured sable outfit, trimmed with white fur and many jewels. His beard is finely trimmed and his eyes are gleaming as he looks at me. I count myself very fortunate to have made such a love match under the circumstances and will fight tooth and nail, if necessary, to ensure that it remains so.

Archbishop Cranmer begins the service but I am too preoccupied to hear or take note of his words. They wash over me. I am aware of Cromwell, standing over to my left and also Norfolk who, like the other, seems to be present on all occasions. My Maids of Honour, Jane and Mary Arundell, Jane Ashley and Anne Barrett, Mary Norris and Anne Parr, are all close at hand, as indeed are all of them. The chamber is hot now and I take a deep breath as we proceed to the vows.

'I, Henry, take thee to be my wedded wife,' the king intones, 'to have and to hold from this day forward, for better for worse, for richer for poorer, in sickness and in health, till death do us part, and thereto I plight thee my troth.'

He raises one eyebrow and I smile at him in return and try to control the butterflies in my belly before commencing my own vows.

'I take thee, Henry, to my wedded husband,' I say in the clearest, boldest speech I can muster, 'to have and to hold from this day forward, for better for worse, for richer for poorer, in sickness and in health, to be bonny and buxom in bed and board, till death do us part, and thereto I plight thee my troth.'

Henry takes me by the shoulders and kisses me. As he steps back to have a quick word with Denny, I look him over and realise, with a little sudden shock, that he is heavier in build and his face is beginning to show signs of excess flesh; how could I have missed the slow changes that have afflicted him since his first visit to Wulf Hall, over a year ago now? I decide that I have been too close to him and seen him too frequently in the past twelve months; recent, horrific events have blurred my sight and concentration on detail.

I am congratulated, bowed to, caught up in a flurry of speech and noise and begin to feel almost faint. When I mention to Henry that I feel weary and might swoon at any minute, he is solicitous and orders that we must return to Hampton Court Palace immediately. I seem to be carried along with the large procession that make their way down to the river and the king's barge. Once on the river, the fresh air and bright blue sky revives me to some extent and I am able to sit back in the big seats reserved for Henry and myself and gaze out at the free flowing river. There are few people abroad on the river banks as we glide past and I recover my brightness of spirit that I felt earlier in the day.

As the palace comes into view I am struck, as I have not been previously, by the sheer size and magnificence of Hampton Court Palace. The gleaming, orange coloured façade, shining in the sunlight, provides a near perfect vista. The symmetry of the building is well- nigh perfect and it suddenly hits me that this fine palace is to be one of my main homes from now on.

'It is a magnificent palace,' I say dreamily to Henry, who has been almost silent throughout the journey.

'It serves its purpose well enough,' he replies abstractedly, watching fish diving and jumping in the water.

'It belonged to Cardinal Wolsey didn't it?' I ask, more to make conversation than anything for my mind is now racing with thoughts about what the next few hours and, indeed, days will bring.

'That traitor, that imbecile,' Henry says, voice trembling with sudden anger. It still amazes and, I confess, shocks me, how quickly the king's temper can flare up when he is riled. I tell him that I'm sorry; I had no intention of upsetting him. It was just that coming round the bend of the river earlier and then catching sight of the palace in all its glory I had spontaneously thought about the man who once owned the place.

'Yes, well, please refrain from mentioning the name of that traitor and blackguard in my presence in future,' Henry says with a countenance as black as midnight.

'Yes, of course My Lord.'

'You have no idea Jane, of the extent of the infamy of that man. He was always a thorn in my side. He opposed my parting with Katherine because of his infernal loyalty to his church and-----well so much that I can scarcely begin and I do not wish to discuss it any further.'

'No, of course not,' I say gently. 'I fully understand.'

'I had occasion to remove him from his prestigious office,' Henry says, forgetting or perhaps oblivious to the fact that he has just stopped me talking about the man. I nod but make no reply. He settles back in his seat for the last few minutes of the journey before we reach the landing stage and alight.

*   *   *   *

I sit next to Henry, under the Royal Canopy. It is a strange feeling, both exhilarating and at the same time, a little daunting. I do not doubt for an instant my right to be here, it is just a little difficult to accept that all this has really happened to me!

His Majesty is in fine fettle. People come and go, offering their good wishes for his marriage and their fervent hope that a son and heir will be born in due season. They are all full of good cheer, good wishes and complimentary towards me and to the king for his 'wise and judicious choice of a beautiful queen.' One ageing Duke and his lady describe me as a 'rare and precious beauty, a true English rose.' I am flattered but know full well that I am no beauty but it sounds good to my ears to hear those words spoken.

When the round of well-wishers are exhausted, the king sits back and orders a tumbler of ale and some rare, sweet white wine from Italy for me. He is content, he tells me, happy in his marriage and sure that I will be much loved by the people before long.

'I do hope and pray that they will like me,' I tell him, looking concerned.

'I cannot doubt it for an instant,' he says, bombastically. 'How could they resist the charm and prettiness of my little white lamb?'

I incline my head and smile at him but make no response.

'A new Parliament opens in nine days' time and I intend to give instruction to ministers on how I wish my position to be perceived,' he says. 'Chancellor Audley will be here directly and he has done sterling work for me in the past.'

I nod once again without speaking. I know from discussions with friends that the man Henry has created Lord Chancellor has helped him at every turn. He supported Henry in his divorce from Catherine, presided over the trial and execution of Sir Thomas More and took part in the trial of Anne Boleyn even though he had fully backed the king's desire to marry her earlier. With Anne's death, he is free to declare Elizabeth a bastard and, his grace informs me, will do so. I find this very distasteful but will not, at this juncture say anything although I do not look forward to an audience with this man.

Sir Thomas Audley prepared and supported the Act of Supremacy last year which gave Henry full control over the church and the country. Like Cromwell, there seems no sacrifice of principals he is not prepared to make or suspect act of parliament he will not support or instigate to gain the king's approval. I watch his approach to the canopy with misgivings but will not betray my feelings.

Audley is heavily built, quite stout really but upright and with a full, well maintained beard and a look that suggests that his eyebrows are permanently raised, suggesting arrogance to all who come into contact with him. He greets us with a subservient smile on his face.

'Sir Thomas,' Henry acknowledges him and indicates with a hand movement that he is free to speak.

'Your Majesty,' he begins. 'I'm mindful that there is a new parliament opening on June the eighth and beg your instruction for any matters you might wish raised or resolved.'

'Yes,' Henry says, stroking his chin. 'There is an important matter that I should be pleased to see highlighted.'

Audley's expression conveys the impression that whatever is required, he is the man to deal with it. Henry tells him that he is rather concerned that the populace in general might feel ill will towards him in view of the recent demise of the great whore. Audley begins to shake his head in denial but the king waves his protest away. He points out that the manner of her death, although necessary, may turn certain sections of the people against him and he does not feel that he deserves such condemnation.

'Indeed not, your Grace,' Audley says, looking shocked. 'Let me think. My speech, I feel, with your majesty's approval, should point up the dark dangers and great intolerable perils that had threatened both you and the crown of England as a result of the Queen's treason.'

'Yes, yes, that is seemly.'

'I could go on,' Audley says, warming to his subject happily, ' to point out that the woman, inflamed with pride and the carnal desires of her body, had, in league with her brother, Rochford, along with Smeaton, Norris, Weston and Brereton, committed vile adultery, diverse detestable and abominable treasons----'

'----Yes, very good. You are on the right lines Audley.'

'And all this to the fearful peril and danger of your royal person.'

Henry nods and smiles and tells Audley that if such a speech be delivered he feels it will go a long way towards proving that he, as king, sometimes has to take extreme measures to safeguard the realm, today and in time to come.

'I should further say, 'Audley interjects, causing Henry to frown angrily suddenly, 'if God, in his goodness, had not brought these treasons to light, what then?'

'Put such a speech together with care Audley,' the king says. 'For the day I open the new parliament.'

Audley bows and scrapes, a sickly grin on his face, as the king turns to me and, spontaneously, pats my hand before turning back to the chancellor.

'Thank you Your Grace, it will be done exactly as you desire,' he says obsequiously, and, appearing to notice me for the first time since he approached, adds, inclining his head, 'My lady.'

I have been watching this man fawning over the king, working like mad to try and please him and gain favour and, until this moment he has ignored me; treated me as though I were not here and do not exist. If the king had not made that brief but important gesture of love towards me, nothing would have been said. Audley looks prepared to depart but Henry is looking thoughtful and has not dismissed him yet.

'Then there is the question of my marriage,' he says, as if thinking aloud, 'just eleven days after the death of the great whore.'

Audley thinks for several seconds before speaking, as the king remains patient but almost bursting for a response.

'Might I suggest, your majesty,' he begins, ' that I speak about you accepting the condition of matrimony, not in any carnal concupiscence but for the good of the realm with a wife, who in age and form, is deemed to be meet and apt for the procreation of children.'

As he speaks the last words, this rather horrible creature, looks at me as if he would like to ravish me on the spot and for an instant, invisible to the king doubtless, there is an expression of carnal lust on his face.

'I do like your thoughts very much,' the king says, brightly. 'Go to it Audley and prepare your speech diligently.'

The Lord Chancellor departs, bowing as he walks backwards until out of the king's sight.

Henry watches his departure in silence and finally turns to me.

'Good man, Audley,' he says gruffly, 'good man. He'll do well for me.'

SEVEN

A veritable uproar can be heard as we approach the great hall. I hear loud music and, almost at the same volume but not nearly as refreshing, voices, raised in jocular conversation and laughing. As the king sweeps in and I follow on just behind him, the voices fade almost to a murmur momentarily as he leads me to the top, raised table where we will sit. The music swells up and I take in the harmonious blend of viols, flutes, recorders, a lute and a psaltery, a harp and the sackbut. They are playing a pretty melody which is easy on the ear, or would be if the voices were lessened. There must be over a hundred people at the tables, all waiting for the food and the commencement of the wedding banquet. I wonder, idly, whatever happened to a small, limited, private gathering that suddenly appears to have swelled to a hundred souls.

The great hall is ablaze with colour. The bright, gleaming colours of the tapestries that hang from every wall are dazzling. So too are the costumes of many of the people, men and women both. The odours of freshly roasted food pervade the hall and I begin to feel quite hungry. Yeomen stand by, ready to assist with the distribution of the dishes to be served and servants linger waiting to serve and run for whatever may be forgotten and required.

Henry marches up to his central place and I sit down next to him as he bangs his fist on the table and calls for commencement. The Duke of Norfolk and his wife are to my right and Denny sits next to the king on the other side. Most of the people we have seen earlier are around us on the big table. As the music swells up and I look at the various faces around me, smiling, laughing or chuckling away as if they had not a care in the world, it all seems suddenly bizarre and unreal. A few short weeks ago I was in isolation, rarely speaking to a living soul from day to day and before that I was a humble lady-in- waiting at the court.

'This tune is one I composed on the virginals a few weeks ago,' Henry says to me. 'Do you like it Jane?'

'Indeed I do,' I tell him contentedly, as the rasp of the sackbut gives way to soft, flowing melody from the viols and flutes. I look at my husband as he turns away to converse with Audley, some way down the table and marvel, momentarily, that he can write such poetry and mellifluous music and still give the order to cut off somebody's head if that person so displeases him. Queen Anne comes into my thoughts again, unbidden and I wish that she would leave me in peace. I catch the eye of Norfolk's wife and she inclines her head to me, a token of respect for my position. I realise that this is now my life and I can expect everybody around me to treat me as though I were some special deity and not a simple country girl from a good but unremarkable family. I feel the same plain, ordinary Jane but I am not and I think, with a little sharp prick of pain in my intestines, I never will be, ever again. Whatever the years ahead may bring, in sickness and in health, as the marriage service puts it, that innocent girl is gone forever.

A servant approaches, staggering under the weight of a huge game bird pie, freshly baked and piping hot. Another puts down a large, round boars head, glazed with fat, surrounded in the dish by dates and apricots. It looks delicious.

'I'm ready now to consume an entire pig,' the king exclaims jocularly.

'And I too,' says Denny. 'So let us call for two my lord.

There is chicken on the table now, decorated with bright red cherries and a roasted peacock which looks bigger than such a bird should. Venison, hare and bustards are added to the cloth covered table as we start with some boar's head, freshly cut by a servant and handed out in order of rank. I pick delicately at the meat on my plate but Henry seems famished by the events of the day and eats heartily, moving swiftly to some slices of chicken with cherries which is cut and placed before him after just a nod towards bird and servant.

I accept a little chicken and some deer, indicating to the server the exact size of the portions I require and he adheres to my requirements with exactitude. Henry is tackling some of the monster sized game bird pie, large chunks of pastry, meat and herbs floating about in a rich, venison sauce. Some of the other lords and their ladies are dipping into this culinary delight but I wave the servant away as he attempts to decorate my plate with some of it.

Henry calls loudly for some bread and it is rushed in, hot from the ovens and with a delicious aroma emanating from it. Then more ale is brought and our tankards filled as I continue to eat sparingly, pacing myself to last the hours of this wedding banquet feast.

The musicians end their tune and strike up again with a jolly, rollicking jig which fills the vast hall with music and enhances the party mood of everybody present. I begin to sip my second tankard of ale and the tapestry colours appear to take on an even brighter, more colourful hue.

I can hardly believe it when servants appear carrying large glazed ducks, surrounded with baked apples and swimming in delicate sauces and place them on the tables. Soon there will not be an inch of space on the surfaces.

'Eat up, my little white lamb,' Henry entreats me. 'This is your wedding feast.'

'I must go at my own leisurely pace my lord, or I will never last out.'

He roars with laughter and continues, indicating to an alert servant that he would like to try some duck. He then tries a small portion of peacock, just to taste what it is like! He says that the flavour is exceptionally rich and the meat ripe and I really should try a little.

'I can eat no more sir,' I say, laughing. 'Or I will blow up like a balloon.'

'There is one more delicacy that you must eat Jane,' he says, winking at me lasciviously.

There is a short interlude as the slowest eaters finish their repast, the debris is cleared from the tables and the musicians play rather gentle, soothing ballads and sad, lost love songs.

Henry is amused about something; there is a twinkle in his eye and I can sense that he has planned something unusual. It surprises and shocks me to discover how very child- like he can be; this man of power and influence, this strong masculine force of nature. Is it not a true enigma? He is obviously on edge, waiting for whatever is to happen, to happen. He begins conversations with Denny or his wife and loses interest suddenly, almost mid- sentence. I know he is behaving strangely because I am newly married to this man and I am observing everything he says and does, most carefully.

There is a sudden roar of delight followed by laughter as a servant appears with a monster sized cake or pie; at first I cannot make out what it is until it reaches our table and is set down. Henry winks at me and squeezes my arm; he is enjoying the moment. Faces around me are all animated, wearing smiles and looking towards me. I glance down at the dish.

It is an enormous pastry based tart which, on the top layer, in various coloured jams, I can make out the words of my motto 'Bound to obey and serve,' and a delicately fashioned reproduction of my emblem: the crowned phoenix, flanked by Tudor roses, rising from a castle. All of this, most laboriously and painstakingly fashioned from different shades of jam! I look down at this marvel of culinary artistry and a broad smile will be seen on my face.

'All this for me sir?' I ask in wonder and suddenly everybody around our table starts to applaud and the king is roaring with laughter and obviously enjoying himself immensely.

'For you, on our wedding day, my queen, my white lamb,' he says jocularly.

I thank him and try to remain calm although it is difficult. Henry bellows out for all to hear that I must have the first slice and a kitchen hand steps forward to cut the tart. I can hardly refuse to eat it but I caution the servant to cut only the thinnest slice for me. It is for me, the final delicacy, and the end of the feast. But as I eat slowly, thoughtfully, I see the servants bringing in Marchpane, made with powdered almonds, icing sugar and rose water on a large dish. It is decorated with gold leaf and looks amazing but I could no more eat any now than fly like a bird. The servants are handing out plates made of sugar and egg white which can be eaten off but also eaten when other honeyed delicacies have been consumed.

The music is now more slow and subdued. A harpist has joined the band of musicians and is playing sumptuous, burnished melodies. A lute player provides harmony. My thoughts at the moment concern the king and his loving gesture towards me. I finish my tart and wonder how the king can be so gentle, generous and thoughtful at some times and at others, despatch five people to sudden, violent death. It is a conundrum that I cannot solve.

* * * *

Couples dance together, side by side, along the length of the big hall. I watch them enviously and wonder how they have the energy after consuming so much food and drink. The musicians are back in the minstrel gallery, playing flowing jigs and other dance like tunes. Henry sits watching it all, faintly amused, quite content, lethargic for the moment, occasionally moving to pick up his tankard of ale and take a swig.

'What now, husband?' I ask softly, as a dance tune ends abruptly and people begin to move back to their seats, if they have them, or to benches or corners with alcoves or just spots on the floor, if they haven't.

'Now you will witness a masque Jane,' he tells me, eyes twinkling.

'What is it, exactly?' I ask, for I have come across them in the past but rarely and never, I do believe, watched one from beginning to conclusion.

'An entertainment lamb,' he continues, still looking animated and expectant.

'What about?' I wish to know.

'Something they have devised for me,' he says, the twinkle back in his eye. 'You must wait and see.'

I do not have to wait long. The musicians come down from their gallery again and arrange themselves to the sides of the big hall. Drums and bells suddenly set up a resounding thud and thunder as several performers run out into central positions. Five are dressed as noblemen and the sixth, a woman, is dressed looking much like the late queen appeared although the costume and gown are rough and badly stitched in comparison to the ones they are intended to emulate. I begin to get misgivings and these turn to positive discomfort as the performers begin a series of dance styled gyrations as the woman goes to each male figure in turn, twisting and squirming and placing her hands and mouth on their privy parts and then bending over to simulate copulation, as each man comes up behind her.

I look at Henry in my extreme discomfort but he is smiling broadly and so much involved in what is going on in front of him that he is scarcely aware of my presence. I have the distinct and uncomfortable premonition that this is all going to get a lot worse before it gets better. A sudden riot of sound and movement explodes and a giant figure, clad head to toe in black, runs out with a huge sword in his hands and, chasing the woman, eventually brings her to the ground and mimes chopping her head off. She is quickly dragged off and out of the hall by two yeomen warders who appear, as if from nowhere but likely, the vicinity of the many kitchens.

There is a murmur of laughter heard around us at this point and I notice with dismay that Henry is laughing; chuckling and drinking his ale and quite enjoying himself. How can he sit here and laugh, I wonder but there is more to come I see, as the female figure returns, this time with her garment cleverly affixed so that it covers her head and she appears to be headless and carrying a paper and glue model of a woman's head, the face hideously distorted. A great roar of laughter erupts and echoes around the big hall. Henry is laughing as loud as any and I gaze at him and feel physically sick.

Suddenly, two more big drums are brought on and there erupts a thunderous, sickening cacophony of music and screams as the swordsman runs around miming the decapitation of the five men, who fall to the ground and remain static in the straw and rushes. A group of pygmies and dwarves run out, all dressed as either hideous goblins or red clad devils with black faces and horns. One of them grabs the woman's head and they begin throwing it to each other or kicking it along the ground as the headless creature tries aimlessly to retrieve it. All this sets off a louder burst of laugher and spontaneous applause.

I turn away from the sickening sight and glance swiftly at the faces around, close and to the left and right of where I sit. Henry is laughing loudly, so too are most of the men, all in fact, except Denny and Suffolk, both of them, to their credit, looking slightly out of comfort.

Some of the women too are looking most uncomfortable but by no means all of them. When I turn back my attention to the performance I see that they have brought on a long, plaster board with orange and red flames of fire painted on it to represent hell. The severed head is being kicked around furiously now as the music swells up and then we see the goblins and devils pulling the headless woman to the fires of hell, kicking and screaming as the drumming and bells rise to a crescendo.

With relief I realise it is all over. Everybody is shouting, screaming, laughing and applauding, not least his majesty himself. I have to leave this hall and I tell Henry that I am feeling a little faint.

'What ails you Jane?' he asks solicitously.

'I have a headache,' I reply. 'I would wish to go out into the grounds to get fresh air.'

'You must have consumed too much of that rich, ripe peacock my little lamb,' he says, not unkindly but in a sombre, casually observed manner.

'I did not touch it sir,' I tell him, 'but it is most likely something else I ate.'

'Yes, yes, away with you then,' he says quietly. 'I'll send two warders to watch out for you.'

'No need, My Lord,' I say, rising but he is not listening. His attention is drawn to some new instruments that are being brought in for a further programme of music. I depart in haste as further musicians, minstrels and helpers are ushered in to contribute to the celebrations. In the grounds the country air is fresh and pure, the last of the foggy, smoking clouds from London chimneys having just drifted past our skyline. I walk slowly along the paths by the lawns and the topiary sculptures all around. I sit on a stone bench.

I realise that I will have to adapt to my husband's constantly changing moods and tempers. He is not predictable. When he is gentle and loving I will press my favours on him and advance my desires, quietly and persuasively. When he is in ill humour and vile of temper I shall do my utmost to soothe him and be sympathetic. The road ahead may be long and hard and fraught with dangers but I can't go back now.

I hear faintly the plaintive song of the lute, viol and the throbbing bass of the gamba. It is a pretty tune, for romancing or dancing or both. It is time for me to return to my husband.

* * * *

June 2nd 1536

In great procession today, to Greenwich, with a convoy of barges and smaller boats to be proclaimed as Queen of England. Henry stands by my side looking very strong and handsome in his Royal finery, his hair and beard neatly trimmed. He smiles at me and I at him and he grips my hand. It is my happiest day in my lifetime. I am proclaimed. I am queen. I am content and joyous.

EIGHT

June 7th 1536.

I am finding it difficult to come to terms with the number of people who accompany us whenever we move beyond palace or mansion. I am used to taking summer strolls alone and unhindered where I can collect my thoughts in peace and tranquillity. Now I find we cannot move within twenty yards of home without the Troop of Gentlemen, the king's bodyguard and various servants and pages to accompany us.

We walk down to the landing stage in procession and board the royal barge. I sit back on the comfortable cushions with his majesty and as the oarsmen make preparation, my husband takes my hand and squeezes it. I am pleased that he is in good humour for, following the evening of our wedding day, when we returned to the king's bedchamber and consummated, at least officially, our marriage, there was a slight altercation before going off to sleep. The king asked me if I had enjoyed the festivities after the marriage ceremony and I had said that everything was to my taste except the masque performance pertaining to the queen's demise. His temper flared, as it is wont to do and he reminded me that the entertainment was presented to us, to provoke laughter and to relieve the pain and hurt he felt following the late queen's infamous adultery and treason. I told him as gently as I could that I felt that it was in very bad taste but this only instigated a fresh outburst of temper and a lecture about the ways of a monarch and how his loyal subjects go out of their way to entertain and sustain him, when he has been cruelly ill-used and hurt.

I look out to see silver fish jumping up from the river as we float gently away from the bank. It is a mild spring morning, not hot, certainly not cold but the sky is blue and cloudless and the sun is making spasmodic attempts to break through.

'It is meet that you make such fine provision in attendance to your wardrobe,' the king says, still stroking my hand in loving manner.

'I always want to look my very best for you sir,' I tell him, honestly.

'Ah but today is different.'

'Sir?'

'This is a beginning Jane,' he says. 'Today you will be seen in public by a few people and first impressions mean so much.'

I shake my head as I listen to the sound of the gently lapping water as the oars stroke it and then I smile. I had chosen a bright yellow gown and a cape with a slightly darker hue, hoping it would please him to see me in it, as it shows off my fair hair and complexion to advantage. It would seem though, that his pleasure in my attire is dependent on the effect it will have on the people abroad this Sunday morning.

'You know how it will please me if the people of this country come to love you Jane,' he says. 'I would not want you unpopular as the great whore was for all my treasury.'

'Then I hope sir, that they are pleased, as I shall be,' I reply. 'But in truth, it was selected to please your Grace.'

The day improves withal. The sun has broken through a drifting cloud and shines brightly on the fields surrounding us and sends sparks of brilliant light dancing on the water.

We alight on a Middlesex bank, close by the region of Richmond. We are offered a canopy to carry us across the field to the church but Henry declines.

'I think a brisk walk will be invigorating,' Henry says, 'on such a morning. Jane?'

'Yes,' My Lord,' I respond. 'It will be fitting.'

We set out across a green field where fresh flowers grow wild and in profusion. We walk slowly, heading the procession and I notice that the king is not limping too badly; an accident some year or so ago during a joust, left him with myriad injuries and a nagging problem with his foot that he cannot shake off. The church, very old and grey stoned, nestles in among a clump of trees and wildly growing bushes. A good crowd of people are already gathered; yeoman farmers, workmen at the back and several high ranking ladies and gentlemen in front. A shout of 'God save the king,' goes up as we draw nearer and various shouts of approval and applause are heard. I wonder, idly, how news of our intentions leaks out so fast; do we have a prattling servant in the ranks somewhere, who goes abroad on Saturday evenings to shout out our plans in local inns and taverns?

We pass in through the stout oak doors and I make sure that I have as natural a smile upon my face as I can muster. I acknowledge the bows of the clerics before we are escorted to our cushioned seats, on a dais, under a hastily erected canopy bearing the royal arms. I must look rather sombre, as the king takes hold of my hand and bids me, in whispers, to cheer up. I tell him I feel fine and there is nothing praying on my mind.

The mass begins and we sit through it in solemn silence. It is the preacher's sermon, long and one dimensional that jolts me to full attention. He begins by praying for our sovereign lord and king, Henry and beseeches God to keep him safe, long to reign over us. He asks us all to be most humble and to pray constantly for the king, who has suffered most grievously in the past few months from the heinous acts of treason and other despicable behaviour, too hideous to go into here, in a place of worship. We are lucky, he tells us, head nodding convincingly, to have such a king, a man determined in all wise, to keep our country out of the hands of foes, to strive fearlessly and relentlessly to maintain high standards of life for the common man and, notwithstanding his own pain and sense of betrayal at the hands of people in high places that he trusted implicitly, to seek and find and marry our new queen, forsaking his own innermost feelings and desires, for the good of the country and the people. We are all, indeed, lucky and should give endless thanks to God and the king.

As we leave the church, with the preacher and many people bowing all-round us, I look to Henry but he seems pre-occupied and barely aware of my presence. His leg is beginning to ache a little, he says, so the canopy is brought forward and he is lifted onto it, to be carried back to our barge. It is only when we reach it, with me walking beside him and he is lifted down carefully and carried to his seat with cushions that I begin to feel any sense of privacy and closeness to him again. I realise suddenly, with a little jolt that most of my life from now on will be surrounded by courtiers and pages, helpers and ladies-in-waiting and my only time of complete privacy with my husband, will be in the marriage bed.

'Well Henry,' I say, as we settle down to return to the palace, 'that preacher was well primed, to be sure.'

He smiles and winks at me and says he has no idea what I can be thinking.

'Do not tell me sir,' I respond. 'That you did not instruct a courtier to have a word with him prior to our visit.'

'It is a fine summer morning by heaven,' he says jocularly, giving me another smile and patting my leg playfully. I could wish that he would always be in this mood and not so constantly changeable. His moods vary drastically from moment to moment and he is as like, at any given moment, to be aggressively violent or simple and even child- like towards me. In those few days that we have been married I have seen towering furies, angry outbursts, cruel destruction, in words, of people in his direct service, petulant posturing over minor trifles and, less frequently, mores the pity gentle loving warmth.

As we float along quietly, water lapping almost silently along the sides of the barge, he tells me that he is looking forward to opening the new parliament tomorrow morning.

'The speeches made in the morning are crucial Jane,' he tells me. 'They will be widely reported and filter down gradually to most homes in the country.'

'You set great store on what the people think of you,' I say, quietly. 'You need the people's respect and, their love?'

'The ravages of civil war left many scars,' he says soberly, his expression suddenly harsh. 'It is God's wish that I, second only to him in overall authority, secure peace and harmony for all my people.'

I know he means exactly what he says and believes in his own destiny and I see in his expression a complete change from the light of heart, frivolous man I was speaking to just a few moments ago. His brow is set, his eyes glint with fervour.

'I'm sure all will be well and good,' I say in conciliatory tones. 'And all the speeches will be to your liking.'

'Perhaps Jane, perhaps,' he says. 'But if I have learned one thing of paramount importance during my reign, it is that nothing, I repeat nothing, should be left to chance.'

I nod and put my hand on his and his frosty aspect gradually thaws.

'The speech that I believe Audley will make and particularly, that part he mentioned to us about marrying for the good of the realm and because you seem strong of limb and well placed to produce a son and heir will, I am hopeful, be strongly supported and promoted by Richard Rich, the Speaker of the house.'

'Rich?' I say, remembering the name but forgetting his function.

'Yes, chancellor of the Court of Augmentations,' he replies. 'He was instrumental in helping to secure conviction of Thomas More when that man became treacherous towards me.'

Now I remember. But I will not contribute any comments concerning Rich for, in truth, I am still sad thinking about the execution of Sir Thomas More for his refusal to deny his church, that which was always my church, and his refusal to swear allegiance to Henry and the new Church of England. This is a subject I will not engage upon, at any price.

'Let us hope Rich speaks as you would wish,' I say and content myself with just that one comment.

'He had better,' the king replies, his brow furrowed. 'Or he'll answer to me.'

The sun is shining brightly on Hampton Court Palace as we glide downstream and approach the landing bay. I sit back, trying to feel light of heart and content for it is now a beautiful summer morning. If the king is in good humour, as he appears to be overall at this time, then I shall be also. He gazes across at me and remarks that I seem a trifle pre-occupied but I shake my head vigorously.

'No, my lord, all is well with me.'

'Well then,' he says heartily. 'Mark this Jane. We will eat well on our return and I have ordered a troupe of fine musicians who shall play for us this afternoon. Flutes and viols, sackbut and gamba, an hautboy player and a harpsichord.'

'That sounds delightful,' I say enthusiastically.'

'And tonight Jane,' he continues, 'we shall lie together you and I, enjoined in love and produce a son and heir for the country.'

* * * *

JUNE 8TH 1536.

I walk briskly down the corridor and find Jane Ashley and Anne Bassett both busily sewing under the window. They are seated on a window seat smiling and chattering gaily as though neither had a care in the world. As I approach my Ladies-in-waiting, Anne looks up to face me and the smile fades from her face.

'It has come to my notice Anne,' I say, 'that you took part in the masque on my wedding day.'

'Yes, your majesty,' she replies, looking sheepish.

'And you were, in fact, underneath the mask of the woman who was representing the late queen?'

'Yes,' she says in a small voice. 'I was.'

I pause and look at them both, sitting now, sewing abandoned, gazing up at me with sheep's eyes and wondering what is coming next. I will be no bully or tyrant and I will not take advantage of my privileged position to heartily berate my ladies; it is not in my nature. There are, however, certain things that make my flesh crawl and the recent portrayal of the late, unfortunate queen, by another woman, is one of them.

'I found the entertainment most distasteful Anne,' I say, quietly.

'I'm very sorry, my lady,' she says, looking crestfallen. 'I meant no offence indeed.'

'The king personally praised her performance,' Jane says, looking a little defiant now.

'Indeed?' I reply, frostily. 'Personally, I still find it abhorrent.'

'Yes, m'lady,' Jane replies, sheepish again. 'I'm very sorry.'

'I would take it as a personal favour,' I continue, 'if neither of you ever indulge in anything similar, ever again.'

They both nod, assure me that they would never, intentionally, indulge in any pursuit that I would find distressing and assure me that they are contrite and will refuse any future assignments even if requested personally by the king himself. I remind them gently that the king is supreme head of the church and government of the country but is also a man and we may expect different modes of thinking and behaviour from the male sex. I suggest to them that we, as women, see things a trifle differently and know right from wrong when we perceive various actions.

They both nod agreement but I wonder, in passing, how much is down to merely wishing to please me and fear of losing a much prized and sought after situation at court.

'One other matter,' I say, noting the bright colours they are wearing. 'I am of opinion that the late queen's mode of dress for her ladies and her own, were somewhat garish and frivolous. I would also take it as a personal favour if you would wear more sombre garments; darker hues of brown and grey. Deep shades of blue perhaps.'

'Yes, your majesty,' they reply in unison.

I am cognisant of their looks of disappointment at my words however. I suggest that I would be more than happy, indeed would prefer it and look upon it as a personal request, if they were to wear bright girdles of pearls; a most attractive and fetching accessory. This brings the red roses back into their cheeks and smiles to their faces and they say they will do so forthwith. I ask them to pass the message on to the other ladies and inform them that if anybody is unable to sport good pearls they should come to me immediately and I will furnish them with girdles.

I relax and sit next to Jane and ask her to show me her sewing. It is of fairly good quality and there is only one small tip which I am able to pass on to her for improvement. Jane laughs, a high tinkling sound and thanks me for my suggestion. Anne is busily engaged with needle and thread and, looking more nervous and ill at ease than her friend, I forbear to offer her any comment. I muse to myself that all these women are almost all my personal choices as Ladies-in-Waiting and I intend to live in harmony with them as queen. I am happy though that I have made my position clear and that the new regime will be different to the old. That is as it should be.

I rise as the hour lengthens and tell them that I will see them after supper and leave them both in a good frame of mind. One does not have to be a tyrant to make one's position clear and to order matters the way one would wish. I return to my privy chamber and commence a little sewing of my own until a page knocks on my door and bidding him enter, am informed that the king has returned from parliament and wishes me to come to his chamber. As I arrive and see him standing inside, resplendent in Royal blue tunic and sundry accessories, I note with pleasure that he is smiling broadly.

'Good news Jane, my love,' he says jocularly. 'The new parliament has pleased me considerably.'

'That is good to hear.'

'It is, Jane, it is,' he continues rapturously. 'Audley more than lived up to his promise to speak in my favour and Richard Rich spoke fulsome praise for well-nigh an hour and forty minutes, comparing me 'for strength and fortitude to Samson, for justice and prudence to Solomon, and for beauty and comeliness to Absalom.'

'Praise indeed sir.'

He frowns. 'Do you think he did not mean every word Jane?'

'No Henry, I'm sure it was heartfelt,' I say swiftly. 'And well deserved of course.'

'Yes, mmm, yes. I hope so.'

He goes on to tell me that Audley had made it clear that Henry had summoned the new parliament to declare the heir apparent and to repeal the act in favour of the succession of Anne Boleyn's issue. The crown was afterwards entailed on the children of Queen Jane, whether male or female. I was safe and would bear the son who would succeed him as King, he felt confident that it would happen, in due course. He is positively glowing with pride and contentment as he speaks these words.

'Best of all Jane,' he continues, elated, 'parliament accepted and endorsed everything I asked for and desired.'

I will not utter a word to dampen his joy. Thoughts about the injustice of declaring his daughters Mary and Elizabeth illegitimate are repugnant to me but there will come a time and place when I can address these issues and make my position clear. Today is not that day, time or place.

NINE

June 8th 1536.

We set out early for the trip to Greenwich. We are carried down to the barge on a canopy, at Henry's insistence. He has what appears to be almost an entire army of courtiers, yeoman warders and sundry others. I have a good sized contingent of my ladies-in-waiting but, with these numbers, much transport is required. When we set off in the royal barge, we are the beginning of a convoy of boats. The weather is dull but fairly warm although acrid smoke of a black and poisonous variety is hovering in the sky above as we approach the city of London.

Henry stretches out his ample limbs on the cushion and breathes a sigh of contentment. His mood changes are frequent and always unexpected but I have learned to soothe his minor moods of disquiet by singing softly to him or reciting passages of his favourite poetry. I can even achieve the almost impossible and turn a bad tempered outburst back to reasonably good humour by reading a poem written by him and, at the conclusion, telling him how much I like it and how highly I regard him as a musician and poet. And in the evening, when we lie together, indulging in gentle copulation with soft, soothing words of love to accompany, always works so very well. He initiates the soft words of love but I return them tenfold!

Many merchant ships are moored along our route, most bound for Europe or beyond with cargos of merchandise from our city. As we proceed down past Blackfriars and towards the Tower, there is a flurry of movement along the banks on both sides as travellers halt their horses and people divert their walks to approach the water's edge and gaze at the Royal procession.

'Wave Jane, make to look bonny,' Henry says. 'This is their first glimpse of their new queen.'

'I will sir,' I tell him enthusiastically. 'I do hope I meet with the people's approval.'

He laughs loudly. 'You need not fear, white lamb, after the great whore, who was most unpopular, you should be received with delight.'

I lean forward so that little of my face and form is obscured under the canopy and wave briskly, ensuring first that I have a big smile on my lips. I continue to wave as the barge drifts slowly past although the people at the waterside seem turned to stone, immobile, silent. I turn back and look to Henry with a pout on my face but he entreats me not to stop or waver. I must, he insists, keep waving and smiling. I renew my efforts diligently.

'Look Henry,' I say. 'They are beginning to wave back.'

'What did I tell you?'

'It's wonderful,' I say, laughing and contented. 'Look at them all now.'

A number of people are gathered at the water's edge and they seem to be joined by more and more as we proceed. Henry leans forward and waves and smiles in tandem with my own efforts. Suddenly a great cheer goes up and I hear a chorus of voices say 'God save the king.'

Then silence for a few seconds that feel like hours as I continue to wave and smile. Then another cheer bursts out and I hear 'God save Queen Jane.'

I am delighted and my smile is broad indeed as I turn to Henry, who laughs.

People pick up their baskets and bundles and some of them move about their business as others linger.

The crowds begin to thin out as we drift past the Tower of London and we settle back, anxious to avoid the bad odours and the swirling chimney smoke around us but powerless to alleviate the ill effects. Soon though, we are past those environs and the dank air of the city is replaced with fresh, country air, pure and refreshing. As Henry seems now to be in good humour I mention tentatively, a matter that has been on my mind a lot.

'Have you given any more thought to my suggestion about bringing your daughter Mary back to court?' I ask, somewhat nervously.

He frowns and does not reply. I say that I realise that it is a delicate matter but it is one that I hope he can see his way to resolving.

'It would best be resolved by leaving her where she is, to rot,' he says, brusquely.

'Oh but sir, she is your own daughter,' I cry out, stung by his response into being a little incautious.

'Yes Jane, she is,' he says in stark tones. 'But she refuses to abandon her Roman church and, worse still, refuses to acknowledge me as the head of the church in England.'

I sigh, sad and heavy of heart.

'Even a daughter cannot be allowed to deny me my position as supreme head of the church and the state. She is too much under the influence of her mother.'

'I thought perhaps that now,' I say tentatively, 'that her mother is dead, this might be the time to bring her back to court.'

'While she maintains her present attitude and beliefs,' he says gruffly, 'that will not be possible.'

'But sir---'I begin, only to be interrupted.

'—Enough Jane, enough. We will speak of this matter no further.'

And so it is, with Henry silent and glowering and myself wondering if I have put him in a bad humour for the rest of the day. We drift along slowly as the approach to Greenwich Palace comes into view. It is another magnificent edifice, much changed by my husband who has added a new banqueting hall, armoury, stables and diverse outbuildings. As we come alongside the landing stage a small group of citizens seems to appear suddenly from nowhere. As we come to a halt and alight, Henry whispers to me to smile and acknowledge the bowing that is going on all around us. The guards stand close to the king but he is in no danger, these people appear happy and smiling.

'God save your majesty,' somebody calls out and another adds, 'and our lovely queen.'

As we pass by a small throng, a woman in rough-hewn clothing with a small, scruffy boy at her side, says 'give us yer blessin' yer majesty.'

'A long and happy life to you,' Henry says and pats the small boy on the head.

I smile at the woman and nod as she curtsies and I pat the boy on the head gently. His head is rough, greasy and dirty and I have to control my natural inclination to pull a face of disgust as we pass on and into the grounds of the palace. Henry looks grim as we walk around but I follow him as he strolls here and there, looking towards the armoury and then heading on down to the tilt yard.

'I loved jousting,' he muses, absently, not really addressing me or anybody in particular.

'Not any more sir?' I ask.

'No. I was thrown from my horse last January and lay unconscious for two hours. They all thought I was dead.'

'Oh how terrible' I say quietly. 'That is appalling.'

'It takes more than a bad throw to kill me,' he says, chuckling. 'Although it caused panic and confusion to Cromwell and the courtiers.'

I can imagine. We head up towards the palace and the king dispatches me to the Queen's chamber and bids me spend an hour sewing or embroidering. I nod assent and he suggests that I gather a few of my ladies to join me. He says he will be in conference for some time and I must amuse myself but he will see me for dinner. He informs me that most of the afternoon will be concerned with affairs of state.

I am escorted to the chamber by a young page and when we are settled, with Anne, Jane, Mary Arundell and Margery Horsman, I take up some embroidery. The ladies are in effervescent mood, remarking on the unexpected number of people we saw lining the route and at the landing stage. Anne tells me that it did her heart good to observe how warmly I was received.

'Yes, 'I say, reflectively. 'It did please me also.'

'Queen Anne was never popular with the people, Margery contributes. 'They hated her.'

'Oh surely not,' I cry out. 'You exaggerate.'

'No my lady,' Anne says. 'They blamed her for turning the king's head and destroying Queen Katherine. She was very popular.'

'Yes, I know,' I say softly and sink into a quiet reverie. We become silent, with only the sound of stitches breaking the peace in the chamber.

*   *   *   *

At supper time in the great hall it is difficult to judge Henry's mood. As soon as he is settled down on the top table, he engages in conversation with the Duke of Suffolk and barely even acknowledges my presence. A large roasted swan is brought in and slices carved for Henry, who has started off with an eel pie. I settle for some slices of white chicken and cherries.

'I do not fear the fucking French king or any of the minions surrounding the bishop of Rome,' Henry shouts truculently, 'but I do intend to step up our barricades and fortresses.'

'All along every coastline?' asks Suffolk incredulously.

'Every last one,' Henry roars. 'I will not risk invasion of these islands and the safety of our people.'

He is getting quite irate, as I note from his red face and glowering expression.

'But the cost, your grace?' Suffolk continues, regardless.

'It will be met partly, be assured,' Henry answers, raising his voice another notch, 'by closing down the Roman monasteries and seizing their revenues.'

Suffolk raises his eyebrows but seems to have finally learned to close his mouth and say no more. Henry finishes his eel pie and waves away the swan slices that have been cut for him. The servant hovers but Henry tells him to get out and bring in a leg of mutton with gallandine sauce. The man retreats confused and heads to the kitchen. I find myself hoping that the squires of the kitchen have cooked mutton on this night or the king's temper will flare up. Another servant approaches and offers lobster or woodcock but Henry waves him away irritably.

‘How went the meeting Henry?’ I ask tentatively.

‘Do not concern yourself with it Jane,’ he says snappily.

I do not pursue it because, for one thing, his abrupt advice not to concern myself has answered my question. It has gone badly which means, in turn, that somebody, possibly Cromwell, has disagreed with him about some policy or other. Most likely it is the king’s determination to close all monasteries the length and breadth of the land and seize all their assets and put it to use bolstering the military. I know from rumours that fly throughout court that this is unpopular with many ministers who are still feeling raw at the parting from the Roman church but are not brave enough to say so. They have all sworn allegiance to the king as head of the church and state and know that Sir Thomas More died for refusing to do so.

‘Will I see you in your privy chamber later sir?’ I ask, for nothing has been said to me about his plans for the evening.

‘No Jane, go back to your own quarters,’ he says. ‘I have much further business to attend to after supper.’

So that confirms my suspicion that things have not gone the way he wished and he will not rest until he changes that situation in his own favour. The servant returns and says that mutton was not asked for tonight’s menu and he regrets that none has been cooked. The king is furious. He demands to know why not, when he, the king, has a taste for leg of mutton. The poor man trembles on the spot but he is saved much more abuse when the squire of the kitchen approaches, bows and apologizes profusely and says he has a fine, rare roasted beef joint, if his majesty would care to try it.

'If I wanted your cursed roasted beef,' Henry shouts, 'I would have asked for it.'

There is an ominous silence and then, after a minute or so that seems like an hour, the servant asks, timidly, if he should bring in the beef. Henry asks the servant if he is being facetious. The man shakes his head but Henry, in a fury, calls for a yeoman warder. When he faces him, the man appears to be trembling although he is a big, well - built fellow who looks strong as an ox.

'Get this man out of my sight,' he commands. 'I should really punish him with a few days in the tower.'

'Oh, but Henry---'I start to say but one look at his red, furious looking expression and I close my mouth. The man is led away and the squire asks the king what his pleasure is next.

'My pleasure is for mutton leg,' he answers. 'But you don't have any.'

'No, Your Grace, I'm very sorry.'

'Bring the beef and make sure it has thick gravy and is very rare.'

'Yes, Your Grace. Would it be your pleasure to have cabbage and onions with it?'

'No, it would not,' he snaps. 'Do I look like a yeoman farmer or a peasant?'

There is an uneasy silence and everybody at table looks uncomfortable. The Duke of Suffolk coughs and Norfolk clears his throat. Henry glares at both of them. To break the silence I suggest turnips to him quietly; I have already found that they represent one vegetable he finds palatable. He glares at me but then his expression softens somewhat and he pats my hand gently.

'Turnips,' he says, facing the squire. 'And a few olives.'

The meal proceeds. Everybody is looking uncomfortable and conversation is muted and spasmodic. The king eats very little of his beef and appears to have lost his appetite. He turns to me and asks me what I would like to conclude the meal. I tell him that sugared almonds with a little jelly would suit my palette and he perks up, just a little and says that would suit him also. We drink ale and consume the sweetmeats that are brought.

When I return to my Queen's chamber, I expect to be there for some considerable time but I'm surprised to be asked by a page to return to the King after just one hour. I enter and find him looking relaxed and having shed some of his heavy garments.

'I thought the business of state would take some time,' I tell him, taking the seat he indicates for me.

'I think they are beginning to see what needs to be done,' he says. 'I've called a halt for tonight and will pick up the reins tomorrow morning.'

I smile and accept the drink he has poured for me. Noting his mood at supper the council have most likely decided to agree with whatever he says to maintain a life of peace. I do believe that his foul tempers are instrumental in getting him what he wants immediately in some situations and, knowing Henry, he plays on it up to the hilt.

As he seems in a much better mood now, I decide to make one more attempt to raise the matter of his eldest daughter, Mary and ask him if he has given it further thought.

'Why should it concern you Jane?' he asks in a surly manner. 'She is nought to you by blood or anything else.'

'No sir, 'but she is your daughter, 'I say and add, softly, 'she is your flesh and blood.'

'Indeed she is Jane,' he agrees. 'Sadly though, there is a long way to go before I can accept her as such.'

I pout and tell him that it makes me sad to see him so at odds with his own dear girls. I know it is not my business and I must not interfere but I feel so wretched about it, I feel I want to help him to put it right. His face clouds over but only for an instant and suddenly changes; I see a smile light up his face.

'Oh Jane, Jane, what am I to do with you?'

'Me sir?'

'Yes, you sir.' He says laughing. 'You are so soft and quaint and concerned for others, white lamb. Do you not think of yourself ever?'

'I am content sir,' I reply, indignantly. 'I have you and your love and everything any woman could desire.'

'Come to me,' he commands.

He takes me in an erotic embrace and we move over towards the king's bed. As he becomes more and more amorous, I halt progress suddenly.

'What Jane, what ails you?'

'What can be worked out and resolved about Mary?' I ask, looking most concerned.

'I really don't know,' he says, in clipped tones. 'I will give it some further thought.'

TEN

June 9th 1536.

The king is not having it all his own way this morning, of that I am sure. I can hear his voice bellowing out angrily from the council chamber from the top of the corridor as I walk briskly down to join my ladies. The voice is even louder as I pass by on my route and the words, 'ships, I must have new ships, I will have new ships, I will not be thwarted in this,' are heard resonantly, probably the length and breadth of the palace. He is back doing battle with his council, something he is most at home with whether it be the French, the Spanish, at war generally or just fighting his own people; it is all one to Henry.

My ladies are at ease in the chamber. Anne is reading, Jane has needlework in front of her and the others are in a relaxed state. The sun shines outside, visible now through the mullioned window. I take my seat and survey the room. Mary Norris appears quite animated and I ask her if all is well.

'Yes, all's well indeed, she says gaily. 'We were remarking before you entered that the king is to have three new warships.'

'How can you possibly know that Mary?' I ask, somewhat peeved at her tittle tattle.

'Oh it's out now, I heard it from Mary, Lady Monteagle.' She tells me happily. 'She is friendly with Norfolk and he told her.'

'Well,' I say, somewhat frostily, 'it is not really for general discussion until the king announces it, is it?'

'No ma'am. I'm sorry.'

The chamber falls silent. Needles move rapidly as stitching becomes focused as everybody concentrates on the work in front of her. I too drift into silent thought; the idea of new warships and fortresses all around our coastlines makes me think, with dread that the king is expecting an invasion, possibly multiple invasions and that means war and bloodshed. I would like to see peace, perfect peace for our island, now and in the future.

'One point of interest Mary,' I say, casually. 'Have they all agreed on three new ships to be built?'

'No indeed,' Mary answers, looking warily at me. 'But Lady M says the king is demanding it furiously, pointing out that any opposition to such a scheme would be tantamount to treason.'

'I see. Alright, thank you Mary.' The subject is now closed as far as I am concerned.

'And what the king wants,' the tactless Mary Norris continues, 'the king gets. One way or another.'

'I think we've exhausted this subject now,' I say, icily. 'And would be well advised to leave it alone.'

'I'm sorry ma'am.'

We revert to silent sewing and embroidery until I hear voices and footsteps in the corridor. It is the halfway point of the morning's meeting and the king, as is his habit, will take a half hour break, strolling round the grounds before resuming. I send Mary for a page.

'I would desire you to approach Master Cromwell,' I tell him, 'and if he is not in conference with the king, or walking with him, inform him that I would like to speak with him.'

I instruct the ladies to take a short, refreshing walk in the summer sunshine and when they are gone, call for some ale. Cromwell, all in black as usual, arrives swiftly, gives a short bow in my direction and stands in front of me, his expression bland.

'Master Cromwell,' I begin, brightly. 'I am sensitive that upon our last meeting I was less than as civil to you, as indeed I should have been.'

'The queen was polite and I was in no way slighted,' he says, tonelessly.

I put him at his ease by offering him a seat and some ale. He accepts with a brief nod of acknowledgement and sits facing me. I tell him that it is a delicate matter that I wish to discuss and he nods again, a barely perceptible movement of his head on this occasion. I tell him that I am concerned about the position of the king's daughters, Elizabeth and, in particular, Mary, the eldest and think it is time for her to be returned to court. I wonder if he could get the king's ear on this subject and advise him accordingly. He frowns, the only sign of animation I have seen on that face in a very long time.

'It will not be easy,' he says.

'No, I didn't imagine it would be.'

'Mary, tucked away at Hunsdon, is not even permitted to write to him.'

Hunsdon house in Hertfordshire is spacious and comfortable and has good shooting which the king enjoys on his visits. It is not that the Lady Mary, as she is now called, by the king's command, is not well placed and in comfort but, rather, that it is unfair that she should be left there, unrecognised by Henry as his daughter and downgraded socially.

'I consider it a tragedy that she is left there,' I say quietly. 'She should be restored to court and re-instated as Princess Mary. As to Elizabeth, she is but a child of three years and will not worry unduly or even know who is looking after her or why. But Mary will feel slighted and depressed in her present situation.'

'It is compassionate and worthy of you that you should feel so,' Cromwell says as he entwines his hands together, something I've been told he does when thinking out deep problems.

I point out that there are many in this land that think of Mary still as next in line to the throne and that she should be able to take her place as Queen of England after Henry dies, if no male heir is born. He sighs and cautions me to tread very carefully with such a view; I may not share it, publicly but I should not even voice it abroad as things stand presently, at court.

'No, you are correct Master Cromwell,' I say. 'But is there a way forward sir?'

He finishes his ale and places it on the table with slow, almost exaggerated deliberation. Then he begins to walk slowly around the chamber, head bent forward as if considering some great problem of state. When he stops and looks at me I see by his expression that something has occurred to him.

'It can do no harm, I think,' he says, 'if I approach the king and seek his permission for Mary to write to him.'

'But will he agree?' I ask. 'What do you think Master Cromwell?'

'He will want to appear magnanimous,' he replies, with the ghost of a smile forming on his lips.

'Yes,' I say. 'I think you are right.'

'It will be a beginning,' he murmurs, moving back towards me. 'Something to get the ball rolling.'

'Thank you Master Cromwell,' I say, amiably. 'I am indebted to you sir.'

'I am always at your service,' he tells me, looking rather self- satisfied I feel.

As he leaves the chamber I reflect that I still do not like the man, much less trust him but, if I can use his influence over the king, which is considered to be all pervasive at the present time due to his securing the speedy execution of Anne, I will not hesitate to use his services. He is a devious individual who will seek to gain favour with me in an attempt to further enhance his popularity with the king but I am not above turning his ambition to my own advantage.

The king calls me to his chamber as soon as his council meeting is concluded. I hurry along and find him at leisure, drinking ale and he wants to know how I spent my morning. Very quietly sewing with my ladies and talking about how best they should conduct themselves, I tell him, as some are new to court He nods, looking very preoccupied and serious.

'I have a fancy to walk further in the grounds,' he says blandly. 'Walk with me Jane.'

'Me Sir?' I ask, surprised. He has not asked me to join him in a stroll before.

'Yes, come with me please.'

The route is Henry's usual one by all accounts. He walks down past the armoury and along past the tennis courts and then heads in the direction of the jousting field. Henry is silent at first as we walk along but as we stop to lean over the rails at the tilt yard, he tells me that Cromwell went off to meet and speak with somebody during the recent meeting.

'I want to know who he spoke with,' he says, speaking quite harshly.

'Is it important?' I ask timidly.

'Of course it is,' he says irritably, voice rising up. 'Intrigue is ever present these days. Particularly since the reformation of the church. I may be in danger. You may be in danger.'

'You can trust Cromwell, surely,' I suggest.

Henry laughs, a throaty, harsh and unpleasant sound. He looks at me and shakes his head.

'I wouldn't trust Cromwell further than he can be thrown,' he says, harshly. 'I keep him close to me but he is as slimy as a snake.'

'But you make use of him,' I say softly.

'I do,' he says. 'But I need to know who he spoke to earlier.'

We continue walking and go down to the edge of the Thames where two large merchant ships have just berthed and are awaiting the loading of cargo. Henry turns and walks beyond them to gaze out and down- stream. I tell him in plain, matter of fact manner that he need not investigate further, Cromwell came to see me. He stops walking, looks astounded, turns to me and asks why.

'I require all my ladies to wear a girdle of pearls,' I tell him. 'Anne Bassett's girdle was inadequate, it lacked the correct number of pearls. I asked Cromwell if he would have a quiet word with her mother, Lady Lisle, to advise her of the right number.'

Henry roars with laughter. He has only had me by his side as wife for several days, he tells me and already I am fussing and fiddling with court etiquette concerning Ladies-in-waiting, like an old hen. I smile and reply that I want to establish my own rules of behaviour and dress code and general court etiquette and what on earth is wrong with that?

'Oh, nothing, nothing at all white lamb,' he says, still laughing. 'What am I to do with you?'

'Treat me well sir, treat me well and love me always,' I reply.

He is not aware of it but the tale of Cromwell being requested to speak to Lady Lisle about her daughter's pearls, is true. It was not the subject of this afternoon's conversation though and I do not want that discussion put in jeopardy at any price.

ELEVEN

June 1536.

We sit under the canopy at White Hall listening to the various requests from courtiers and others for over an hour. Henry turns to me as the last one goes on his merry way and sighs. He finds it all very wearying he tells me and will be pleased to step out and walk around the grounds. The king expresses the hope that we are clear at last but I remind him that Cromwell has requested a word with him.

'What does he want?' Henry asks irritably. 'I can see him anytime, he's always hanging around like a sick and worthless puppy dog.'

'I've no idea, 'I say but it is not true.

Cromwell enters, moving slowly and deliberately and after a few words of needless praise for the king's ego says that he has heard that the Lady Mary would wish to converse with him. Henry snorts and says that no such conversation can take place and that young woman should look to her behaviour and her past treachery and eventually request the opportunity to beg his forgiveness for her utterly reprehensible behaviour and way of life. Cromwell agrees enthusiastically and is shocked at her sheer presumptuousness but wonders whether the king might give her permission to write to him.

'For what good reason?' Henry asks truculently. 'Have I not given her every opportunity in the past to mend her ways and behave like a true daughter of a generous and magnanimous sovereign?'

'Indeed you have sir,' Cromwell replies. 'I wondered if you might consider giving her an opportunity to write and beg forgiveness for her stubborn stupidity and see you for the gentle, forgiving, loving father that you really are?'

'She tries my patience too much Cromwell.' I want to beg him to relent, to allow her to write but know full well that he would only become more stubborn and probably lay into me for interfering. I remain silent.

'You are right,' Cromwell says. 'She simply doesn't deserve so generous and forgiving a king as you are sir, she asks too much.'

'Disobedient, ungrateful girl that she is.'

'It is true,' Cromwell mutters, shaking his head.

'What do you think Jane?'

I tell him, gently, that no girl could have a more loving, kind and generous father and her behaviour really entitles her to no concessions or consideration. But knowing him for the warm hearted father he is, I fully expect he will grant her request, underserving though it is. He nods his head all the time I am speaking his jowl bobbling passionately. He turns to me and says he knows I would like him to be generous, even though it be undeserved. I nod agreement.

'I'll do it for you Jane,' Henry says at last. 'There is no gentler more loving wife in this kingdom Cromwell, know you that. Send her my blessing and permission to write to me.'

Cromwell nods and with a few more words of sycophancy, takes his leave.

'Walk with me Jane,' the king commands suddenly.

I go with him and he enters the bowling green. His previous generous gesture, as he sees it, is past and he is already questioning his own decision. He is muttering darkly about Mary's refusal to accept him as supreme head and her ongoing loyalty to Rome. He storms off suddenly and I follow, anxious not to vex him at such a delicate point in my attempts to get Mary her rights. He begins to get in a state of anxiety as we wander down to the grounds and walk through a sunny parkland.

'I see danger all round Jane,' he says. 'If that girl rallies her Catholic and Imperialist friends to destroy me, what then?'

'She wouldn't sir,' I say, softly, shocked. 'She is your daughter, your own flesh and blood.'

He mutters that she cannot be trusted and he would be foolish to entertain overtures from her until she renounces the Roman religion and accepts him as supreme ruler; head of church and state. I try to assure him that she will soon come to her senses once she is able to write and communicate with her father but he becomes angry and calls me a naïve fool. It seems that I have overstepped the mark although, in God's name I do wish I knew where the mark is sometimes!

'She will never change,' he roars. 'And you Jane are a fool to try to help her and a thorn in my side while you continue to do so.'

He is working himself up into a bigger and ever bitter rage and I feel powerless to halt the flow of his venom. I start to protest my good intentions always towards him and his but it is useless. He tells me angrily to be gone to the Queen's chamber and stay with my ladies while he goes and recalls Cromwell to reverse his decision about writing. I watch him stomp off in a rage and shake my head wearily. Where do we go from here?

*   *   *   *

Supper in the banqueting hall at York Place, White Hall and the king is in quite jocular humour. Earlier he did lie with me and whispered words of love and affection, twirling strands of my hair round his finger and saying I was the best and only love of his life. He praised my soft, white complexion and luxurious fair hair and told me he loves to gaze into my blue eyes. His lovemaking was uncharacteristically warm and gentle and he was concerned that I should be content and pleasured and have no pain. I am content!

My Lords of Norfolk and Suffolk and the Bishop Sampson have been summoned to sup with us and are seated round the big table. Henry presses all three to enjoy the delicate taste of the peacock and advises that a good roast mutton joint will be here directly with gallandine sauce and boiled leeks for contrasting flavour. The three eat heartily, making a feast of the peacock but the king seems listless and without appetite and I can tell that there is something weighing on his mind. He picks delicately at some white chicken and cherries but spends more time drinking ale from a large tankard and calling for it to be refilled.

'I have a duty of the utmost importance, 'he tells them. 'That I wish you to carry out tomorrow.'

'Of course Your Grace,' Norfolk says. 'Anything within our power.'

'I wish you to travel to Hunsdon to see the Lady Mary.'

Sampson nods and smiles, a very weak smile. Norfolk looks suddenly alarmed but retains his composure almost immediately. They are all three very attentive to the king now and the roles are somewhat reversed; he begins to eat a little more heartily with the arrival of his much loved roasted mutton and the other men are paying little attention to their food. Not being involved in the conversation, I call for some chicken and begin to eat.

'You are to inform her,' the king says, raising his voice and looking very angry suddenly, 'that I regard her as a monster in nature. I find her wilfully disobedient, ungrateful, angering her father and sovereign and arousing the indignation of Almighty God.'

Suffolk nods agreement, followed by Norfolk and the bishop says that he will do his utmost to bring the lady to God and suffer her to honour her dear and just father. Henry nods impatiently and goes on to say that he requires them to recall to Mary his gracious and divine nature, his clemency and pity, his merciful inclination.

'You are required to stress my displeasure at her imbecility,' he continues.' and you must be sure to depict me as ever ready to take pity on all offenders who are ready to repent.'

'I will point out all those things and more,' says Norfolk, boldly. 'I shall remind her that she is a traitor and could, by a less compassionate sovereign, pay with her life.'

Henry nods his head slowly, still wearing a frown of concentration. He waves his hand at the steadily accumulating dishes of hot food that are piling up on the table and bids all present to eat heartily. The king, still not satisfied with what is in front of him, calls for venison and the servants bring out deer and hare, decorated with cabbage leaves and thick red gravy. The visitors finish their first courses and accept platefuls of venison, along with Henry.

'I am not an unreasonable man,' Henry says wistfully. 'Many would say I am over generous in my desire to forgive the Lady Mary.'

'Indeed they would sir,' Suffolk says obsequiously

'She must acknowledge me as supreme head of the church,' Henry continues ruminatively. 'That is paramount.'

'Or face death on Tower Green,' Norfolk whispers.

'You need not mention that,' the king says, quietly.

It shocks me to the very core that he is obviously considering such a punishment; for his own child! I feel my appetite evaporating swiftly and pick ever more delicately at the food on my plate as the other four eat with appetite. In my most despairing moments I simply cannot reconcile the gentle lover who twirls my hair round his finger with such delicacy of touch with the man who, at times like this, appears to be a selfish, uncaring monster. How on earth are these two distinct personalities merged in one bulky male frame?

As the meat courses disappear or are, at least, reduced to bones and rubble on the table, Henry invites his guests to eat sweetmeats. All three decline and after drinking the health of the king and his queen, as they put it, put down their tankards and bow their way out of the banqueting hall, walking backwards, having stated their intention to ride to Hunsdon at first light tomorrow morning.

'For you Jane,' the king says, sitting back expansively and wiping his chin with a napkin. 'Some sugared almonds and gingerbread?'

'No thank you.'

'Some preserved fruit perhaps?'

'I couldn't eat another morsel,' I say coldly. 'Thank you.'

'What ails you little white lamb?' he asks, voice vibrant but gentle.

Nothing ails me I report and when he presses me I say, merely, that I am just a little under the weather today and will be fine after a good night's sleep. Nothing will induce me to mention the king's daughter again tonight although I wait patiently and with genuine, concerned anticipation, on the outcome of the visit of my lords of Sussex and Norfolk and the Bishop Sampson.

TWELVE

June 11th 1536.

I walk slowly down through the lush grounds of Hampton Court Palace towards the Thames. It is a pleasant day with some sunshine, warm and comfortable without being too hot. The river flows peacefully on with fish jumping and a feeling of peace and calm pervades my mood. I am hopeful that the problem of Lady Mary, as I must reluctantly call her, will be soon resolved. The king awaits a reply to his latest letter but she has been evasive in the past weeks and his temper has fluctuated according to what he has learned about her. Cromwell has advised him that she will be sensible and appreciate the kindness and thoughtfulness he has shown towards her. I hope that she will not antagonise him for I fear for her comfort and safety if she does.

I move towards the bridge and pause by a stone seat to sit for a while. A herd of cows are being ferried across the bridge by a broadly built farm worker. They move slowly, laboriously but fit in with the peaceful mood of the day. A bell tolls in the distance.

My initial concern for Mary has been intensified in the past few days as news has reached me that Elizabeth is also in need of being restored to favour in the king's eyes. Lady Bryan, her guardian, has, Cromwell tells me, been voicing deep concern because the little mite has 'neither gown, nor kirtle nor petticoat, nor linen for smocks, nor kerchiefs, sleeves, rails, stychets, handkerchiefs, mufflers, nor begins.' The good woman also let him know that the little princesses' teeth were causing her great pain, causing the lady to give her her own way 'more than I would.' It seems a parlous state of affairs and I am shocked that the king allows it, if it be true.

I complete my walk down through the village where few people are abroad and start on my return journey. The guards that Henry has assigned to me are keeping their distance, as I required them to do but in any event, I have not, I think, been recognised.

I reflect sadly that I must advance the cause of the little Lady Elizabeth to the king, when I can catch him in goodly mood but not, I think, until the fate of Mary has been established. She is, after all, in most people's eyes, even if they dare not speak it, next in line to the throne if there is to be no male heir. It saddens me very much that he has had both girls declared bastards as he refuses to acknowledge the validity of either of his previous marriages.

As I approach the king's chamber my heart sinks as I hear a loud, angry voice raised. The king barely notices me as I enter and Cromwell, standing in front of him and, it appears, almost trembling as his grace pours out his invective.

'The Lady Mary,' Henry bellows,' writes to me that she lives in my mercy, next to Almighty God.'

'She means no offence,' Cromwell says, almost in a whimper, his voice is so strained and emotion charged.

'No offence?' Henry roars, his face red as paint. 'Next to Almighty God! Which Cromwell, as I'm sure you are well aware, means that she has not condescended to acknowledge me as Supreme Head of the Church?'

'She will sir, she will,' Cromwell says quickly. 'I will visit her again and make the situation plain.'

'The situation has been plain for years Cromwell, make no mistake. And be advised that if I have occasion to punish her, I will punish you and Norfolk, Suffolk and the Bishop Sampson who have all betrayed me vilely in this matter.'

I sigh, explosively, unable to control my feelings. The king turns to look at me, fury in his expression. He seems to be waiting for me to speak and so, intimidated, I say softly that I have prayed and am still praying that the Lady Mary will see reason and appreciate that he is anxious to forgive her and restore harmony to their relationship. He shakes his head and says that people will have to realise that he will not be thwarted in this matter. I beg him to show mercy and compassion but this just triggers a fresh outburst.

'Do not interfere Jane,' he shouts. 'This is not within your realm of influence.'

I stand in silence.

'Get out,' he roars at Cromwell. 'And do not return until you have resolved this situation satisfactorily.'

Cromwell departs hurriedly, after bowing and keeping his eyes on the ground.

Henry watches his departure, his whole frame twitching with nervous irritation; unable to control his fury or his temper. He complains bitterly, in a loud and raucous voice that he is surrounded by imbeciles that will not do his bidding. He pauses for just a brief moment and then begins pacing the large chamber, spitting out invective about his daughter Mary. She will not be allowed to continue to follow the illegal Catholic faith and refuse to take an oath of allegiance.

'Better people than her have refused such an oath,' he says angrily. 'And look what befell them.'

'Oh please, my lord,' I say, tearfully. 'Don't say such things.'

'Do not presume to tell me what to say Jane,' he bellows.

'I cannot help myself,' I tell him. 'She is your eldest daughter and deserves your love and protection.'

For a moment he just stands perfectly still and glares at me, eyes glinting with angry passion. Then with a quick movement he moves forward and slaps my face with such venom that my eyes water and the harsh sting in my cheek burns fiercely. He does not speak and I am incapable of speech. After what seems a long time he turns and marches briskly out of the chamber. I reach for a handkerchief to dab my sore eyes and stem the free flowing tears and sit down on the nearest chair. For my own safety I must endeavour not to argue or question anything he says or does again.

* * * *

June 1536.

The Lady Mary stands in front of me, a forlorn looking figure indeed! She is a mere twenty years old but a stranger might put her age at nearer thirty five. Or even more. Her face, once bonny, framed by dark brown, almost black hair, is thin looking and parched. Her pallor is greyish white and her eyes, listless and lacking any sparkle, stare out bleakly at the world. She looks so forlorn, so bereft of peace of mind or gaiety that my heart goes out to her before a word is spoken.

Master Cromwell has delivered her to my chamber and bids me look after her until she is called to take her oath. The king has summoned her immediately after receiving her latest letter, in order that she may repeat its contents to the king and council and take her oath.

I bid her be seated and send a page for some good quality ale that we may drink and talk together for some time. The king is out arranging for some falcons and other birds to be made ready for him tomorrow. He is keeping his own council people waiting and will not hurry on his daughter's account. I tell Mary that I am pleased to receive and see her.

'Oh, and I you, Gracious Queen,' she replies. 'You have been so good to me.'

'No more so than you deserve Mary,' I tell her honestly.

'Oh, you are my friend,' she says, eagerly, with some small colouring appearing in her cheeks. 'My Gracious Queen and mother.'

'Great heavens above,' I say. 'I am honoured but to call me mother seems so strange. I am but eight years your senior.'

'You are, I think, my saviour,' she says soberly, the expression reverting back to solemn sadness. 'Ever since that day you visited me, barely two weeks before the execution of that woman.'

The page returns with our ale and sets it down for us. Mary takes a drink immediately and I realise, with a little jolt, that she has travelled from Hunsdon with the rough, pitted tracks shaking her bodily and is now hot, tired and much in need of refreshment. I raise my tumbler and clink it against hers and make a toast to a happy future. I too drink heartily.

'So,' I say, brightly, 'your last letter pleased his grace.

'At last,' she says with a sigh and a wan smile.

I tell her that I am delighted and praise God that it is all resolved at last and hope that, in due course, she will be restored as Royal Princess, a title she is entitled to by birth. She bids me shush and says if the king's spies should overhear that, her dear friend and gracious queen will be in severe trouble. I shake my head as though it is all of no consequence.

'I said in the letter that I most humbly prostrated myself in front of him, as his most humble, faithful and obedient servant, terming him merciful, compassionate and most blessed and I acknowledged him as Supreme Head of the Church, disavowed the Pope as a pretender, and declared my mother's marriage by God's law and man's law, incestuous and unlawful.'

'Well that should satisfy even Henry,' I say quietly. 'It is most brave of you Mary.'

'Indeed. I just hope I do not burn in hell for it! Ambassador Chapuys advised me that God regards more the intention than the act.'

'I'm sure that's true,' I say gently. 'We are all forced to make statements we would rather not, these days.'

I notice that she is beginning to look nervous once again and remind myself that I must keep her talking and take her mind off the upcoming interview in the council chamber. I talk vaguely at first about the uncertain times and our uncertain futures but then I get around to something more specific.

'The king is hopeful of a boy child as heir,' I say briskly. 'But if I fail to deliver, and it is in Almighty God's plan that I do, you would be first in line after the king's death.'

'Oh no,' she says smiling. 'My father is robust and strong indeed and may outlive us all.'

'He becomes weightier by the day,' I say, smiling, 'and will do well to reach sixty I wager.'

I see that Mary is becoming more animated by our conversation so I continue with the idle speculations. I tell her that when Henry goes, many people think that we will all revert back to the true religion. She cautions me to be careful. Walls have ears.

'I will be a loyal subject,' I tell her.

'I can't see it,' she says, shaking her head. 'The king will leave his crown to the Duke of Richmond.'

'No, no, that cannot be,' I say, smiling. 'The boy is a true bastard, the son of one of Henry's whores. Even Henry can't change that. There will be no illegitimate king in England.'

She looks thoughtful and says that in any case, Richmond does look very sickly and has always been in poor health. She doubts that he will live beyond thirty. Much more animated now and gaining a little colour she says that if she is ever Queen of England, I shall be Dowager Queen and have a place of honour at court. Always. I have done my job I think and cheered her a little. I send for more ale and fill our tumblers. Mary says that she hopes my support of her has not caused problems for me with the king. I tell her that things were a little fraught before her latest letter arrived but he is calmer now.

'He can be a bully,' she says, frowning. 'But not to you I hope, dear Jane.'

'He did strike me, two days ago,' I say, quietly,' and I was very upset. Last night he wanted to lie with me but I told him I regretted it very much but couldn't, as I had begun to bleed.'

'Oh I'm so sorry Jane,' she says, obviously genuinely upset.

'No, no, all is well,' I say, smiling. 'Things are getting back to normal slowly.'

She looks haunted temporarily but I grin at her and tell her that I know how to look after myself. I rarely make the same mistake twice.

'Take heed though,' I say in a whisper. 'I am not bleeding yet but the king knows nothing of women's bodies or times of the month. Nor will he ever know.'

We both laugh and I tell her I can be devious too. When it suits me. And she need have no worries over her faith. God knows her worth and will forgive.

'Do you love him Jane?'

'I do,' I tell her. 'I don't understand why but I do.'

We sink into a quiet reverie and very soon the call comes for Mary to proceed to the council chamber. She looks ill at ease suddenly and I take her arm and walk along the corridor with her.

'Take a deep breath,' I say, 'and repeat the words of your letter and take the oath in a quiet but firm voice.'

As we approach the chamber, a door is opened and she is ushered in. I return to my own chamber safe in the knowledge that Mary has been sensible and acknowledged her father in all that he demands. Now, I pray, she will be safe.

THIRTEEN

June 1536.

We ride out very early today, bound for Hudsdon House in Hertfordshire to visit Mary. It is already very hot and will get much hotter as the day proceeds. Henry leads the way, coaxing his grey horse to a steady, comfortable clip and ensuring that I can keep steady pace with him. The procession follows us as we ride out through the fields of green and leafy trees of Highgate. The high sun, Henry tells me, indicates a scorching hot day ahead so we are well advised to arrive as early as possible and gain shelter from the burning rays.

Apart from our immediate party of guards and servants, nobody knows of this trip. Henry wishes the visit to Mary to be secret, as rumours of one sort or another are likely to occur if it is announced in advance. I am a little apprehensive, wondering how Henry will treat the daughter he has had so little contact with for so many years and considering that their last face to face meeting was in a council chamber where she renounced the faith she was born into and had practised since birth.

My white horse is beautiful; Henry tells me that he selected it specifically for me, checking out and rejecting dozens of others. He tells me this morning, being in goodly humour and seeming to be in a mood to patch up any bad feeling that might still exist between us, that he had to have a milk white horse of the most delightful shade for his little white lamb! Am I to feel flattered and well-loved and forget all my hurt at his vile outbursts of temper and exhibitions of cruelty? On such a morning, with early mists dispersing, the sun shining and the sky as blue as Safire, I do confess to a forgiving mood.

Henry bids me increase my pace and we sprint off across two wide fields, keeping parallel to the rough track that delivers us to our destination. I can easily keep pace with the king's burst of speed and handle my horse proficiently. As we slow down to a canter, he nods to me in acknowledgement of my prowess and I give him a smile in return.

'You trained and learned well in horsemanship,' he says, as we trot along, side by side now.

'My father was keen for me to ride,' I reply. 'And I took to it like a duck to water.'

As the imposing façade of Hunsdon comes into view, we slow down to an amiable trot. Henry has built upon the original house to fashion a palatial building, with Royal apartments and a moat and drawbridge to ensure privacy and unwelcome intrusions. He has also, I understand, spent much time here in the past, hunting in the deer park and holding banquets in the newly built house.

At a signal to the gatehouse occupant, the drawbridge is raised and we trot into the courtyard. Attendants and grooms appear suddenly as though out of nowhere and it is not very long before we are greeting Mary in the long hall. She smiles and curtsies to the king but he takes her by the shoulders and kisses her forehead gently. She seems surprised and momentarily put off balance by this but recovers swiftly and moves towards me. I embrace her openly and kiss her cheek.

'I fear that too much time has been lost,' the king says when we are settled. 'I regret having been separated from you for so long daughter.'

I am surprised but delighted to hear his first remarks. Mary beams.

'I too regret it father,' she says sadly. 'So very much have I missed.'

'Fortunately we have much time to make up,' he says. 'To put things right.'

'Oh yes, I hope so,' Mary says eagerly and beams again at her father.

She orders a servant to bring us wine and refreshments and two girls appear carrying the wine, tankards and a plate of sugar almonds, sweet fruits and little white marzipan balls. The king drinks heartily and I too find myself thirsty after our ride in the gradually searing heat of a June morning. Henry gobbles up several almonds, a sweetmeat that he particularly enjoys, possessing a sweet tooth. I pick delicately at some fruit but Mary shakes her head when I enquire about her joining us. Doubtless she has breakfasted much later than the king and myself.

'It is a pleasure indeed,' the king says, jocularly. 'To meet with you here and talk and drink and make merry.'

Mary smiles contentedly and I sit back wondering again how the king manages to change from angry tyrant to gentle, loving father so seamlessly. Is his mind and body split asunder depending on his constitution at any given time?

'I hope the wine is palatable to you father,' Mary says with a slight frown creasing her brow. 'It is a fair French wine and the best we have in our cellars here.'

'It's lovely,' I say. 'So refreshing.'

'Well, it won't compare with what you have at court I fear,' she says.

'We are pleased that you offer us your best,' the king says, still in jocular mood. 'It will serve well enough.'

He pats her hand like a loving father should and nobody could guess, looking at him now and listening to him, that a few days ago he was wondering what fate to meet out to her if she did not take his oath. He tells her that she shall have no further worries about money for she should have as much as she would wish.

'For your little personal pleasures.'

'Well, thank you father. I'm sure I don't deserve such generosity.'

'Now you must not say such things,' he admonishes her heartily. 'Or think them. Must she Jane?'

'No indeed,' I say, with feeling.

'About those little pleasures,' he says, eyes twinkling. 'Here I have a thousand crowns for you to use as you will.'

She thanks him profusely and I hand over my own present to her, a diamond. She claps her hands in delight and says it is beautiful. One talent I possess above all others is an ability to spot and acquire good jewels, with diamonds and pearls being particular favourites of mine. I am so pleased that she likes it.

'Now how do you occupy yourself,' he asks suddenly. 'Through long summer days and endless winter nights?'

'I keep fairly active father,' she assures him. 'I play tennis in the summer and walk in the deer park frequently.'

I am pleased to notice that there is a sign of roses in her cheeks and she has lost a lot of the drawn and pinched look she had on arrival for the council meeting. Her eyes too have more of a sparkle than the last occasion that we met and it is obvious that a great weight of worry and despondency has been lifted from her shoulders.

'I play the fox and goose game in the evenings,' she continues, smiling. 'Frequently.'

'Fox and goose?' Henry asks, puzzled.

'It is a board game,' I tell him, laughing. 'Where the fox has to eat the goose. Or try to. We played if often at home in Wulf Hall.'

'You surprise me Jane,' he says merrily. 'And you too Mary.'

'I must always be the fox,' Mary tells us. 'I insist upon it.'

Henry expresses a desire to walk around the house and check that all the alterations and additions he ordered on his last visit have been carried out satisfactorily. I offer to accompany him but he says he would rather go with a courtier and a servant, as he may wish to instruct them in the finer details of construction he still requires and add or subtract from work already in progress.

'You ladies may discuss the finer points of foxes and geese,' he says, grinning mischievously.

As he goes off with what, in effect has suddenly become a small train of attendants, Mary and I relax a little and she calls for more wine. She tells me that dinner will be ready soon and she has ensured that roasted leg of mutton will be served

'With gallandine sauce.'

I laugh. 'You remembered that?' I say.

'Oh yes, from days long gone by.' Her face clouds over. 'Happier, family days.'

'Well, we must live in the present now,' I say quietly.

'Yes, of course,' she answers. 'I've got woodcock and snipe and pigeon. I know he always liked delicacies at dinner.'

She tells me about the house and the various chambers she uses and the ladies that look after her. Her mood is full of gaiety and the day is proving to be a big success, our visit undertaken in relative secrecy notwithstanding.

'I am so very grateful to you Jane,' she tells me, solemn faced. 'For initiating my return to favour.'

'Well, we've only just started,' I reply. 'We must see about returning you to court and getting you re-instated as a princess of the realm, as you are entitled.'

'Oh, now, let us not be hasty,' she says briskly. 'I'd rather not risk the king's disfavour by asking too much, too soon.'

'We'll bide our time,' I assure her. 'Have no fears on that account.'

She becomes silent and I too for a while. I mention casually that I would like to bring the child Elizabeth back into the king's favour; she is hidden away at Hatfield and in sore need of clothes and other accessories. I notice that Mary looks uncomfortable and enquire what ails her.

'I'm sorry,' she says, 'I have an unreasonable aversion to that little child I'm afraid but that horrible creature, her mother, treated me so abominably when she was queen.'

'It's hardly little Elizabeth's fault though, I say, gently. 'She is a bonny little girl.'

'Yes, I suppose so. I really must try to be more tolerant.'

'She too has been deprived of her inheritance,' I say, thoughtfully. 'And is, after you Mary, in line for the throne of England. If I fail to produce an heir.'

Mary nods and after a very brief pause, smiles. At that moment the king reappears, looking hot and flushed from his walks on this hot summer day and announces that he is feeling very hungry now and is hopeful that dinner will be served forthwith.

We do not speak so much at dinner and the king appears to be in a reflective mood. At first I am concerned that something, some trifle perhaps, has put him out of humour. He enjoys his leg of mutton as usual but only eats a small portion and slices of the game birds provided.

'What ails you Henry? I ask softly, as Mary is in conversation with one of her lady companions.

'No, Jane, I am not out of humour,' he tells me. 'Just the thought of loss compounded by today's journey.'

'Loss sir?'

'The lady Elizabeth, that tiny tot,' he says, still in reflective mood. 'I have not seen her little face for so very long.'

I brighten up and look at him and fashion a big smile on my face. I suggest, tentatively, that we go out to visit her but he frowns and looks vexed. He tells me that he is busy for a good few days ahead with birds of prey, hunting and matters of parliament all clamouring for his attention.

'You could go Jane?' he says as a question.

'Yes,' I answer, quite eagerly. I have been concerned about her ever since I arrived at court.

'Only to check on her health and lodgings,' he says, more coldly. 'She is illegitimate but I feel a certain responsibility towards the tiny mite.'

'I would be pleased to go and see her tomorrow,' I say, decisively.

After we finish eating, the king expresses a desire to take an hour of rest. A bedroom is hastily prepared for him and I find myself speculating yet again on the many sides of this man's character. The bold warrior of old, strong of arm, strong of limb and powerful of build would never, surely, have admitted to feeling tired after a modest dinner? He is though, in his forties now and age is creeping up on him. He also has an ulcerous leg wound, agitated and made much worse by the heavy fall during jousting last January. I think to myself that I must keep an eye on the king's health from now on and try to arrange a physician's visit.

Riding home in the late afternoon, through rich pastures of green in Hertfordshire, the sun less intense but still burning red marks into our brows, I note the king's further melancholy. I wonder if he would really like to postpone the visit to little Elizabeth until he is able to accompany me.

'No Jane, it is meet that you go alone,' he says, as we fall into a slow jog past a rural tavern where people have spilled out into the pitted road to watch our progress as we trot past.

'But you sir, would like to see her,' I say. 'Would you not?'

'It is a two edged sword,' he tells me sadly. 'I do feel concern for her but she reminds me of that cursed whore, she who I will not speak of.'

'I understand,' I say gently. 'I'll travel alone.'

He pats my leg, smiles, calls me 'white lamb' again and then sets off at a fast gallop across the fields of Highgate, leaving me, surprised, to tug on the reins and set my own white horse off in pursuit of his.

*   *   *   *

June 1536

I start out even earlier this morning, anxious to fulfil my mission and return to join the king at supper. The weather is intemperate, lacking the early sunshine of yesterday but warm and fresh withal. A damp mist covered field and hedgerow at first light but is clearing slowly now, evaporating in drifting clouds towards the greyish sky. I ride hard and quite fast, confident that my guarding companions will keep up with me. I reach Hatfield in very good time and I am shown into the oak panelled room on the ground floor where Elizabeth's guardian receives me. She bids me be seated and provides much needed refreshments.

'I am glad to welcome you, Your Majesty, she says. 'Your good name and compassion precedes you.'

'Thank you,' I say and smile. 'Let us hope that I am worthy of it.'

She is a broad built, handsome woman with grey streaked hair and a rather round face that shows her to have been a beauty in her youth. She is well attired in a crimson gown with velvet facings and overall, a healthy pallor. I ask about Elizabeth.

'Oh she is well enough,' she replies. 'A lively, bright child, always involved in whatever childish game she indulges in.'

'The letter you sent to Cromwell Lady Bryan,' I begin, slowly, 'indicated concerns about her.'

She suddenly wrings her hands together and looks at me imploringly. She tells me she is concerned about the shortage of clothes the child has and how worn some of them have become. She also says that she needs a bigger allowance of coins for bed-clothing, coverlets, and many sundry items.

'If you could use your influence with the king,' she says. 'The poor little princess should not want for anything. She is the king's daughter after all.'

'I'm none too sure I have much influence in that quarter,' I tell her, smiling. 'I'll do what I can of course. Trouble is, Lady Bryan, he does not acknowledge her as a princess and insists upon her illegitimacy due to the illegality of his marriage to Anne.'

'Oh God be praised,' she answers, 'she is his daughter, no child more so.'

'Lady Mary is in a similar position,' I remind her.

She has no sympathy with that one she tells me, a true bastard if ever there was one, the daughter of Aragon, the Spanish pretender. I shake my head, musing over the wide variety of prejudices people have and tell her that both girls are in similar situations and, in my view, equally deserving of sympathy and consideration.

'I meant no offence Your Majesty,' she says, looking stricken. 'Forgive me.'

'You must leave it with me,' I tell her. 'I will see what can be done.'

She takes me to the playroom where little Elizabeth sits playing with spinning tops and clay marbles, watched over by a buxom nurse. The child looks up at me and I smile at her but she remains fairly stone faced. I suggest politely, that I be left with Elizabeth so Bryan and the nurse depart. I go over to her and sit on the floor and pick up a clay marble.

'Hello,' I say brightly. 'You must be Elizabeth.'

She nods to acknowledge her identity but does not speak. She seems to be looking at me with a mixture of curiosity and mistrust. I roll a marble and hit one of hers, sending it off to the left. I watch her closely as she prepares and then sends her marble rolling towards one that I have set up. She is a bright eyed, intelligent looking child with red hair and I smile as I recognize something of Henry in her expression and in the way she concentrates on what she is doing.

'Are you the queen?' she asks suddenly.

'I am, yes,' I reply.

'My mama was the queen.'

'Yes,' I say softly. 'That's right.'

'Now she's gone to heaven.'

'Yes,' I say. 'She has.'

She looks sad, thinking about her mama no doubt but then she seems to shake off her melancholy and concentrate on playing marbles. I play a game with her and we do not speak again for a short time. As I play with her and watch her childlike movements and the toss of her head if she misses contact with a marble, I suddenly feel a wave of guilt that I flirted openly with Henry when he was still with Anne and their marriage had not yet fragmented. What on earth was I thinking? I should go to confession but I dare not considering the subject of my sinning.

We set up the marbles and I spend some time playing with her in the nursery and when we hear the bell announcing dinner she leaps up and takes hold of my hand as we leave the chamber.

'Dinner time,' she says brightly. 'And it's fish today.'

'Fish today,' I repeat solemnly. 'Always fish on Friday.'

FOURTEEN

Arriving back very early due to a fine ride, with clement weather that was neither too hot nor cold, I seek the sanctuary of my own chamber and some of my ladies-in-waiting. Mary Norris is looking animated when she arrives, following my summons. She did not ride with me earlier, complaining of a 'bad belly,' but she seems lively and fit enough now. I take up some personal brocade work on a new but plain gown that Henry has given me, after first gazing out of the window to watch the flight of a blackbird, dipping and swaying gracefully through the air. I ask Mary if she is now fully recovered.

'Oh yes,' she tells me, contentedly. 'It was just a sore belly.'

'The king is in bad humour,' Anne says suddenly and I look up sharply, as this is not what I desire to hear.

'What have you heard Anne?' I ask, trying not to frown or look unduly concerned.

'I just heard shouting from the council room,' Anne says, looking defensive suddenly.

'Do you know what about or what was ailing him?'

'No,' she whispers.

'Come along Anne,' I say, persuasively. I know her too well and am aware that she knows a lot more than she is offering. I tell her that I want to know all she has heard, even if most of it be merely rumour.

'All I know Your Majesty,' she begins, slowly, 'is that Ambassador Chapuys is reported to have been sending sharply worded requests to the king to renounce his church and go back to the old one. The king was shouting and cursing him and instructing Master Cromwell on how he should put the ambassador in his place.'

'It seems to me you heard a lot,' I say, smiling. 'And all that just as you passed by a door. Merciful heavens!'

Anne blushes scarlet. But I do not care to question or reprimand her for snooping or standing listening outside closed doors. It wouldn't stop her anyway with me being out of sight and out of mind. I am more concerned with the king's frame of mind and, specifically, his temper.

I find out as I am summoned to his presence in his privy chamber. He looks in foul mood as I enter but he greets me, stony faced and trusts I had an agreeable journey. 'How about you sir?' I ask but I am almost afraid of the answer.

'That cursed thorn in my side Chapuys has been causing problems,' he complains, voice raised angrily. 'I wish I could have him thrashed.'

I sympathise and try to soothe him with soft words and assurances that he will be able to deal with it all, no man is more competent to do so but he brushes my platitudes aside with anger and puts down my arms that I have attempted to place on his.

'That is not the worst, curse it,' he says and begins pacing the room agitatedly.

'What Henry?'

'My son, Henry Fitzroy is very ill.'

'Oh, I'm so sorry,' I say. I have only met Henry once, when he was at court during the days of Anne and I was one of her ladies-in-waiting. His mother is Elizabeth Blount and she was the king's mistress during his marriage to Katherine of Aragon. The birth of his son was known to the commoner peoples but I also know that Henry is very fond of the boy and often expresses the wish, to me and others close to him, that he could see more of him. Alas though, he is truly illegitimate and must be kept apart from his father much of the time. The king has honoured him though and created him Duke of Richmond.

He is a callow youth of seventeen years, pasty faced and with doe eyes and a long nose. I think he must resemble his mother Mistress Blount for I see no likeness to Henry in him. He is though, the son that Henry craved for and that he could not have in wedlock with either Catherine or Anne and he thinks very highly indeed of the boy. He is also consumptive, doubtless the cause of his present malady. No expense however, will be spared on his treatment with Henry's physicians offering various pills and potions.

Henry has stopped pacing and sunk down on a chair and he is holding his face in his hands. I walk over and sit down gingerly, close to him. 'Are the physicians in attendance?' I ask very quietly.

'They are,' he says, gruffly. 'I have instructed Cromwell to give them every facility and to report to me directly if they do not give him the very best that they are capable of.'

'They will,' I say. 'They will, with all speed and conscience.'

'I cannot lose him Jane,' he says, looking up at me from behind his hands, his face a pathetic expression of vulnerability and pleading, as though I had the power to ease his pain, cure his son's consumption and make his world happy and contented in one swoop. 'He is of utmost importance and concern to me.'

I promise to pray to Almighty God, every day for his safe deliverance and ultimate good health. I tell him that I am confident of Henry's swift recovery and long life. I take hold of his hand in mine and squeeze it but he pulls away, roughly, disentangles our hands and tells me angrily that simplistic platitudes will furnish no recovery, he is beginning, he says, to think that he is doomed; no male heir from his wives, who turned out to be illegal anyway and if I fail him what then? He must be doomed he says again as I try hopelessly to reassure him. God has forsaken him, he the king, his next in command, left him to struggle and suffer unbearable pain like a fish, caught on a hook.

'What am I to do Jane? He asks miserably. 'He is my only hope if you cannot produce a boy child.

'I sincerely hope and believe I shall so do,' I tell him, earnestly. 'But now?' I cannot help asking, 'is Henry your only hope?'

'I hope that he can succeed me and take his place on the throne as the next Tudor king.'

'Can that be sir?' I ask. 'Surely the question of illegitimacy cannot be overcome.'

'Oh indeed it can and will be,' he answers savagely. 'Do you not recall Jane, the act of succession which I required parliament to pass on June the eighth? Does it not give me full and plenary powers and authority to dispose, under my seal or by my last will, made and signed in my own hand, the imperial crown of this realm, and all other the premises thereto belonging, to such person or persons as shall please me? And I have a promise, by one common assent, that after my decease, parliament will "—faithfully promise to accept and take, love, dread and only obey such person or persons, male or female, as your majesty will give your crown unto; and wholly to stick to them as true and faithful servants ought to do."'

I am amazed that he has remembered all of it and much of it in the original words of parliament.

'A pretty watertight case,' he says boldly. 'Would you not agree Jane?'

I can only nod agreement, thinking back to the day he instructed Lord Audley in what he was to put before the new, hand -picked parliament and how faithfully they gave him the freedom to be head of the state, the church, and the people of England and pick his own successor at random. Henry now has full control over everything that happens in this land.

It is time for supper. He halts the conversation immediately and bids me get ready to go into the great hall. Henry shows some appetite for eels and picks out some salmon and perch to follow up with. I take a small portion of baked trout and as we sup I tell him about my trip to see Elizabeth. 'She is such a sweet little girl,' I tell him enthusiastically, 'and oh my, how she has grown in the past few months. You haven't seen her for such a time Henry.'

'Nor likely to for some time yet,' he says, chewing away contentedly on the trout.

'Would you not consider bringing both girls back to court?' I ask, hopefully.

'I don't think it will be possible,' he says, pausing for a moment from his supper. 'Both girls are illegitimate. Or rather they will be when the present act completes its progress through parliament.'

I cannot hide my disappointment and continue eating slowly and without interest or purpose. Henry coaxes me to try a little crab meat but I resist as he tucks into some and adds mussels to his plate. I drink some ale and we finish our meal as a troop of musicians come in and set up their instruments on the rushes. They start to play, a melody that sounds like one of Henry's but he appears to take no interest. Something is weighing on his mind. He signals to the musicians to lower the volume and leans over to me.

'Are you still bleeding Jane?' he asks anxiously.

'No sir,' I reply, sheepishly.

'Ah, that is good,' he says. 'Tonight I would wish to lie with you and we must hope that Almighty God blesses our union with a baby boy.'

Back in his chamber he is solicitous towards me, trying to make me comfortable and giving me sweet wine which he has had brought in for me. I drink slowly, watching him carefully for his moods are truly unpredictable. He becomes amorous, taking my hand in his and squeezing it delicately. 'Such delightfully small white hands,' he says. 'Such delightful soft white flesh all over.'

'Yes, My Lord?' I say, puzzled and a little confused.

'Do not fret little white lamb,' he says, laughing. 'You are my love, my one true love, do you know that Jane?'

'Am I sir?'

'Indeed you are.'

As we lie together he tells me that he will no longer fret about Richmond, his son. God will preserve him, he feels sure and if not, nobody on earth can do anything about it anyway. Tonight, he assures me, is about love making and tenderness and, if we are blessed by God in his ultimate wisdom, a son and heir for the English throne. He becomes more graphic concerning our lying together; he tells me in urgent whispers how gentle he will be and all the privy parts of my body he will caress and kiss. No other woman, he tells me gushingly, has ever meant anything to him, not in the way that I do. Do I believe him?

He is extremely gentle and considerate. Is this the same man who screamed in anger a few hours ago? And do I believe him? I want to believe him, I want to very much indeed.

*   *   *   *

Our carriage is halted temporarily in Piccadilly as a drover walks a herd of pigs across the street. Henry is impatient and calls to a knight to send the man and his beasts packing; he must get them out of the way or the king will run his sword through the man's belly and slaughter the pigs where they stand. Drastic but it does speed up movement considerably.

We are heading for St. James's Palace to visit Henry Fitzroy, the king's son. The latest intelligence informs us that he is much improved. What the king's physician could not achieve, his majesty's apothecary could, it seems. Pills and potions with certain herbal properties have been tried and seen to be effective although, we understand, the boy is still very weak. Henry is in a state of fear and apprehension considering the ongoing weakness and suffering of his son. He has been in foul temper for some days and many a servant, courtier and lady of my circle has endured stinging words and threats of punishment. Henry sits next to me muttering constantly that his poor boy is sick, almost beyond hope and what on earth has he done to deserve such suffering; he is but seventeen years of age and should be in the prime of life rather than lounging in his bed, rarely able to move. I make sympathetic noises from time to time but, really, when Henry is in this sort of mood nothing will comfort him.

We arrive and rushing in to avoid a sudden swirl of rain, are shown up to the boy's bedchamber. Henry kisses his pale cheek and I do likewise and we settle down by his bedside. He tries to smile but seems too breathless to exert many muscles. Henry asks him if he feels any better today.

'Improved since yesterday,' he answers. 'And a goodly improvement since the day before.'

'That is something,' his father says gruffly. 'Although your pallor is still grey since I saw you last. Is the apothecary helping you?'

I tell him he is looking a lot better, not because he is but as his father is not exactly tactful, I feel that he needs cheering up. 'The apothecary fills me with herbs and pills and heaven knows what but I do doubt overall it is much help or improvement,' he says, listlessly.

'Is he here?' Henry asks abruptly.

'Yes, he is down in the kitchen mixing up a potion,' the boy says slowly, his words seeming to be forced out painfully.

'I'm going to take a look around this place,' Henry announces, rising, 'and have a few words with that fellow.' He goes out before his son, raising a restraining hand can halt his progress. I say to young Henry that he must rest easily, not talk too much if it is painful and reserve his strength. He smiles and says he will be alright in a moment, when he gets his breath back. I nod and wait in silence as his wheezing gradually recedes and he seems to have recovered somewhat.

'I wish he wouldn't upset that fellow,' he says. 'He is doing his best.'

'Henry is just concerned about you,' I say softly. 'He wants the best for you, always.'

'Not for me,' he says, wheezily. 'He just wants a potential heir to the throne.'

I tell him that he is mistaken, the king is merely concerned for his welfare and his speedy restoration to good health but he does not look as if he believes a word I say and I must admit I have my own misgivings. I keep those feelings to myself though.

'No, no, he doesn't give a fig for me or anybody else,' he says truculently. 'Only for himself. As always. He made me have leeches to bleed me although I told him it only made me feel weaker. And he only gives me the court assignments he can't bear to take on himself.

'I can tell you Jane, I'm still haunted and having nightmares from having to stand on Tower Green and watch Anne's execution. He made me attend although I begged to be excused. I stood there, close by and saw her, all pale and white, shivering although it was a warm morning. Shivering with terror as the moment approached. She tried to be brave but she couldn't do it; she shook with fear and tears ran down her face and they prepared her and lifted her into position and then, an awful flash of steel as the blade cut through her little neck and her head flew off. Blood in torrents; I tried not to look but I was transfixed.' He shudders.

'Oh, poor boy, poor boy,' I say, in heartfelt tones. I want to embrace him and comfort him and take away his pain but it would not, perhaps, be seemly. Instead I take hold of his hand and squeeze it and say that he should never have been put through such an ordeal.

'Tell my father that,' he says with a sneer.

'I will talk to him,' I assure him. 'And make my feelings known.'

‘Good luck Jane,’ he says and laughs but that only brings on a severe bout of coughing and I have to rise and go to rub his back soothingly. The king returns abruptly and runs through a list of potions and medical remedies he has approved with the apothecary and instructs young Henry to see that he takes them all without fail. The young duke nods agreement, reluctantly, going by his expression but, it would seem, bowing to the inevitable and being too ill and weary to resist.

I wish him a speedy recovery to good health and his father bids him to be brave and take all of his medicine and pray to God daily and nightly for his deliverance. It is not what I would have said to a poor boy in terribly bad state of health and I give Henry a withering look as we depart but, of course, he does not look at me or see, or even sense, my displeasure. In the carriage he asks me how I thought the boy looked, as we dip and sway over deep craters in the road.

‘He is far from well,’ I say, honestly. ‘We must pray constantly for him.’

‘God will, I hope, be merciful to me,’ he intones gruffly. ‘And spare the life of my boy.’

I decide that I must ask, even though it might trigger an outburst of anger. ‘Why did you send him to witness the execution?’ I ask. ‘Surely he is too young?’

‘No Jane,’ he responds with steel in his tone. ‘He is the king’s son, possibly heir to the throne and he must learn to face difficult assignments in the name of the crown.’

‘Yes but Henry,’ I say, blood suffusing my cheek. ‘To witness such a harrowing event and him so young. And his constitution so weak. Couldn’t you have found a more suitable representative?’

'No, in God's name, do you not understand?' he roars. 'He is the nearest male blood relative and my son. He will need to show his mettle in future.'

I shake my head sadly but will not pursue it further. My motto is 'Bound to Obey and Serve' but there are times when I feel the restraints of that vow pressing in hard upon me. He reminds me that we are touching on that which, he has warned me frequently, must and will not, be discussed. I maintain a frigid, icy silence. As we reach White Hall the rain falls again in torrents and they bring out canopies to shield us from the downpour.

FIFTEEN

July 1536

A time for reflection. I sit under the big window in my chamber and listen to the chatter and giggles of my ladies but not really paying any attention to their inane outpourings. I have my own thoughts, my own private sorrows and at the moment they are not for sharing. It is little more than six weeks since Queen Anne died so horribly and only just over that when I became queen. Much has happened in the interim. My main concerns have been for the young Mary and the even younger Elizabeth, the king's daughters, still kept in isolation.

When I approach Henry to ask if they may be restored to the court he is at first evasive and later adamant. 'It is not the appropriate time Jane,' he says fiercely. 'And you must be patient and bide your time.' When will it be appropriate I ask coyly later and he flies into a rage and requests me not to interfere in matters of state, of which I know nothing. When the time is right, I may be sure, he will acquaint me with the news. So he says anyway. I do not pursue the matter further; not for the time being at any event.

The young Duke of Richmond's health does not improve much. He goes up and down and is given ever new potions to try, all initiated, I feel sure, by the king in league with his most trusted apothecaries. Some days he is up and his cheeks blooming but mostly he continues to deteriorate. I suspect but cannot prove that much of his gradual decline is due to the shock of watching the execution of Anne. He told me that the king had suggested to him that Anne had tried to poison him shortly before her own death but he said

'I do not believe that for one minute. She was never that cruel.' All of which serves to re-inforce my view that he was bitterly hurt and harmed by watching her sad demise from such close quarters. He and Anne were quite close.

Word has reached me that my father has been unwell recently and I must go to him as soon as it suits my lord, the king. He is an old man, sixty two years old and no longer strong or in good health. I find it difficult to forgive, as my mother has done, his adultery especially considering the manner of it but will not bear a grudge or think ill of him. He is my father and I love him as such.

My family have benefitted much since I married Henry. My father and my brothers; Edward has been created Duke of Somerset and Thomas is now Baron Seymour of Sudeley. My mother is comfortable and content whether she should be or not. I am content and at my leisure as Queen consort and Henry assures me that I will be crowned at Westminster, 'with all due haste and ceremony.' So be it. I will await the event patiently.

Henry continues to confuse and puzzle me. He struts about bullying all and sundry from the lords and ladies at court to the rawest stable boy. He is short of temper with me frequently and disagreeable most of the time. And then he will surprise me with little gifts of jewels and become amorous and gentle in the evening. His bulk increases daily but when dressed up in his finery and with trimmed beard and sparkling blue eyes, I find myself melting to jelly in front of him. Sometimes he is a monster, at others a god. Physically, he overwhelms me, in more ways than one. When I try to put it all into perspective I think about the young King Henry; the constant warrior, the unvanquished, fearless leader who led his troops into battle, fought harder than any of them and risked his own life for his country.

The present Henry is not the man he used to be but his reputation precedes him and he is still an imposing, impressive figure. And, God help and save me, I do love him.

Henry writes to Francis, the king of France and they both issue veiled threats, one to the other. However, the king is worried about invasion constantly and very fearful that the Catholic countries will team up to combine against him in a war he cannot win. To this end he is increasing the number of ships of war and fortifying every possible strip of coastline land. He fears invasion by sea more than any other.

His favourite ship, the Mary Rose, named after his sister, is being re-fitted completely and will lead the fleet once again. When I ask he tells me he is as ready for war as anybody and nobody fights with the passion and skill of the English. But he fears overwhelming odds, the force of numbers that France, Spain and Rome could mount against him.

We have spent a few days at Richmond Palace, a favourite of Henry's. He seems calmer there, more content and less likely to break out in a fury or become impatient with servants who make silly mistakes. The royal rooms are glorious with the beamed roof painted azure blue and studded with gold Tudor roses. The crenulated beams are magnificently carved and the rooms in general open, bright and with large panelled windows. It is good, too, on warm days, to walk in the gardens there; past the fountains and high walls and on past the chapel and the library. I like to linger by the carved animals that are studded around these lovely gardens and then go back into the royal apartments, with their lush tapestries, murals and oak panelling and just rest on a recliner and drink mead.

Too many times though, it seems that wherever we locate, Greenwich, White Hall, Hampton Court, Windsor or Richmond, I am left to sew and embroider or wander abroad through the grounds, at my leisure, with my ladies in attendance only to find myself, at twilight, soothing the brow of the king, His Majesty weighed down by affairs of state or worries of imminent invasion. In most instances however, I can calm him down and do seem to possess a magic potion of love and affection that puts him in a somnambulistic state after agitation. I hope to be able to facilitate this method in the coming months as he becomes more and more belligerent with every passing day.

* * * *

To some of the big houses in Berkshire and Buckinghamshire for the King's Summer Progress. It is an annual event of course and entails the monarch's hunting dogs, the chapel royal for religious services on the road and musicians to entertain him and his physician and apothecary to tend to his health. It is a large procession of carts and waggons, horses and flags waving merrily in the summer breeze.

The Knight Harbinger looks pre-occupied, sitting astride his horse and well he might, as the responsibility of securing accommodation at every house we visit, including arranging the best apartments for the king and myself and putting everybody in order of rank, is his and his alone. Put somebody of lesser importance in a bedchamber close to the king and there is an almighty outburst. Rarely though, from Henry himself who, as long as he and his wife are comfortable, lets the accommodation crisis run its course.

The weather has not really been kind. We have endured swirling early morning mists, thick as peacock soup, torrential downpours which, in turn, have made mud swamps of the roads and cold evenings, unseasonable though they be. These last have been most troublesome to the servants and page boys forced to sleep in hastily erected tents in the gardens of the smaller mansions.

Henry has been in good humour for several days now, sharing tales of battle with old knights who fought with him in war, engaging in bawdy tales over mulled wine in the crepuscular light of early evenings and laughing heartily at ribald jokes, told by ancient Dukes and commanders of armies. Now he sits with me in the carriage, jerking and jumping over rutted mounds of rain soaked earth on the roads, if I may describe them as such, of Wiltshire. True to his word, Henry has ensured that we are including Wulf Hall in the progress and I am to see my stricken father. Letters have reached me from Lady Margery, my mother, that he is much improved since last week but still very much out of sorts.

'This continual jumping up and down is intolerable,' Henry complains irritably. 'I would have a less sore posterior if I went back on my horse.'

'Then do so my lord,' I say jocularly, for I am in hearty mood in spite of the continuous buffeting of the cart's wheels.

'What about you though, white lamb?' he asks, obviously in considerate mood today.

'I prefer to remain here,' I say. 'I can last out the few miles to Savernake, even though my rear end will be like bruised mutton.'

He halts the procession and has his horse brought to him. We proceed at leisurely pace with the voices of some of the musicians singing a madrigal; a far more agreeable sound than the crunch of wheels on stiffened mud and the constant noisy shaking of the carts. The trees of the forest, as they come into view, have a plethora of differing shades of green with just a little pale sunshine gamely glinting through branches, spasmodically.

When we approach the drive up to the courtyard of Wulf Hall, the sun has come out fully and is bathing the grass and gravel leading to the buildings. We are greeted effusively by a contingent of staff and servants, headed up by my mother and father. Although my mother looks in good, rude health, my father, heavily wrapped in warm robe and shawl, looks bowed and frail. It is mid-summer now but he obviously has to be well covered to keep out chills and draughts at all times. His hair and beard, now snow white, remind me once again of his advancing years. Henry greets both of my parents heartily and acknowledges their bows and curtsies.

'Sir John,' he says standing square in front of him.

'Your Grace,' father responds. 'Welcome sir, indeed.'

'I trust you are shaking off your recent malady satisfactorily,' he adds.

'I'm much improved thank you, Your Grace,' father says courteously.

We are shown to the most luxurious and sumptuous set of chambers in the mansion, those that I have seen inside but never occupied as daughter of the house in previous years. Henry bustles about as he always does on arriving at a new location; seeking out the best velvet chair and ensuring that the view from the bedchamber window is bright and agreeable to him. It is usually a sign that the chambers and ante rooms supplied are satisfactory when he sits, clears his throat loudly and, if the journey has been torturous, as this one surely has, promptly nods off into deep sleep.

I settle down in my own chamber and send for Mary Norris. I ask her if all my ladies on this progress are settled comfortably and she assures me that they are. I thank her, despatch her on her way and seek out my mother. She was a beauty in her day but I am disturbed to see all the lines on her face now and the grey and white streaks in her hair.

'How has father been?' I ask, as soon as we are settled comfortably in her oak panelled bedchamber.

'He was very bad,' she says bleakly. 'I won't lie to you Jane, I've been very worried.'

'And now?' I ask gently.

'There is improvement,' she says firmly. 'But he still has much shortness of breath and a hacking cough which will not go away.'

'Oh,' I say, inadequately. 'I must go and see him shortly.'

She bids me wait awhile as he usually takes a bed rest at this time of day. He is still quite weak and will have found it a strain going down the hallway to greet the king and myself but could not be persuaded not to go. She makes a shrugging movement of her shoulders and raises her eyebrows to indicate the hopelessness of trying to stop father doing things he shouldn't. She tells me he has hardly made any journeys to Savernake in the past month and he has not been out hawking or even onto the bowling-green. Her eyes light up though, quite suddenly and she bids me tell her all my news of court. I tell her about Hampton Court and the endless richness of the many apartments there and about the great hall and the music that is played day and night. She smiles, delighted and I tell her, in more sober tones, of my concerns for Mary and Elizabeth and what has transpired to date.

'Oh Jane, you must not press the king against his will,' she says, looking anxious in the extreme.

'I know what I am doing mother,' I assure her, austerely.

'Yes but, daughter, you speak of him refusing to restore Mary to her rank,' she replies. 'And you must not vex him if he is adamant in this.'

'Slowly and surely,' I tell her. 'At first he would not even let her write to him. It was seemingly impossible for there to be any reconciliation whatsoever but look what has been achieved already. Next step will be arranged in due course but I will bide my time.'

'Oh please Jane,' she says, imploring me. 'Do not put yourself in danger for the sake of others. Do not vex the king in any matter.'

It takes me some time to soothe her and assure her that I am in no danger and will not pursue any matter if I know the king to be against it. The plain fact is that the king and I have a genuine love match and I can tread where others fear to go. This alarms her afresh but I again convince her that I will never take risks or, more importantly, the king's love for granted. I know what I am doing at all times.

Father is a different matter entirely. He lies back on the bed his face, hair and beard almost blending into one shade of white. I think at first that he is sleeping and should not have expressed a desire to see me but then I notice a flicker of movement in his left eye and he looks up at me, straining to focus his sight on my face.

'Jane,' he whispers.

'Yes father. I can come back later if you are too tired to speak?'

'No, no, do not move,' he says commandingly. 'My brain is active even though the flesh be weak.'

'Well, do not tire yourself unduly,' I say firmly and he smiles, appears to rally quite a bit and sits up in the bed, placing the pillow behind his head.

'Is that my little girl?' he asks, mock severe. 'Commanding me not to do something?'

'I'm most concerned for your well -being father,' I say.

'I'm alright,' he says brightly, 'I'm a tough as leather soldier and fighter and not one to give way to a milksop malady.'

'That's the spirit,' says the king, striding in unexpectedly. 'As a fierce old warrior we would never give in to light illness or coughs eh? How are you feeling now Sir John?'

'Better your grace, a lot better and brighter and all the happier to see you sir.'

Henry turns to me, laughs loudly and then tells me that this father of mine is a brave soldier who was knighted in the field by his father, Henry VII and also fought with him, Henry. He was present at the sieges of Therouanne and Tournay and meetings between him and the king of France. He was a very brave, selfless soldier in his day, none braver or more trustworthy. Most, if not all of this I know but I try to look suitably impressed by new intelligence.

'And what of the Field of The Cloth of Gold eh?' the king asks jocularly and my father appears to perk up instantly at the mention of this old place of meeting between Henry and Francis I, the French king. My father was there too. He smiles and nods his head vigorously as Henry reminisces.

'Tomorrow Sir John,' the king booms, in his most regal and commanding voice, 'we shall go hunting together round Savernake.'

'I wish verily that I could sir,' my father says, sadly. 'Unfortunately the flesh is rather weaker than the spirit and I would only hold up proceedings.'

'Ah, unfortunate indeed,' Henry says, looking slightly irritated. 'It will be good sport and the weather seems as though it will hold.'

'Father will delight in joining the hunt as soon as he is fully recovered,' I say softly although Henry ignores my words completely, just as though I hadn't spoken. He looks to my father and says perhaps a little hawking on the following day, a mild enough pastime surely and he may rest as the birds fly. My father nods in agreement but he will not be joining in any hawking if I have anything to say on the matter. He is ill, tired and in need of rest and, perhaps, a little fresh air that stops short of active participation in sports.

'For the present though,' the king says expansively, his voice vibrant but not over loud, 'you must allow me to send my best apothecary to attend you. He has potions that will set you on your feet in no time.'

'Thank you, Your Grace, it is most thoughtful of you,' father says weakly and I can see that the visit has gone on too long and is wearying him. I suggest that we leave father to rest and recover now. Henry nods solicitously, aware of my presence at last.

'One other matter,' he says before we depart. 'I'll have my page bring you a tankard of posset. It is a healing drink, much used in France, consisting of milk and wine.'

'Your Grace is most kind and considerate.'

'May Almighty God aid and speed your recovery,' Henry says as his parting words.

As we reach the king's quarters he begs me come in and sit with him awhile. I ask coyly about my ladies and wonder what they will think if I am away from my chamber and most likely, in their minds at any rate, dallying with the king. He says let them think what they will, their minds are like privies anyway, all of them and he laughs at his own humour. I sit with him, as he settles in the velvet chair and I take the much smaller one near to it.

'It was gentle and kind and generous of you,' I say to him. 'To be so concerned for my father's health and well-being.'

'Anything in the world for you, little white lamb,' he says and looks as though he means it. Again, I feel I am seeing yet another side of this complicated man. Henry tells me he will pray hard and frequently for my father's full recovery; he doubts that Almighty God will not listen to a king of his eminence and will feel duty bound to answer his prayers in the affirmative.

* * * *

After supper the musicians troop in to my father's banqueting hall and set up the virginals. There are flute and recorder players, a cornetist, an hautboy practitioner and a man with a sackbut. We are all at leisure after a fine supper that my father has ordered and my mother supervised. The music goes on for some time until Henry, in the absence of my father as host, dismisses them and carries on playing himself. I listen entranced as he plays recorder and then flute and finally the virginals. The music is rich, melodic, evocative and much of it, I suspect, composed by Henry himself. I am almost overwhelmed by the delicacy and beauty of his playing and the look of delighted concentration on his face as the notes tumble out. One tune, which I am sure is by his own hand, is so sweet and pastoral that I feel, just for a minute, that I am sitting in a field of soft grass and flowers and the sun is beating down on me.

This cannot be the same man who sends men and women to their death on Tower Green, and rants and raves and screeches. It can't be. Can it?

SIXTEEN.

A raw morning, early chill and a thin mist over field and hill although we are well into summer. A grey day, lacking sunshine and even much warmth at this hour of morning. I leave my father tucked up in his bed still and my mother supervising the smooth running of the household and join Henry in his most joyous pastime: the hunt.

It is exhilarating to feel the breeze on my face as our horses race through field and past thicket, into woodland glades and dense forest patches. The greyhounds run and snap and bark and we follow their paths, searching out the prey. Henry looks wild and free in his hunting attire and I see him smile at me, red cheeks puffed out as he concentrates on keeping the horse steady on course and getting himself prepared for the kill. He winks at me as he pulls ahead and charges after his dogs and I pull heavily on the reins and steel myself to keep within his sights and stay very much in the thick of it.

As the light mist gradually dissolves, the air becomes warmer and more like a summer morning although the breeze from the speed of our horses is tangible still as we ride hard. Suddenly, a cream coloured hart comes into view, running at speed and zigzagging all the way across a field; I see Henry in joyous pursuit and I worry momentarily for he is not as quick and fleet of movement as he used to be. Then I observe the movement of his bow as he lines up, shoots his arrow with deft skill and speed and the animal falls to the ground.

I catch up with Henry and dismount and as he prepares to fire another arrow into the beast, to complete the kill, I avert my eyes, turn around and look the other way; I cannot bear to witness the final killing shot. The courtiers all crowd round to congratulate his majesty and he issues brief instructions for removal of the carcass back to Wulf Hall and further demands for picnic food to be brought to where he settles.

Henry takes my arm and leads me in the direction of a clearing at the side of a patch of woodland. Here pallets are laid swiftly and He smiles at me, looking much pleased with himself.

'Well done,' I say; it is expected of me.

'It was an easy kill,' he says, unable to keep the excitement and pride out of his voice. 'It appeared suddenly as we were almost on top of it.'

'All the same you should take care my lord,' I say, frowning. 'You are no longer young and your bad leg could take much worse if you fell from your horse.'

'I've been hunting since the age of ten Jane,' he tells me. 'I can almost do it in my sleep.'

'Well I was worried for your safety,' I say with a pout. 'I couldn't bear it if you were badly hurt.'

He wraps his big, muscular arms around me and kisses my forehead. I must not fret he tells me and he indicates with one instantly freed arm, where he wants the various food, drink and spoons laid. We settle down on the now fairly warm grass. It is a dull, cloudy day but the temperature continues to rise, slowly.

'So you care for your Henry, your lord and master,' he says, jocularly. 'You were concerned for my safety white lamb?'

'I was indeed sir,' I tell him and I can't stop myself pouting.

'I still have the gift as a huntsman' he says, winking. 'It will not desert me Jane.' The servants bring cold leg of mutton, a venison cake, onions, artichokes and tankards and a large jug of ale. We set about eating and drinking and I find I have quite an appetite although it is not yet near noon. Henry makes short work of a large mutton leg and washes it down with a huge draught of ale. I join in but eat much more slowly and with delicacy. He starts to tell me about the thrill of the chase and how the anticipation of finding and killing prey has always excited him, as a youth and right through to the present day. He compares it with battle and games and other sports and says it is almost as exhilarating.

I nod and try to show interest but I don't really want to think about death and destruction; not even the fate of a poor animal, caught at the end of Henry's arrows. This man I am married to, this impressive prince, all six feet of him, craves constant excitement and vigorous occupation. He is as good and as competitive at games and sports, as he is at fighting in wars but sometimes, it seems to me, can scarcely tell the difference. He would get much the same thrill, I wager, winning a game of tennis or killing a stag, as piercing the heart of an opponent in battle. And always, always, he must win.

'Tomorrow is for hawking,' Henry says suddenly, digging out a chunk of venison cake with his spoon. 'Will you join me, Jane?'

'I think sir,' I tell him soberly, 'I must remain at Wulf Hall and spend time with my father before we move out.'

'Yes, yes, that may be as well,' he says, nodding. 'Let me know if my man's potions and special drinks have helped his condition would you?'

'Yes Henry,' I say, smiling.

The progress is coming to an end so the next day is likely to be our last at Wulf Hall. I hope I can leave with my father well on the road to recovery and looking less listless and pale of face than he has this last four and twenty hours. My mother too looks strained and grey, her face is lined and she is doubtless feeling the pressure of my father's ailments. I hope fervently, to leave my folks in much better health than I found them on arrival.

* * * *

I move steadfastly along the corridor towards my privy chamber and a quiet hour or two with my needle. I have a colourful gown of bright yellow and a wish to embroider some gold brocade upon it. My ladies will be in attendance for anything I might desire and the king is out hawking. I peered through the small panes of my bedchamber window and saw a hawk, flying high and then swooping down suddenly, gracefully, to settle on Henry's outstretched glove.

My thoughts of two or more hours of leisurely embroidering are shattered however as I encounter Lord Cromwell just outside his office. He is now made Baron of Wimbledon by the king. He inclines his head to me in greeting and I give a barely perceptible movement of mine in response.

'Might I encroach on your time madam,' he asks civilly. 'And request an opportunity to speak with you?'

'Certainly Lord Cromwell,' I reply, cheerfully and walk into his room. His desk is spread thickly with bundles of paper, sealed rolls and stacks of quills; most of the contents being state papers no doubt as he is now first minister and secretary to the king. He pulls forward a chair for me and politely settles me into it before taking his place behind his massive oak desk.

'Bad tidings I regret to report,' he says, grim faced.

I feel a sharp little pain in my bosom and a grip in my belly, wondering what is amiss now. He seems to take an age to proceed when I ask what is wrong.

'Henry Fitzroy, the Duke of Richmond is dead.'

'Oh no.'

'Rather sudden, I am advised,' he continues, stone faced and showing no sign of any emotion of any kind. The young duke died earlier today after a fit of coughing and spluttering and there was nothing, according to Cromwell, that the king's physician could do. He begins to twist his hands together slowly, deliberately in a manner that I have observed many times when he is less than comfortable or at ease.

'I should go to the king,' I say. 'He will be suffering.'

'I thought, with regard to that,' he says, slowly, watching my face carefully, 'you should be forewarned. He is much upset.'

'Yes, thank you Lord Cromwell.'

'It will most likely put much pressure on the king and also on you my lady,' he continues tentatively and he drops his eyes to stare down at his desktop.

'Yes, well, thank you for your concern,' I say, more confidently than I feel. 'Nothing however that we cannot handle I'm sure.'

It is only when I have left him floundering, as he rises to his feet while I depart, that it occurs to me that he is being insolent in even broaching such a delicate matter. His reference to 'much pressure' can only refer to the succession and need of a male heir to the throne although he, Cromwell, should know nothing of Henry's plans to legitimise Richmond before today.

I walk swiftly to the king's chamber and enter to find him alone and sitting morosely on his velvet chair. He is weeping silently, his big shoulders shaking rhythmically and he hardly appears to notice that I have entered the chamber. I wonder how long he has been like this; when last I saw him he had a hawk landing on his outstretched arm.

'Jane,' he mutters and rises to his feet and embraces me, holding me close to his chest for what seems an eternity.

'I'm so, so sorry,' I say softly into his chest.

'The poor boy is dead,' he mumbles. 'And he so very young.'

'Yes.'

'What have I done for God to abandon me like this?' he roars, disentangling himself from me and striding off across the room. He suddenly picks up a plate and hurls it with force at a tapestry, causing a tear in the fabric. I try to console him and tell him that I am with him to support and love him but he is temporarily inconsolable. I leave him to rant and rave for a moment and go off to send for wine which, I instruct, must be left in the ante chamber. When it comes I get the page to pour two goblets and I take them in and bid Henry sit with me and drink. He approaches, eyes red rimmed, sits and takes a large draught of wine, drinking it down like ale. I fill his goblet and he drinks again and thrusts it down and weeps again, openly, a fresh flood of tears. I am becoming emotional myself now and begin to cry, in sympathy with him no doubt but I do feel a sense of loss for a young life and overwhelming sadness.

'He was my boy,' Henry says pathetically. 'My only boy.'

I want to comfort him now; I want to forget all his past misdemeanours and cradle him close to me to take away his pain and hurt. He snuffles a bit and then shakes his head and mutters about undignified behaviour and sits up straight and glares at me.

'God is punishing me,' he says, bleakly. He wishes to destroy me. He will not give me a son and heir and he has taken away the one boy I could have legitimized for the crown.'

'It is very sad,' I say. 'But we will recover Henry, you and I and we will have a boy child.'

'And if we don't?' he asks interrogatively, raising one eyebrow.

'Mary is next in line to the throne,' I say, softly.

'She will not reign, she will never reign,' he says contemptuously. 'A mere woman will never occupy the throne of England. Even if she were not illegitimate she could not do it. What are you thinking of Jane?'

I shake my head and say that we will have to produce a boy then, he and I. He starts to pace around the chamber, thinking out loud. There must be a funeral but not a state occasion, it would not look seemly. And he cannot attend. He will ask Lord Norfolk to make arrangements for burial at Thetford Priory, near where he lived. He sends for Norfolk.

'The boy shot a deer dead with his arrow,' Henry says in a quiet voice that is almost a whisper. 'He was just six years old. Did you know that Jane?'

'No sir,' I say. 'But he was a bright boy indeed. Ahead of his time.'

'Just six years old,' he repeats, as though he can scarcely believe it, even after all these years.

We are quiet for a moment, sitting awaiting the arrival of the duke. Then Henry grabs my hand suddenly and says we must put all personal feelings and desires aside and concentrate all our efforts on producing a son and heir. I do not think very much of the idea of lying with Henry in intimate embrace, over and over, with nothing in mind but the creation of a prince of the realm; I shall have to steel myself to submit to him under the most distasteful, for me, circumstances but will not vex him now in his hour of grief.

'It is imperative that we lie together regularly now,' he says. 'Every night for a month, at least.'

'As you wish My Lord.'

'For the future of the realm Jane,' he says, pompously. 'For England and the people.'

I assure myself that Henry is calm now and over the worst of his state of shock. He is quiet, saying little, drinking wine. I say that I will leave him to make arrangements with Norfolk and I will return to my privy chamber and my ladies. I walk down the corridor briskly but not briskly enough to avoid almost bumping into Cromwell as he returns to his office. He inclines his head to me and I acknowledge him but we pass by and do not speak.

The thought of lovemaking purely for the purpose of producing a prince is playing heavily on my mind and causing me some distress thereof. I could refuse my favours of course but what horrors would that instigate. I think about Anne Boleyn, the queen that was and is no more; she could not produce a son and look what happened to her. She produced a girl, Elizabeth and a stillborn and she was accused of adultery and treason and lost her head.

And who set her up for execution and gathered all the evidence of adultery against her and did the same for five men who were close to her? And who stood on Tower Green, close to her, to watch her die? That would be Thomas Cromwell, the same man that sits in his office along the corridor here, now or wherever we set up court; sits there like a cold black spider waiting to do the king's next bidding, whatever that should be and whatever life or lives are to be forfeited. Full of venom and poison of all shades, he is to be feared and respected for, if he can bring down one queen------but I must not think like this. I must set my mind straight for the future that lies ahead.

In my privy chamber I gather my ladies around me and tell them the sad news although I get a distinct impression that Mary Norris already knows. It is something about her eyes and the glint in them. Anne and Jane are full of condolences and look suitably sad and melancholy of expression. I continue with my brocade embroidery and there is an air of stillness save for the sound of knitting, embroidering or sewing all around.

Mary Norris seems unusually animated and I ask her what is on her mind. She approaches and settles down close to me. She asks me what my view is with regard to the monasteries. I ask her in what respect she asks.

'The rumour around court is that they are all to be closed down,' she says, watching my face warily.

'Where do you pick up such gossip Mary?' I ask. 'I doubt it is accurate information.'

'I think it originated with Lady Lisle,' she says blandly. 'And that source is usually impeccable.'

'Well, you had better not spread it further,' I say, irritably.

It is generally known that a few of the smaller monasteries with very small incomes have been closed down and their monks transferred to other sites. But all of them, which must run into several hundred?

'They say the king has instructed Cromwell to close them all.' She continues.

'I rather think that I would know about it,' I tell her sharply. 'If that should be the case.'

Henry has mentioned to me, in passing, that there are too many small monasteries that do not provide any income and are unnecessary and would be best put out of commission. I did not think, at the time, that he meant to imply any major re-organisation.

I continue to embroider and engage in light conversation with my ladies but I am listless and anxious to find out more about the monastery situation. I feel the Holy Roman church is being systematically expunged from the face of England's green and pleasant land by Henry in his determination to be head of church, state, government and everything of significance in the land. I do not wish to offend Almighty God but I have been assured, some time ago, by an honest and devout cardinal, that I will not be punished at the day of reckoning, if I remain true to the holy religion in my mind and soul, no matter what I am obliged to say in public. If only Sir Thomas More had felt able to accept such wise counsel!

I dismiss my ladies in perfunctory manner and walk down the corridor to Cromwell's office. I walk in boldly and he rises from his desk as he sees me approach. He indicates a seat in front of his desk but I am seated in it before his slow moving arm returns to rest.

'My Lord Cromwell,' I begin. 'What can you tell me about the current state of the monasteries in this land?'

'Perhaps Madam,' he says slowly, punctuating his words in stark tones and looking grim and disturbed, 'you should address your questions to your husband, the king.'

'My husband is in mourning,' I say, raising my voice. 'And not in need of any distress at the present time. I am addressing my words to you sir.'

He looks fierce and angry and a flush suffuses his grey features. My heart beats faster as I contemplate that he is being challenged and does not like it but I am the queen and he will not dare to anger me. He has already overstepped the mark with the import of his admonishing words. He sighs and folds his hands together in front of him. I remain very still, facing him, determined not to show any hesitation.

'I have been instructed, madam,' he says very slowly. 'To have all the monasteries checked and investigated for irregularities and to report back to the king.'

'And the closures?'

'Very few, as yet.'

'So there could be many more to come?'

'I honestly couldn't say,' he pauses, 'at this juncture.'

'What sort of irregularities?' I ask, still facing him squarely and keeping my expression harsh and questioning. He says that the irregularities are many and varied and some of the abbots, monks, friars and nuns have been replaced or the buildings closed and the inhabitants sent to other monasteries, still open. Some have been dismissed and sent out into the world to seek other occupations.

'These irregularities,' I persist. 'Specifically?'

'Since you ask madam,' he says, quietly. 'Sexual perversions.'

'Yes, well that must be stopped,' I say, feeling my face redden.

'Indeed.'

I have no idea about such things occurring in monasteries and Cromwell will be aware of that. Does he seek to humiliate me though; of this I can't be sure so decide not to make further reference to it. I ask for further intelligence but he is obviously reluctant to supply it and I find myself struggling with him when I should be in a dominant, commanding situation. He is polite, if stony faced and I am powerless to accuse him of any insolence, real or imagined.

'These small incomes, from the unwanted monasteries,' I ask cautiously,' where do they go now?'

'Those being kept open or those closed,' he asks sarcastically, 'madam?'

'Both,' I snap.

'To the crown of England,' he says, swiftly, voice raised slightly and obviously rattled that anybody, myself included, should question him on such matters.

'I see,' I say quietly and sit regarding him as he again begins to fold and unfold his hands. There is a short silence before he finally looks straight at me and speaks.

'As I've said on occasion before,' he says, 'I am not your enemy.'

No you are not, I think to myself, at least, not until the king tells you that you are!

'Of course,' I say abruptly and leave the room without further comment.

SEVENTEEN.

To Henry's bedchamber at Greenwich in what has become quite a ritual of late. Although it is not unusual to spend time together in the evening, as husband and wife, of late we have been practising Henry's suggestion that we lie together every night with nothing on our minds but the procreation of children. Specifically a son and heir to the throne of England.

I may find it harsh and unnatural and not the circumstances under which I would normally agree to amorous relations with my husband but then I am in a particularly peculiar position due to the king's necessity, as he understands it, to produce a son.

I have come to view these evenings as times to use, wherever possible, to my own advantage as well as Henry's. He is in amorous mood from the start but I am more circumspect. I also attempt to slow down the rate of progress from quiet meeting to lying down in bed. On this day I find him restless but thoughtful too, a rare combination in the king of England.

'There are rumours flying,' I begin. 'About the monasteries and their fate.'

He frowns at me and his expression turns to one of anger and irritation. 'You need not concern yourself with monasteries Jane,' he tells me.

'But I would know, or wish to know a little sir,' I say, pouting at him. 'About the workings or changes occurring. So that I may talk intelligently and not say the wrong things in conversation with various people.'

He tut tuts and frowns and generally acts irritated before telling me that he feels I would be better off attending to matters appertaining to sewing, embroidery and like things with the ladies-in-waiting in my privy chamber. All I really need to know however, if it will quiet me down and leave him in peace, is that several small monasteries have been or will soon be, closed down and the revenues from them placed in the privy purse for help in the purchase of armaments in case of threat of invasion of our island home.

'And the larger monasteries sir?' I ask tentatively but note with dismay that it causes a look of thunder to form on his brow.

'All you need to know little lamb,' he says, with a colossal effort at humouring me and keeping his own temper, ' is that I am dealing with it, it will take time, possibly years and all will be to the good of England and the English church.'

'Oh but what about the bishops and monks and people my lord?' I ask. 'Will all be spared through your mercy?'

'Listen carefully white lamb,' he says, face twitching and obviously making an effort to control his annoyance with me. 'All, with few exceptions will be closed down. Some, a few, will make payments to me and be allowed to continue. Those that persist in preaching the Roman church gospel and spreading discontent, will be forcibly closed and their bishops will be executed if they resist. This land is my land and my church will prevail. Do you fully understand?'

I tell him, humbly that I do understand; he is a wise king and knows what is best for England and the people. I note the look of satisfaction on his face as I speak these words. I continue, picking my words very carefully, that I realise he is acting in the interests of the English people and our new sovereign church although I am hopeful, given his reputation as a wise and compassionate ruler that he will show mercy and forgiveness to those that are misguided enough to oppose him. I do worry also, I tell him, about the poor people, the wretches that are starving and without work who go to the monasteries and are helped with alms and hand-outs and are sometimes given shelter when they need it most. Knowing his concern for fairness and goodness in all things I suppose he will be keeping open a few where this function of hand-outs and succour to the poor must be maintained?

'Yes, you are correct in your assumption Jane,' he tells me, calmer now and without a scowl darkening his brow. 'I will allow a few, those that do good works, to stay open. Provided that they make a small contribution to our coffers.'

'Naturally,' I say, smiling.

'But Roman bishops in large monasteries that defy me will be shown no mercy. Already I have had to put one to death and spike his head on the monastery gate.'

I shudder as I think of the poor wretch who has fallen foul of the king but I can do nothing now to save him and I realise I must safeguard my own position for the present time at least. Henry is looking pensive.

'I know you will be merciful to all but the most obdurate,' I tell him.

'Indeed I will,' he says, looking more tranquil now. 'Am I not always?'

'It is just that I worry,' I tell him, frowning. 'About foolish people who do not think before acting.'

'Enough of this about monasteries,' he says, sweeping the subject aside swiftly. 'Can we not continue with our usual serene evening sojourns?' I nod swiftly and he says it is not really for me to question any of his activity in this regard, I may depend that he will settle it all in good time and goodly resolution.

He orders some fine, sweet French wine, goodly spiced with herbs and fragrances that he has had brought in especially for the Royal cellars. If I will drink a goblet with him, we may make ourselves comfortable for the evening and attend to matters of the flesh a little later. I'm still not in the mood and the sour taste of the hounding of the bishops and monks in the monasteries is troubling me yet but I do not want to vex or trouble Henry further so I smile and say 'of course, My Lord. Of course.'

The wine is poured and we make ourselves comfortable to sit back, drink and be merry. It is at times like these that the king becomes friendly and frivolous and very warm towards me; a lead in to the more serious business of the love act. Of course there are times, with him, that he becomes impatient to proceed and fumbles and presses his way to a beginning and frequently leaves me in tears afterwards although he is scarcely even aware of my condition once the act is completed. Tonight is not one such night and the only impediment to a contented sequence of events is my own frame of mind, one that, under the circumstances, it is seemly that he remains in ignorance.

'Are you content and at peace, little white lamb,' he asks, as I recline, only rising up to sup my wine.

'I am sir, indeed,' I reply.

'Will you have sweetmeats?' he asks, solicitously. 'With your wine?'

I nod an affirmative and he calls for sweetmeats. I nibble a sugared almond or two when they arrive and Henry consumes four or five in one go. He is sitting very still and staring at me with that rather bemused but fond expression on his face that I know so well from the times when he is beginning to feel amorous in the extreme.

'Oh Jane,' is all he says.

'Sir?'

'You are indeed the light of my life,' he says softly.

'Am I sir?'

'Affairs of state weigh mighty heavily,' he begins, pompously. 'But after a day of battling in the Privy Council with lords and members of my parliament, it is refreshing indeed to gaze upon your pale, white face and fair hair. You are a blessed balm in a sea of troubled conflict when councillors have tried my patience once too often.'

'Thank you,' is all I can manage in response.

'Only you Jane, only you,' he continues warming to his subject. 'All other women I have known have been nothing to me. Nothing but a base pain and aggravation that is.'

'I choose merely to be a good wife,' I tell him, honestly. 'To obey and serve and to love unrestrictedly.'

Shortly now, it will be time for the lovemaking. He presses me to eat a scented, honeyed sweetmeat and I take it and put it delicately in my mouth, the white, sugary flakes attaching to my lips in a manner that I know he finds---- stimulating, shall we say?

I smile and he moves in close to me, his lips approaching mine but I pull back, teasing him. I raise one white delicate hand to stop his progress and take another small, soft bite of the cake, carefully ensuring that a few further flakes attach to my lips. I know by the way he is looking at me that he is growing impatient and in need of further progress but I keep him at bay a few more minutes before he reaches over and touches my bosom, his big hands gentle on my soft flesh.

'Patience sir,' I cry in mock horror.

'Now Jane, now,' he says, speech slurred by his emotive state.

When the teasing has to stop he is anxious and his fondling becomes intense, fevered almost. His probing fingers inside me, causing much wetness are all he needs to tell him that I too, crave the physical act at last and there follows a speedy build up to conclusion. I am still somewhat disturbed in mind but my confusion recedes a little as I let natural instincts of the flesh take over. My last thoughts, as indeed I suspect his also, are of the possibility of my growing quick with child.

* * * *

Henry in foul mood, shivering with anger and resentment at the Duke of Norfolk's shoddy treatment of his illegitimate son, Richmond. Apparently, as Henry explained to me briefly, between bouts of cursing and threatening the duke's life, the man allowed the young duke's body to be carried in a sealed coffin to Thetford in a cart, covered in straw and hastily buried there, in the priory, where other members of the Howard family lie at rest.

'I should have that vile man put in the tower,' Henry raves. 'Then send him to the block and relieve him of his useless head.'

'I think you are too much the compassionate prince,' I tell him plaintively. 'In your worthy all-embracing compassion, you will surely forgive him Your Grace? The man is a fool and made a terrible mistake but I can't believe you will not be merciful.'

'Why should I forgive him?' he asks tetchily. 'Does he deserve forgiveness?'

'No sir,' I say, 'and he does not deserve such a forgiving, gentle man as his king.'

'My boy will have to be re-buried with due ceremony in a fitting place.'

'Yes, yes, that is the solution. It is as you say,' I agree, enthusiastically. 'You always know the right thing to do Henry, it is instinctive with you.'

He grunts and then stares at me, long and hard. He rambles on about fools and vagabonds surrounding him and all in high places, places they do not deserve to be in. He will bring them all down to earth and remove all their privileges. As to Norfolk he has to think long and hard about the fate of that man and he will sleep upon the problem. I assure him that he is right to show such consideration to somebody unworthy and undeserving of his natural goodness and leniency. I tell him I am certain that he will reach the right solution, couched in mercy and hope fervently that he really will.

After due consideration and the passage of five days Henry is no further forward; he is possibly even angrier. I hear from the ante room, his conversation with Cromwell and he is not a happy man. Cromwell has no reason to like Norfolk, the two are in direct competition for the king's favour and the highest positions in the land. All the same, Cromwell is forced to point out his adversary's finer points.

'He is your finest warrior, after yourself of course,' I hear Cromwell say. 'He is always a useful man to have in battle.'

'That may be well,' Henry says, anger in his voice, 'but the insult to my poor son, am I to just forget that and let him go free?'

'I would not presume to advise you sir,' Cromwell says, in his usual sickly tones, used when in conversation with Henry. 'You, with your gracious and divine nature, know well how to deal with people like Norfolk.'

'But you think him more use to me than would justify punishing him eh?' Henry asks.

I move on about my own business, feeling anyway that I should not be listening in to such conversations and convinced that what I have heard so far will persuade Henry to restrict further punishment. I do not like Norfolk and have always found him a rough, brutal, horrible man; one that I recall, brought me from Chelsea to the king the night before my betrothal.

When I catch up with Henry he is still seething at the way he is being treated; firstly he complains again about Norfolk and then about Spanish Ambassador Chapuys who has written once more to him, urging a return to the Catholic church, with all possible speed and conviction, for the greater good of his soul.

'How dare that imbecile speak to me that way? 'he roars. 'Does the man not realise I am head of a church of equal significance and importance to the one he serves? Has it not yet seeped into his brain that I will never go back to the Church of Rome and neither will my country?'

'Do not trouble yourself Henry,' I implore him. 'The ambassador will come to his senses in due course and recognise you for the head of church and country that you truly are.'

When the duke of Norfolk is announced and ushered in to the privy chamber I ask to be excused but Henry tells me to stay where I am. Anything that infidel has to say he can say in front of him and his queen and there's an end to it. I remain seated.

Norfolk bows to the king and inclines his head to me. His brow is dark, his expression a mixture of fear and deep resentment and I think again, what a vile man he is. Henry asks what he has to say for himself and he fawns, kow tows and generally debases himself, offering to make amends in deed and spirit, to do the king's bidding in every manner henceforth and only hopes the king, in his infinite goodness and wisdom, will see fit to forgive such a wretch as he.

'Why should I forgive you?' Henry demands to know, loudly. 'You have made a mockery of me and my poor dead son. You are a hound of hell My lord, the Almighty God will not forgive you so why in heaven's name should I?'

'Give me the chance to redeem Your Grace,' Norfolk says gruffly but with a shake in his vocal timbre. 'I do not deserve it, God alone knows but I ask it humbly, notwithstanding.'

'You will put this matter to rights as soon as possible.'

'Yes, Your Grace.'

'Not trusting underlings, however eminent they be; you will be there in person, until it is resolved, on the spot.'

'Yes, Your Grace.'

'Hmmm.' Henry paces the chamber irritably as Norfolk stands, head bowed, not daring to look up at him or to catch my eye. He is perfectly still and as far as I can see of it, his face is cowed, bleak. Henry leaves the room abruptly and I am left sitting and watching the wretched Norfolk in front of me, neither of us able to move a muscle. After what seems an eternity of silence, Henry returns slowly into the chamber and takes up his former position.

'You will go to the chapel and do penance. You will pray for the full forgiveness of Almighty God and his right hand man, myself, and you will do it plainly and openly in front of a witness.'

'Yes, Your Grace.'

'I will send Cromwell to witness and ensure you carry out my wishes exactly.'

I see Norfolk flinch at this prospect but he nods acquiescence.

'Now get out of my sight.'

Norfolk departs. Henry calls for a page boy and when Cromwell appears he instructs him to do his bidding and go immediately to the chapel. Cromwell nods and I notice him put up a hand to hide his joyous smile before taking his swift departure. Henry asks me if I am about to depart for my own privy chamber and I smile and say 'yes.'

'Wait a while, with me, will you?' he asks. 'I need your soothing presence to calm my troubled soul.'

'Of course,' I reply. 'I am here for as long as you need me sir.'

'Only you Jane, only you can soothe me.' He continues unctuously. 'Those other whores were useless whenever I was under intolerable pressure from fools and councillors alike.'

He calls for wine for us both and bids the boy pour two goblets. He puts mine to my lips as you might do for a child and I sip the liquid gently, peering at him bright eyed over the rim of the vessel. He smiles; he is calmer now; at last!

'Am I not a fair and judicious monarch Jane,' he asks, frowning with vexation. 'Am I not gentle, forgiving and generous to all my subjects?'

'You are sir,' I tell him, smiling. 'Of course you are.'

‘So why do so many of them play me false and so often?’

‘They do not appreciate what a gracious, divine and merciful king they have,’ I say, softly. ‘They are fortunate indeed.’

‘Stay with me this afternoon white lamb,’ he says gently, entwining his hand round my fingers. ‘You are a blessed balm, a sea of calm in a desert of disaster. I need you more for myself than your ladies-in-waiting. They may wait. I will not let you go.’

EIGHTEEN

Summer 1536.

I do feel that the question of restoration to their royal status, for Elizabeth and, more urgently for Mary, is of paramount importance. On the rare occasions I catch the king in good humour and mention it to him however, he refuses to discuss it. Most recently I approached him prior to one of our evening 'love nest' sessions, as he calls them and he became agitated in the extreme, acknowledging that I had been right to effect a reconciliation with Mary but assuring me that it could go no further than that.

He has given his seal of approval to a visit to Greenwich. And that, little as it is, represents progress as far as I am concerned. If he is to remain obstinate and unyielding in this matter I must adopt gradual chipping away to facilitate eventual change tactics. A visit here to Greenwich followed by a trip to Hampton Court and as many visits to White Hall as can be managed.

Mary is seated in my privy chamber working on some embroidery that I have set up for her. She likes the work, she tells me and will try more back at her home. Anne and Jane are fussing around, offering her sweetmeats and wine and admiring her embroidery. Mary Norris questions her relentlessly about facilities at Hunsdon, perhaps not realising that Mary regards the place as a semi-prison and is reluctant to say much about the house and grounds.

'I'm very grateful to you Jane,' she tells me earnestly. 'You've worked tirelessly in my interest, these past months.'

'I regret I've only been able to achieve so little and so late,' I tell her, pausing to halt the progress of my needle for a while.

'No, no, you have done more than anyone could ask,' she says, enthusiastically. 'Am I to see my father this day?'

'Indeed yes,' I tell her, smiling. 'He is looking forward to the meeting later.'

Henry has been locked in heated discussions with his council for nearly two hours. Cromwell has been giving him a hard time, I am informed, over the speed and progress of closing down the unprofitable monasteries; the first minister recommends slowing down the procedure to avoid bad feeling building up with the people throughout the country, many of them still sympathetic to the institution and the Roman church they serve.

I suggested he take heed of Cromwell's words in this instance, only to be reprimanded severely for venturing an opinion on affairs of state. I tell him he has all the time in the world to deliberate but he replies that I should have a care; action needs to be taken now for there is much revenue to be collected from that source, revenue that will facilitate change for the country as a whole and help to swell the coffers for the provision of reinforcements of our coastal areas, to repel invaders. It is all one anyway, Cromwell will have his way in the end, after he has carefully arranged it so that the king thinks it was his idea initially.

'I just wish I were able to speed the progress of re-instatement,' I tell her, with a frown on my brow. 'For you and the Lady Elizabeth.'

'Do not fret Jane,' she says. 'It will all resolve in due course anyway. In any event I will only be in line of succession after any children that you may bear.

'If I have any,' I reply, laughing.

'You will Jane,' she assures me. 'I know you will.'

We are summoned to the king's chamber and find him in expansive, almost jolly mood. He greets us both affably, complimenting Mary on the bright colours she is wearing and admiring my white satin kirtle with red cloth lining; I have learned what clothing to wear that pleaseth him.

'We are pleased to receive you daughter,' he tells Mary. 'You must visit often.'

He seats us, one on either side of him and asks Mary if she is comfortable where she is living and whether he can do anything to increase her comfort and way of life.

'A little more freedom would be welcome father,' she begins, tentatively.

'Freedom?'

'To ride out, to visit friends and possibly little Elizabeth at Hatfield.'

He stares at her for a short time and then his face breaks out in a grin. He says he can see no reason why she should not ride out as far and as frequently as she might wish. The king's daughter should, after all, be a good horsewoman. Mary thanks him and mentions that she would like to think that she is not being watched carefully all the time.

'A king must know what is happening with all his subjects, children included,' Henry says jocularly. 'But I can instruct servants and others to be more discreet.'

'Thank you father.'

'And she must visit us at White Hall and Richmond Park and Windsor too, mustn't she?' I ask.

'Indeed,' Henry says, still smiling.

He frowns, looks at his eldest daughter and suddenly asks her if she has enough support and space at the house, just as if he has only this minute thought of it. Perhaps that is the case. Mary says she has good apartments and bedchamber and can ask no more.

'Hmmm.'

'No, really father, I am well situated.'

'Perhaps one or two extra ladies- in- waiting, or servants?'

Mary shakes her head. She begins to look a trifle exasperated as though she has been left almost a house prisoner for so long that all this sudden attention to her needs is too much, too late. Perhaps that also is the case? Henry is still going on about extra ladies, saying that he gets requests daily for women to be admitted to court, from Lady Mounteagle and Lady Lisle among others. If I do not need any more, he says, looking directly at me, he could easily divert some to Mary.

'No, sir, I am well provided for. Courtiers, ladies, servants, stable boys.'

'Perhaps a move back to court is all that would make Lady Mary really happy,' I say, sheepishly and feel my heart start to thump in my chest. Henry gives me a withering look and I avoid his gaze immediately. He stands up and suggests a walk down to the gardens and some tennis.

Although growing in girth gradually and some would say rapidly, the king is still impressive in his tennis clothing, his shirt open at the neck. His height ensures a strong physical aspect and his features are clear and bright, his eyes shining. He has chosen the toughest looking, physically most impressive young courtier as an opponent as both Mary and I both declined a chance to play in a doubles line up and we are seated under a canopy with goblets of mead and sweet meats ordered for us by the king.

The young man plays well, returning hard hit strokes easily at first and delivering well but he is soon seen to be no match for Henry. The man that was England's strongest warrior in battle has still managed to retain a powerful ability at games and a unique determination to win at all costs. The solid ball is hard indeed and I flinch on the occasions when it hits Henry full on the thigh or arm and, even, when his opponent receives a fierce knock. Neither man will ever shout out or break off play.

Henry wins, as I always knew he would and strides back to the canopy to join us, hands the young man a bag of coins and despatches him on his way. He calls to a hovering servant and asks for a large jug of strong ale and settles down next to me, perspiration dripping from his forehead. He looks to another servant but I call the fellow to me and ask for linen soaked in rosewater.

'I will wipe your brow sir,' I say in my most seductive voice and he smiles contentedly.

'What would I do without you Jane?' he asks and winks at Mary.

I wipe his brow gently and he takes up his goblet and drinks the contents in one extended draught. He nods to the servant who immediately refreshes his goblet. I smile, content for the moment in the warm afternoon sun. Mary looks pensive.

NINETEEN.

The royal barge is being loaded in a hurry to transport us all to Windsor Castle. A fleet will follow us as there are many in the king's party and he will not travel without them. Henry is rushing around barking out instructions to courtiers and servants alike; no discrimination!

'When are we to set sail?' I ask, flustered by the suddenness of it all.

'Any minute now,' he shouts, 'God's teeth, why does everybody dally at a time like this?'

'Why the urgency Henry?' I ask.

'It is the plague in London,' he tells me irritably. 'It is all over the city.'

'Oh,' I say, confused again.

'It is all over Westminster,' he says, rushing out to the ante room to collect a personal trifle. 'Even in the abbey.'

Henry has a morbid fear of the plague which, although it tends to spread over many parts of the country, is always at its fiercest and most debilitating throughout London and environs. So many people die so quickly when it spreads that it is almost as though they never existed. We all troop out to the barges and note that a sizeable number of people have gathered on the banks of the Thames and are waving at us. I return their greetings but Henry does not appear to even notice that they are there. It seems that he will only be comfortable when we have put many miles between us and the city.

The oarsmen work frantically, pulling hard to get up a reasonable speed and sending up waves of white spray as we progress. Henry will not sit still.

'Calm down My lord,' I say, smiling at him from my seat.

As we pull up to the landing stage at Windsor, with the castle above and behind us, he is off quickly and making for the gateway and the drawbridge to be lowered to gain admission. Orders are barked out to the yeomen guards and it is soon possible for the king to gain entry. I leave the barge more slowly with my escorts, helped off by Cromwell who is standing by to assist.

'Is the king usually as concerned as this about the plague?' I ask.

'Usually a lot more so,' he replies, allowing himself a rare, wry smile.

I am escorted to the North Wharf terrace along the outer wall of the upper ward. There is an outside staircase to the king's apartment which I am led to, so he must have requested my immediate presence. As I mount the wide staircase I note the magnificent view of the river and fields below. The king is already settled in a favourite velvet chair and, it seems, a lot calmer now he has escaped from the city.

'Come in Jane.' He bids me and I take a seat next to him.

Are we safe now sir?' I ask ironically.

He ignores my levity and speaks calmly but with a serious expression on his face.

'You know we spoke about your coronation in the abbey?' he begins.

'Sir?'

'Archbishop Cranmer, Cromwell and I all agree,' he says soberly. 'It would be foolhardy to go ahead with preparations while the plague rages.'

'Oh,' I say, understanding the solemn mood.

'It will go ahead Jane,' he says. 'Be assured of that. But not this year. Next.'

'I understand,' I tell him softly. 'All is well.'

He nods his head contentedly. That little bit of business over, in his mind, he can proceed with matters of state or other pressing needs. He says he supposes I will wish to see if my ladies are settled in happily and at ease with their quarters. Which is, of course, my cue to leave him at peace in his privy chamber and get about my own business.

My ladies are, indeed, content; all are assembled in my chamber, some in window corners, busily utilizing the light for sewing or embroidery; some reading studiously and two more chattering merrily; the latest court scandal no doubt?

Mary Norris and Margery Horsman are the two conversationalists, the two I would have expected. As I approach, Margery rises, half curtsies to me and moves off to the window corner. Mary smiles sheepishly at me.

'I do hope sincerely I am not interrupting any talk of prime importance?' I say, ironically and she merely shakes her head and looks down coyly into her lap,

'So tell me the latest, do.'

'You may be vexed,' she blurts out suddenly and blushes.

'Really?'

As many times before, I have to tell her that having started something and aroused my curiosity, she had better get on and inform me of the substance of her discussion.

'Well I know it is none of our business,' she begins, sheepishly. 'It is just that I was surprised, as was Margery, to hear a rumour that Jane Parker, as was, Lady Rochford, has made overtures to return to court.'

I manage to nod and try to look composed as though it is no surprise to me but, in truth it is. More of a shock really, if truth be told. Lady Rochford, George Boleyn's wife and sister-in-law to the late queen Anne, was instrumental in sealing the fate of both of them; her ex employer as Lady-in-waiting and, horrible thought, her own husband. What sort of woman can send her man to the block, as well as the Queen of England? Her evidence at the trial was crucial however and I recall being relieved when, after the executions, she was whisked away somewhere, out of harm's way. The charge of incest between Anne and her brother George was a sensational part of the proceedings but one in which I, for one, saw Rochford as the architect of that infamous allegation.

'Where did you hear this Mary?' I enquire harshly.

'Oh it is court gossip, the usual,' she says.

'Well nothing has been decided with reference to that person,' I say coldly. 'And it is best if you do not discuss it further.'

'Of course. My lips are sealed.'

'Please ensure that they stay that way Mary,' I say. 'This is not a subject for gossip. Within the confines of this chamber or outside it.'

With great difficulty I control a desire to rush to the king and demand to know all about it. I do not want any of them to know that I have not been advised of this situation. I go over to the window corner and resume my own embroidery, engaging in very light conversation with Anne Parr, Jane Arundell and Anne Bassett. It is, however, burning me up inside. I have always had a strong dislike of the Rochford woman, particularly when I was in enforced close company with her in Anne Boleyn's household. The thought of her returning to court as one of my ladies, fills me with horror.

I do not broach the subject at dinner; Henry will not tolerate contentious subjects when he is eating, as I have already found out to my cost. Back in the privy chamber he wants to get amorous but I remind him gently that it is early in the day.

'With you, white lamb,' he says, cheerily, 'anytime of the day or night is the right time.'

'May I speak seriously with you, My Lord?'

'I think I shall go out to the archery early tomorrow morning,' he says, gaily. 'To hone up my skill with the bow.'

'Yes sir,' I reply, 'but I would speak of another matter.'

'Yes? What is it my love?'

When I mention the name Jane Boleyn, his face clouds over. He clears his throat and I tell him that I was disturbed to find two of my ladies gossiping about her overtures to return to court. 'Yes lamb,' he says cheerily. 'It has been put forward.'

'But I know nothing of it,' I say, aggrieved. 'I hear it as court gossip.'

'That is regrettable,' he tells me, seriously. 'Although no decision has been arrived at.'

'I do not like that woman,' I say, sharply, my voice breaking slightly.

'She did me a service some time ago,' he says quietly. 'And I would wish to return the favour.'

I recall that she once did Anne a favour by removing a woman from court that she took a strong dislike to. Someone that Henry did like, perhaps more than he should have! On that occasion Henry was very angry and put Rochford out of court for a month. Now I am fearful thinking about what service she has done for him that, by contrast, merits his favour and reward. Unless it refers to the downfall of Queen Anne and that murky story does not bear thinking about, much less discussing.

'Is she to be one of my Ladies then?' I ask coldly.

'As I indicated,' he says brusquely now, 'no decision has been reached yet.'

'I would prefer not to have her near me,' I say icily but I note with dismay that his face goes very red, the veins in his neck bulge and he gives me a withering look.

'Sometimes Jane, people have to put their own feelings to one side and accept what must be for the good of the realm.'

'Is that what I must do, My lord?'

'Leave it Jane, leave it,' he says, rising and beginning one of his angry paces round the chamber. 'I will advise you as soon as I have made a decision.'

'Very well,' I say coldly and beg to be excused. He is not happy but signals with a brief gesture that I may leave his presence. I go to the chapel and spend twenty minutes in silent prayer, alone with God and my thoughts.

Candles are burning brightly as I kneel by the altar. I find myself uttering solemn prayers and using words that I used to employ from the Holy Roman Church. Nobody is about; I am alone in the chapel and nobody but God and I know how I conduct my private prayers. I look around the chapel to ensure there is no other person in sight and then, briefly, I cross myself in front of the altar.

To try and cheer myself or, at least, feel a little more content, I order the charcoal burner to be fired and a bath prepared for me. I decide to spend an hour in my privy chamber, reading but do not send for female company; with servants always close at hand I require no other ladies at present. As to the bath, I can lie back with castill soap, camomile scented water at hand and luxuriate as I stare at the gold battens decorating the white ceiling. Two servants wrap me in a hot towel as I finish and, already I feel renewed, refreshed, my skin tingling and my cheeks glowing red.

The king sends for me as evening progresses and torches and candles are lit throughout the palace. I go to him but our conversation is fragmented, strained and eventually we settle into near silence. At supper our chatter is light and frivolous, without real content, just words for the sake of words almost. The king eats with less than his usual heartiness, only doing justice to a particularly succulent venison cake of which I also partake.

Back in the king's privy chamber he bids me sit next to him. I comply.

'What is it, what ails you white lamb?' he asks solicitously. 'I cannot stand to see you out of sorts.'

'I'll be all right my Lord,' I say with a smile. 'I already I feel refreshed from my bath and my mind is less troubled.'

'But I would wish to have your mind completely untroubled,' he says. 'Is it the thought of Lady Rochford?'

'I do not like her, to be sure,' I say, frowning. 'And would prefer her far away.'

'Let me look into the matter,' he says, brightly. 'I'll see what I can do.'

'No, please do not trouble My lord,' I say. 'I would not wish to interfere with the progress of state matters. No, let her come if that is your wish. I ask only that if she be disagreeable, I may deal with her in my own way?'

'But of course lamb,' he says, grinning. 'The ladies of the bedchamber are your domain and yours only.'

We settle down, side by side, the atmosphere lighter and I feel much more content. I will not let Jane Boleyn upset me, she is not worth it. And I have cleared the way to deal with her should she become troublesome. Henry makes it known that he is feeling amorous and is cognisant of our need to continue to try and produce a male heir.

'Oh,' I say, disconcerted by the cold calculating nature of his desire.

'What is wrong Jane?' he asks, concerned now. 'Are you bleeding? You are not bleeding are you Jane?'

'No sir,' I say, forcing a smile. 'I am not bleeding.'

'Then come to me, to be loved, little white lamb.'

I go to him to be loved.

TWENTY

Autumn 1536.

It is warm and peaceful in the orchard. I sit under the high red brick wall and gaze at the fruit on the trees, still unpicked. Summer has departed but left a hazy, pastel shaded autumn, cool, never cold but comfortable. The sun shines intermittently, never hot, only warm. A blue sky threaded with milk white clouds indicates that rain is far away; for the moment at least.

Soon the bad weather will come and winter will chill us all. That is what makes these balmy days of late summer sun, so acceptable and why I choose to take my leisure out of doors wherever possible. Henry approaches and I am alarmed to see that he is red faced and angry; he has been in ill mood for some days now, struggling to increase the speed of the monastery closures and to get full approval for yet more warships and protective battlements around the shores of southern England. Curiously he does not fear invasion from northern ports and word is abroad that there is much discontent internally in those parts.

As he reaches the stone seat where I sit, I see how very angry he is. My heart sinks.

'I am betrayed and insulted,' he roars, 'by my own cousin.'

'Pole?'

'Yes Pole, Reginald Pole, a man who refuses an archbishopric and prefers instead to wallow in his books in Europe. I ask him for a book on Unity of the Church and he sends me a scurrilous invective. He says that during the twenty seven years I have reigned, I have continually plundered my subjects and if I was liberal in anything, it was certainly not in the things that make for the common weal. I have robbed every kind of man, made a sport of the nobility and never loved the people. He bitterly attacks my right to royal supremacy over the English church and stoutly defends the pope's spiritual authority. How dare he?'

I put my hand on his arm and gently squeeze it. He must take no heed of such bitter nonsense I tell him.

'Take no heed? Such foul insult and contempt cannot go unpunished. He further accuses me of troubling the clergy and tearing like a wild beast, the men who were the greatest honour to my kingdom.'

'Whatever possessed the man?' I ask.

The devil possessed him, that's clear enough,' Henry fumes. 'And God has forsaken me that is clear enough also.'

I shake my head, despairing of how I can calm him down but he continues to rave about being a kind, compassionate prince, merciful to all subjects, gentle of nature and all he receives in return is insult and vindictiveness, and he feels sure, God has abandoned him.

'He will die,' Henry roars. 'He will lose his head and I will spike it on London Bridge for all to see. He will not mock and insult me and escape full punishment.'

Pole was most likely set up to do this by Rome, specifically the Pope. The church has tried all manner of means to bring Henry and England back to the true faith but I do not discuss my ideas with Henry; he is too distressed at the moment and it would only encourage a fresh outburst.

'Oh he will die for this,' He continues, 'kith of mine or no. He will die,'

'Yes sir,' I agree quietly. 'But I wonder if you should speak first with Cromwell?'

'Cromwell? I don't need words from that quarter. Although he would see the justice of my decision. The man has condemned himself in writing.'

I nod my head and Henry is silent as we sit listening to bird song. The sun comes out briefly and then fades again. The king rises, without word and walks off alongside the high red wall. I wait patiently until he returns after a short interval.

'I may speak with Cromwell first,' he says softly.

'Yes?'

'It will in no wise alter my decision though.'

'No.'

Cromwell arrives early, well before supper time. He acknowledges my presence briefly and Henry tells him about the offensive words and his decision. Cromwell nods and inclines his head, listening intently but showing no more than a plain emotionless mask.

'Yes, I see Majesty,' he says soberly. 'I wonder though if it might be misinterpreted.'

'How so?'

'Well, if you take the man's life it could be seen as revenge pure and simple and his words seen as truthful. You are a wise and magnanimous monarch and will not wish to be seen by the populace as being as Pole has scurrilously described you.'

'No, of course not. What other action is open?

'I wonder sir, if it would not be best to send word to him that you are not displeased. Invite him to return to England. Offer him a post. That way you show him up as a fool and a liar. A vagabond.'

'I can't do that. You are a fool Cromwell. He must die. I'll have his head spiked before winter comes.'

Cromwell merely shrugs. The king gives him a withering look and walks out of the chamber without further word. Cromwell prepares to take his leave but I detain him with a wave of my hand.

'What now Lord Cromwell?'

'Leave him for an hour madam.'

'And then?'

'He will return and do as I have suggested.'

'Are you sure?'

'I'm sure. Once he has convinced himself it was his own idea.'

I raise an eyebrow.

'In any event he can't touch Pole and he knows it. He will not return to England. He can, of course, harm members of Pole's family here. His mother for one.' Cromwell looks thoughtful for a moment, frowns and taps the palm of his left hand. 'Of course he may do so.'

Cromwell continues to surprise, shock and sometimes amaze me. I still think he will come to a bad end whether that be at the sharp point of a nobleman's sword or on the block. He has lived all his adult life by the sword in one way or another and will surely die by it. I am convinced though that I am right to seek his help whenever necessary; he was close advisor to the king all through Queen Anne's time and I will be well advised to utilise that gift of his. He did though, engineer her departure from this world so I must tread extra carefully, always.

Henry is quiet on his return to the chamber and continues that way through supper. He silently works his way through goodly sized portions of roasted mutton with gallandine, venison pie, chicken and cherries and finally, almond sugared sweetmeats. He is still quiet, if thoughtful, as we return to his bedchamber prior to our ritual evening preparations.

'I have given the matter of Master Pole much thought,' he announces suddenly.

'Have you?'

'I have decided not to take his head,' he continues blandly. 'I have worked it out that he will look like a poltroon if I say I am not offended by his words and I will be seen for the gentle, gracious and divine sovereign that I am.'

'Indeed you are Henry,' I say, smiling at him.

'The Bishop of Rome and his followers will not get to me by this foolishness.'

'I'm sure you've made the right decision. As you always do.'

'The man is a thorn in my side nevertheless,' he says sanguinely. 'He would do well to look carefully to his future conduct.'

I try to distract Henry with gentle whisperings in his ear and talk of love and affection but it is hard work. The attempts to unnerve him by the various church people who support the pope in Rome are having their effect and he is frequently irritable or at least, distracted by the very thoughts of invasion of our island. As we prepare to lie together, he bids me come and sit, unclothed, on his knee. I do so and as he kisses my cheek I recall another occasion when I sat on his knee, with my clothes on but I couldn't have caused a bigger sensation without them. At that time Queen Anne, discovered us and, in a fury, slapped my face so hard that I still feel the sting to this day.

'You look sad, little lamb,' Henry says, solicitously. 'Why so?'

'I was just thinking of people now gone, no longer with us,' I say reflectively. 'It made me feel low.'

'Do not mourn the dead,' Henry says grimly. 'Leave them where they lie, buried.'

'I'll try sir,' I say, softly, 'I'll try.'

Henry, amorous, is all hands and mouth, everywhere. He squeezes and caresses my titties, nibbles my ear seductively and fondles the soft flesh of my rump with his big, sensuous hands. At last his mind is off acts of treason and insult, attempts to undermine him as head of his church and real or imagined slurs. I caress him in return and we become locked together in an act of passion. I let myself go in thoughts of love and tenderness and he, in the grip of blind passion, thinks, if he thinks at all at such times as this, most likely thinks of begetting a son and heir to the throne.

TWENTY ONE.

Breakfast at White Hall with Henry making light work of some boiled eggs, white flour bread, salt beef cake and a large jug of mead. I eat two eggs and a little bread but nothing else. Henry calls for more mead as his jug empties but pushes away his plate and will eat no more. He belches suddenly, puts a hand to his mouth and begs me excuse him. I smile.

'Lady Rochford is due here today,' he says quietly. 'She is instructed to present herself to you in your chamber at eleven hours of the clock.'

'Is she indeed?' I enquire. 'Is she aware of my rules of dress etiquette?'

Henry smiles expansively. 'She is made aware of your requirement for girdles with no less than one hundred and twenty pearls sewn in.'

'Well the others observe it,' I say. 'There is no reason for Lady Rochford not to.'

'I make no further observation on the subject,' he says, grinning and spreading his hands expansively.

He says that he intends to spend the morning at archery practice. He feels he has been neglecting his prowess as a bowman of late due to the constant worry and irritation of letters from Europe; Spain, France and Rome in particular trying to beg, cajole or bully him into returning the country to the true church. He tells me that they will never wear him down and he is no longer upset by them but I know, or sense, that deep down he is much upset and worried as he was the most solid defender of the faith in his youth and a catholic by birth and conviction until his marriage to Anne. He spends much time in the chapel praying and confessing to the priest and I would dearly love to overhear some of those outpourings.

He tells me he has kept the new church much like the old; he retains the mass and confession and is anxious not to upset older people who prize their religion and worry about the state of their souls these days. He will, he says, uphold the old religious ways and methods of prayer and praying; only the head of the church has changed, he himself and he is a pious man.

'In my youth I could hit the centre of the target nine times out of ten,' he tells me, looking thoughtful.

'And today, My lord?' I enquire.

'Much the same if I practice regularly,' he says jocularly. 'Maybe eight out of ten.'

We go our separate ways after breakfast. I find my ladies in a state of excitement over the imminent arrival of Lady Rochford. Anne Bassett is talking about her as the woman who sealed the fate of the late queen almost single handed.

'That is not true Anne,' I say, sternly. 'She was just one of many who gave evidence.'

'I only say what many others are saying,' Anne replies belligerently.

'Yes, well, we will have no more talk of it, if you please. She is to be treated exactly like anybody else in this chamber, is that understood?'

Many heads shake in unison. I bid them all attend to whatever business occupied them before I came in. There is much movement of ladies into positions followed by studious clicking of crewel needles and looks of concentration, real or studied, on all the faces around me. A few elect to read but they peer over the tops of their volumes at me when they think I am not observing them.

A servant announces the arrival of Lady Rochford and I bid her install the woman in the ante chamber. As I enter I see her standing in front of me, in a blue velvet gown with fur trimmings, her fair hair neatly positioned and her headdress firmly held in place. She is quite pretty I must reluctantly accept but I do not like the faintly supercilious expression she wears. She gives a brief approximation of a curtsey as she sees me.

'Lady Rochford,' I intone quietly.

'Madam,' she replies, softly.

I study her girdle which has, I think, the correct number of pearls attached. In any event I will not be counting them now. She allows herself a smile. 'Well Jane,' she continues, 'we meet again and this time you are the queen I serve.'

'Yes,' I say, contentedly. 'Did you think it might have been you?'

She smiles crookedly. 'The king and I have had our moments Jane,' she continues, 'but he is my half second cousin, which you will be aware of.'

'Yes, I am,' I say quietly. 'And Henry has strong views on incest as you will be more than aware.'

She blushes scarlet. 'I see you are not the quiet, retiring little mouse most people think,' she says archly.

I ask her if she is aware of my requirement for ladies-in-waiting to wear girdles with one hundred and twenty pearls attached. She says she is and asks if I would wish to count hers. I inform her that it will not be necessary. I am merely making my point.

'I think we understand each other now,' I say, smiling.

'We do indeed,' she agrees.

I invite her into the inner sanctum and she makes the rounds of my other ladies, most of which, she already knows. She settles down next to Mary Norris and I notice that they engage in conversation, rather strained as it sounds, from where I sit but no sign of malice on either face. I get on with my embroidery; I have a smock to finish and would wish to have it ready in less than two more days. There is no sign of anybody feeling uncomfortable so I am hopeful that she will, perhaps, fit in. By the time I leave for dinner everybody is chattering away merrily.

Henry has arranged for dinner in his privy chamber and I wonder if he has a specific reason or, perhaps, an announcement to make that is for my ears only. He bids me sit and joins me and calls for dishes to be brought in immediately. I begin to eat, slowly and delicately, in my usual manner, happy to find my Lord and master in good humour; it happens infrequently enough to be sure.

'Well Henry?' I say, raising an eyebrow.

'Jane?' he replies, spearing some venison and onion onto his plate.

'You obviously have an announcement to make,' I tell him. 'I know you well by now.'

He continues eating; there is nothing that can distract him from good food so I bide my time, drink some mead and select a little chicken for my plate. He smiles.

'I know how concerned you are about the closing of the monasteries,' he says sanguinely. 'You should know however that I am making a major concession in that particular field and one, I think, you will most heartily approve.'

'Tell me more,' I say.

He is, he tells me, re-founding two religious houses, one of monks and one of nuns. Bisham Abbey and the nunnery of Stixfold. They are to be re-endowed and re-staffed completely. I nod and smile and look to hear more of this somewhat surprising news.

'The point being,' he begins, speaking expansively and obviously enjoying himself, 'they will be renamed in the king's own name and their purpose will be to pray for the welfare in life and the eternal rest after death of myself, my wife Queen Jane and our heirs and ancestors.'

'That is wonderful,' I say. 'I thank you, My lord for the thought and the honour.'

'As I've said on many occasions,' he says, smiling expansively, 'nothing is too good for my little white lamb. You are the love of my life Jane; have I told you that before?' he asks ironically.

'Just once or twice,' I reply with a smile.

''Tis true.'

It occurs to me that this is an expensive operation and one that will be financed from the coffers of many other small monasteries that have already been closed down but I will not risk an outburst or change of mood from his Grace by pursuing the point. I content myself by hoping that the two new monasteries will not be unduly harsh on the national treasury.

'The coffers are equal to the requirements,' he responds.

'I'm pleased to hear it,' I say and it is true.

'And now, white lamb,' he says, jocularly. 'We have a duty to England to ensure the continuation of the line of Tudor to the succession which, in its execution will, I hope and pray, afford us both great pleasure.'

'But sir,' I protest in mock horror,' it is only twenty minutes past noon of the clock.'

'Indeed it is. But I have arranged for dinner here in my privy chamber and we will not be disturbed for the remains of this afternoon.'

'What can you have in mind for the next several hours?' I ask ironically.

'Let us drink more mead, at our leisure, sit back and contemplate the tapestries upon the wall here. I feel assured that something will occur to us.'

TWENTY TWO.

Henry with his arm outstretched and a hawk on his thick glove. I watch as the bird flies off, wings fluttering speedily before it reaches a certain height, stops then glides gracefully for a few moments before flying off again.

The look of pleasure, compounded with satisfaction is always good to see. Certain pursuits like hawking and archery demand his full attention but are deeply satisfying to the king. He is good at these pursuits and that is surely the main reason for his pleasure.

I walk over to him as the bird returns to his outstretched arm. He in turn takes the bird back to the aviary where it is taken by the attendant and settled in. Look well to their feeding and comfort, he instructs and the man nods and touches his forelock.

'Well Jane,' he says, turning attention to me at last. 'Walk with me, if you will, I would wish to converse.'

The king is attired in a bright red tunic which does much to brighten my field of vision; it is a dull day indeed, grey and with early morning mist still hovering but, thankfully, dry after a two day spell of rain. We walk on through the orchard and past the stone statues that make such a pretty vista in this garden.

'You should know Jane,' he begins. 'That I have settled on my Ten Articles of Faith, as they will be presented to the clergy and the people.'

I nod acknowledging his words and we continue walking, slowly.

'I have taken out anything that I feel is too radical or, even, words and phrases that might upset people who previously followed the doctrine of Rome.'

'That is good sir,' I say, contentedly. 'And very good for the people.'

'Well, yes, that was my main concern,' he adds. 'The church factions continue to argue, scrap and fight among themselves. They all want to present religion in their own way and will probably never agree. They must and will accept my ten articles however, for they are law.'

I nod once again as there is little I can usefully say. I cannot say that I would wish for the church to return to its previous Catholic principles with authority coming from the true church leader, the Pope, much as I might wish to. It seems unlikely that will ever happen again. Henry's articles will be his commands, his interpretation of gospel and his, full authority at all times.

'The articles actively discourage pilgrimages, veneration of relics and the reporting of miracles by saints,' he continues. 'Superstition and excess will not be tolerated. And the entire set of articles have been compiled and put into effect by Archbishop Cranmer and Cromwell.'

'Have they?' I ask.

'It is phrased however,' he says, grinning contentedly, 'by the king and by the authority of the king and no other. In other words my sole authority and not that of parliament or the bible.'

We walk back slowly towards the house where Henry will have yet another council with his ministers and Cromwell. He will deal with the latest round of letters and messengers from Europe seeking to change his ways or otherwise undermine his authority. Because of his latest changes to the rulings of the church and his decision to have two monasteries dedicated to himself and his queen, he is feeling in relatively good spirits. And to my advantage.

At his apartments he turns to me and bids me to go about my business.

'You will want to check that the Lady Mary is settled and happy with her accommodation?'

'Indeed,' I say with a broad smile. 'And I want to thank you heartily for bringing her and the little Lady Elizabeth back to court.'

He spreads his hands wide and grins. 'It is what you've wanted ever since you arrived at court. Do I not give you everything you ask for white lamb?

'You are very good to me sir,' I tell him.

'Yes, I am. I should say though, it would be better for all concerned if you thought mostly about the children you will bear for us rather than those of others.'

'Yes but they are your daughters sir. And as they belong to you, so I feel they are mine also.'

With a second admonition to think positively about becoming with child myself, he lets it go. I promise him I will conceive and it will be a son. I do feel confident that I can deliver but I don't even want to think about the consequences should I fail. Before I leave him I ask, tentatively if he will consider having the Lady Mary joining us for dinner before too long.

'I see no reason why not. She is here and she is part of the family now.'

'Thank you sir.'

'You may bring her in today if you wish.'

I thank him and hurry on my way in case he changes his mind. In my privy chamber my ladies are in earnest, animated conversation and I do not need to ask the main topic. Margery Horsman is installed now as my chief lady-in-waiting and I go to her and greet her heartily. I kiss her cheek and hug her to me.

'Margery,' I say, 'I'm concerned that Mary should feel at home in every possible way now that we have her here at court.'

'Of course Jane,' she replies, looking concerned. 'What would you have me do?'

'Nothing out of the ordinary,' I assure her. 'She has been exiled and moved around from pillar to post for so long now that I just want her to feel at home and, well back where she belongs. Yes?'

'Yes,' I understand,' she says calmly. 'I'll do all I can to make her feel welcome.'

'She will have all her own ladies and servants but I just don't want any friction between them and,' I indicate the occupants of the chamber, 'the rest.'

She assures me that she will keep an eye on all of the ladies, looking directly at Lady Rochford as she speaks. I smile; Margery and I have always been intuitively aware of what each other is thinking and feeling. I have a quick word with Anne and Jane and then make my way down the corridor to Mary's chambers. I am shown into her private room where she sits very quietly, looking somewhat lost. She jumps up as soon as she spies me and we are soon in a firm embrace. She dismisses a lady and a hovering servant and the two of us are alone.

'I can't believe I'm here, at last,' she says, smiling broadly.

'We did it,' I say, grinning.

'You did it, dear Jane, my dear good mother.'

I frown and then pull a face. 'I'm flattered,' I say sombrely. 'But would much prefer to see you as a sister.'

'Oh yes, sister, my dear good sister,' she says blithely.

'Shall we walk awhile?' I ask.

We wander out, arm in arm like two real sisters who have lived together and known each other for many years. Mary's face is flushed and smiling and I note how much improved she looks to the day I first saw her at Hunsdon. I am careful to walk level with her with never a hint that she should be two paces behind me and as the big doors are opened for us, we go through together. Henry may be obstinately refusing to restore her to her rightful place as a princess of the realm but I am determined to treat her as an equal in all ways. We pass through the orchard and linger under a fruit tree; the weather now is clear and warm if not particularly bright.

'My father calls you white lamb,' she says, grinning.

'Oh you've heard that,' I say surprised.

'Not from his lips,' she says, smiling. 'From one of your ladies.'

'Now I wonder where she heard it.' I say, frowning. 'Mary Norris?'

'Yes, that's the one. Is it true Jane?'

I explain the origin as best I can. Henry notes my preference for white or pearl satin or damask with gold trimmings and, with my fair hair, he claims that I remind him of a soft white, new born lamb. It has become a term of loving endearment and I cannot find fault with him over it. Mary laughs, a high tinkling sound like little bells ringing and it is good to see her restored somewhat, to high spirits and general contented demeanour.

'He can be most charming, warm and loving,' I muse reflectively. 'But he can also be a beast.'

'Yes,' she agrees and a cloud passes momentarily over her face.

'Sorry,' I say swiftly. 'I should not have said that'

'Oh yes, it is true,' she says brightly. 'I know well enough. I recall the days we lived together, with my mother and myself, at court.'

I indicate a stone seat over by the high, red brick wall and we move over to it and sit, side by side. I can't resist asking her how things were in those days when he lived with Katherine as queen and her as Princess Mary although I wonder if I have gone too far in my curiosity. She shakes her head and tosses it defiantly.

'He was mostly distant,' she says, thoughtfully. 'My mother and I only saw him at meals and for short interludes in the evenings. His intimacy with my mother was only at night, behind closed doors of course.'

She takes a pause, looks sad for a moment and then continues speaking.

'As a small girl I do recall he was most affectionate. In the early days when I was but three or four. He would sit me on his knee and rock me to and fro and set up games of marbles and play with me on the nursery floor. He was very different then both in appearance and character. A tall, very slim, very handsome and athletic looking man who could charm any woman with just a glance and a twinkle of his big blue eyes.'

'Yes,' I say softly, recalling early days at court as lady-in-waiting.

'Until that terrible Anne Boleyn bewitched him.'

'Do you think she did?' I ask, earnestly.

'Oh I do,' Mary says, emotively. 'There was witchcraft in that woman from the start. She led him on, flattered him but kept her distance when he was bewitched by her. It sent our world crashing Jane and started a train of events that has seen tragedy after tragedy ensue. She herself paid the price for her witchcraft but what is done cannot be undone.'

I think for a minute about Queen Anne and her tempestuous nature, her wheedling her requirements out of the king by stealth, by coyness or by clever subterfuge. I think about their brief love affair, some of which I witnessed from a distance as lady-in-waiting to Anne and how it went sour when she gathered many friends and followers about her, male and female but, significantly, mainly male. I know it vexed the king considerably and he looked lost and, I surmise, felt threatened. And yet, much as I came to dislike and even fear her I cannot, deep in my heart, believe she was ever adulterous while married to Henry. Perhaps in thought but not in deed.

Mary, understandably, will see things very differently in view of what has happened to her but I will not challenge her views and deeply held opinions. It would not be seemly and in any event, I regard her as my close friend now.

'Well,' I say cheerfully, 'this is a new beginning for us all. And the start of your complete re-instatement.'

'Oh I do hope so,' she murmurs optimistically.

I tell her that she is to join Henry and myself and sit at the dinner table with us. She claps her hands delightedly and says that she hadn't expected that, not yet. We rise and set off together for the king's privy chamber where dinner will be shortly delivered.

'And this afternoon,' I say, warily, 'I visit your half-sister Elizabeth in her nursery.'

Mary walks silently by my side for some way, not responding. I fear I have upset her with the mere mention of little Elizabeth but recall that she expressed a desire to visit the child when at Hunsdon.

'Yes of course,' she says at length. 'The child is here as well. And of course, she has as much right to be here as I do,'

'I do believe Henry is very fond of her although he seldom expresses any feelings about her.'

'I must confess I used to feel very unkindly towards her,' Mary adds frowning. 'She supplanted me in my father's affections and I was pushed into the background.'

'All is well now,' I say optimistically.

In the king's chamber he greets her robustly, kissing both cheeks and bidding her to sit just below me at table, almost facing me. Mary takes her place after handing the napkin for washing first to the king and then to me. We all eat heartily. At the conclusion of the meal, before the musicians are called forth, he asks Mary if she would be good enough to send a letter to Emperor Charles.

'I would consider it a favour,' he begins. 'If you would write to the effect that, being better instructed by consultation of books and holy learned persons, but principally by the holy spirit, you freely, willingly and without fear or restraint, have acknowledged and approved the statutes made by parliament declaring your mother's marriage unlawful and myself, the king, your father, head of the church.'

Mary looks pained for an instant but recovers swiftly, smiles and nods.

'And request Charles to permit the truth to have place and not hinder it, in order that the king, who treats you kindly, may not have occasion to change toward you.'

'Yes, Your Grace,' she says softly.

'It is long and I'll prepare a draft for you before writing,' he says, smiling.

I look to Mary and raise my eyebrows as the king looks away from table and Mary returns my gesture. Then we smile at each other. I do believe, blasphemous or otherwise, she would shake hands with the devil at this moment to keep her father happy and herself in favour at court.

*   *   *   *

I ask permission to visit the little Lady Elizabeth in her nursery, unsure of the king's current feelings towards his child. He looks thoughtful for a moment, repeats the name Elizabeth as though he has forgotten who she is for a moment and then nods.

'Yes Jane, proceed,' he says. 'Kindly inform me if she is in want for anything.'

I nod and proceed as directed and call at Mary's chambers to see if she would wish to accompany me. She does and we go along, as before, arm in arm in our new, sisterly fashion. The newly decorated nursery is fresh with murals on the walls of knights and ladies and sundry pictures of animals at play. In the centre of the nursery, little Elizabeth is seated, sending her spinning top spiralling around speedily, a look of concentration on her young face. A nurse is in attendance but we bid her take a break from duty with a walk in the grounds.

'Hello,' I say, approaching and settling down next to her with Mary close behind. 'Remember me?'

'The queen lady.'

'Yes, that's right. And I've brought your sister Mary.'

Mary greets her and kisses her and the child looks momentarily frightened as though in fear of her half -sister.

She frowns and says Mary was told to brush her hair and bring things for her and look after her. 'Is that why she's here?'

'No, not anymore,' I say gently. 'You will have servants and others to do those things. Mary is your sister and your friend.'

Elizabeth looks a little confused and doubtful but Mary settles down next to her and sets the spinning top whizzing round at a furious speed. The child looks on, momentarily fascinated and then turns and glares at Mary. I whisper to Mary that it will take her a little time to get used to things as they will be now and she nods and tries a weak smile. The spinning top comes to a halt and Mary sets it going again at speed. Mary stands up.

'I think I'll leave you to get to know her Jane,' she says, quietly. 'For now.'

I nod. 'She'll be fine in a couple of days. Give her time to settle in.'

'Yes,' she says, 'goodbye Elizabeth, I'll see you again soon.'

I settle down on the floor next to the little girl as Mary departs. I set the spinning top going once again and we continue playing until the child tires of the game. She asks to play marbles and I fetch them from the toy store and we begin playing. I contrive to let her win the games until, ringing the changes just for once, I beat her. She clenches her fists and glares at me furiously. Well, well, I think to myself, you are a determined little mistress, are you not? When you grow up you will be a hard taskmaster to deal with, to be sure!

Henry comes into the chamber, unaware as I am of his presence until I see him standing beside me. He kneels down beside Elizabeth, smiling at her.

'Do you know who I am, little one?' he asks, softly.

'Father,' she says, smiling.

He nods and takes hold of her little hand. He tells her that she is going to stay here and live with us, with him, her father and with me, her new mother. Elizabeth looks up at my face doubtfully, frowns and then manages to compose her features into a weak smile.

'The queen lady?'

'That's right,' I say jovially, 'the queen lady.'

Henry roars with laughter suddenly, a big burgeoning, throaty sound that shows him in more jovial mood than I have seen him for some considerable time. He even kneels down and throws marbles for a couple of minutes. Finally, he kisses his daughter's forehead and stands up, facing me.

'Well Jane,' he says, soberly. 'I have my family together at last. My one true wife and love and my two daughters.'

'I'm glad sir,' I say sincerely. 'I too am content. If you are'

All would seem to be well but there is just one thing that causes me to think and wonder anew. The nurse returns and, as he spies her, Henry goes over and has words with her. I watch him shake his head, nod and then walk back to me. His face is dark and angry.

'Do not, under any circumstances ever,' he begins truculently, 'ever dismiss the nurse again. Visit Elizabeth as often as you will but keep the woman in the chamber at all times.'

He strides out without waiting for my response.

TWENTY THREE.

As I enter the ante room to the king's chamber I hear him in conversation with ambassador Chapuys. He sounds heated somewhat and although I do not have the intention to eavesdrop on their conversation, something in Henry's tone makes me curious. I stand very still in the ante room.

'It is a worry, I can assure you,' Henry says.

'Perhaps, Your Grace, you think too much on it and stepping back from the problem would cause it to right itself.'

'My worry is my age,' Henry answers. 'I sometimes feel I'm already too old and will have no children by the queen.'

'I'm sure you are mistaken sir,' Chapuys replies diplomatically. 'A strong man like yourself, in his forties, should have no trouble fathering infants.'

'Well, it isn't happening, not yet,' Henry says.

I listen, concerned that he is becoming so impatient; I am young and have many years of childbearing ahead of me. And Henry is fit enough and man enough to father them. How to approach the king and attempt to re-assure him though, that is the question. He will not be pleased if he finds I have overheard a private conversation.

The voices though become much louder and Henry's most fraught and angry. He is taking Chapuys to task about the emperor of Spain treating with the pope again. The king sees, in his mind, plots against him and people from all countries lining up with the pope against him, Henry. The change of subject is abrupt and if Henry was genuinely worried about the chances of having a child with me, he is now furious and off on a different subject entirely. I will not listen further and will bide my time before I try to convince him that we can and will, produce a male heir.

I have another mission. Henry has informed me that he sees Mary's place here as serving me, as queen and although it is not my idea or what I would want, I must acquaint her with the king's desire. I walk purposefully to her chamber. She is seated, sewing and looks up, delighted to see me.

'Jane, just the person to help me here,' she says. 'My stitching leaves something to be desired.'

I sit alongside her, show her how best to proceed and inform her, gently, of the king's wishes.

'Oh, do not fret Jane,' she says, looking only momentarily disconcerted. 'I am content here and content to serve you in any way I can.'

'Well, it isn't any of my doing,' I say. 'Or anything that I would want.'

'You should know,' she says, looking grim indeed, 'that when I was first sent away from court, as my mother fell out of favour, I was treated like a servant. I was actually put to eat meals with the servants. To be here now, with father and you, dear Jane, is luxury to me.'

'That makes me feel a little better, but not much,' I say, sincerely. 'And when we are alone, you and I, we will continue to behave, as sisters, always.'

'Yes,' she says, with a broad and warm smile. 'But never put yourself in jeopardy for me Jane, you must promise me.'

I promise her and leave her to go to my own privy chamber. I see Margery who I trust and we go to sit in a window corner. The ladies are all busy in one way or another, sewing, embroidering or chattering in little knots of two or three. Even Lady Rochford seems busily engaged, at least deep in conversation with Anne Bassett.

'Is that one behaving well?' I ask and Margery's eyes follow mine to the obvious candidate of my question.

'I'm not too sure,' she says, frowning.

'What problem with her Margery?'

'Oh it may be nothing really,' she says urgently. 'I overheard her talking to Mary and asking if you knew Sir Thomas Wriothesley.'

'I know of him of course,' I say softly. 'He is clerk of the signet under Stephen Gardiner, the king's secretary.'

'Yes.'

'You think it was a sinister enquiry?'

She does not know she says. It might, she concedes, be a casual enquiry about someone fairly prominent in the king's inner circle. But, she continues, watching my expression carefully, he is a handsome fellow.

'You think if she contrives to introduce me to him,' I say, 'she might then go to the king with stories of my adultery.'

'Oh, it's a bit far -fetched Jane,' she says lightly. 'Is it not?'

'Well,' I say grimly, eyebrow raised.' Look what happened to Queen Anne.'

'We cannot afford to trust that woman for a minute,' Margery says coldly.

I re-assure her that I will not be compromised or caught in an awkward situation. I have the king's love and respect and I will never let anybody like Rochford lead me into a trap. Knowing most of what happened to Anne Boleyn only strengthens me and helps to make me self-protective in every situation. I am confident.

'Well I hope you know what you are doing Jane,' she says, doubt in her voice. 'Go to the king with stories of adultery and him so jealous and who knows what ensues. And she is the sort of woman that would fancy her chances as the next queen.'

I wink at her and say 'trust me Margery, 'I know how to keep Henry happy.' I leave her with admonition to keep a very close eye on Rochford.

My next port of call is little Elizabeth's nursery; I do feel a responsibility to the child as it was mainly on my recommendation that she is returned to court. As I arrive I find that Mary is ahead of me and sits in the centre of the nursery with the little mite. I sit with them and join in the game of marbles that is in progress. Mary smiles at me. I am pleased to see that she is going out of her way to be a friend to her little sister; with their history together and the unfortunate positions both have been put in by their father in past years, this is most encouraging. I play the game with them both for some time before departing to walk in the grounds.

The king is approaching me as I walk towards the fountain. He looks resplendent in bright yellow tunic and contrasting dark robes, trimmed with velvet. He has a fine white feather in his cap and he smiles expansively as we meet. I am seduced all over again by his twinkling, bright blue eyes and I return his mute greeting enthusiastically.

'Walk with me Jane,' he says cheerfully. 'If you will.'

We walk on through the orchard and past the armoury and tennis court buildings and he is silent until we round a bend and move along a winding path leading, circuitously, back to the house.

'I am vexed Jane,' he says, serious now and his smile evaporated. 'The closing and re-appointing of small monasteries proceeds with deadly slowness. Most accept their fate but there are those that attempt to resist using force.'

'Oh, 'I say. 'That is unfortunate.'

'More than that, it is totally unacceptable. They should look swiftly to Cromwell and his officer's instructions or find themselves in the tower at best or with their heads spiked on monastery gates at worst.'

'Can you not show mercy sir?' I ask, nervously. 'They are so set in their way of life.'

'It is treason Jane,' he says roughly. 'And as such unforgivable.'

I shake my head sadly, thinking of all the many hundreds of monks, nuns, friars and their abbots and heads who find their way of life terminated. The lucky ones may be re-assigned to larger, more profitable abbeys and reclusive places of worship but the unlucky ones are turned out into the streets to face a way of life they are singularly ill prepared for. To argue forcibly with Henry will, though, only make him ill- humoured and more determined to pursue his plans more vigorously. I want to take issue with him but common sense and self -preservation forbid me to do so.

'They must be put down,' he continues, an irritable edge to his voice. 'Or we are faced with revolt and possible revolution. The safety and security of the realm is paramount Jane, as always; you would do well to keep that constantly in mind.'

'I know My lord,' I say, quietly. 'I know.'

He takes my arm to lead me slowly back to the palace. Once installed in the king's privy chamber he calls for a large jug of his favourite sweet French wine and we settle down in comfort. He tells me, solicitously that there is method in everything he does and he would wish me to fully understand. He has to watch constantly the intentions of Italy, France and Spain and avoid war if possible but be prepared to make it or fight it if necessary for the safety and independence of the realm.

'I remind the French constantly,' Henry says, 'that if they cling to Rome for devotion, they must consider the abominations that have grown from it. How they have encroached upon Princes who by God's word are heads and supreme ministers of justice in their own dominions. I wish them to compare the advantages they have from England and the Bishop of Rome, who is nearer his end than the other, and when he is gone our realm shall continue the same it was and is. England, in other words, can be a better arbiter of Europe than any church with pretentions to be a military power, if only because a hereditary monarchy is more stable than one where the sovereign is elected by a college of bribe-taking cardinals.'

'Yes, I do see the logic of that,' I tell him, quietly.

'England's role therefore, is not to ally itself with Charles or Francis but to keep its principal fluid and remain always high minded and impartial.

I nod, wishing to make myself amenable to his determined strategy knowing anyway that nothing will detract him from his own sense of dominating sovereignty.

'And Cromwell, viper that he is, nevertheless is well schooled in implementing everything I want and will have for England and the English people. He fought and scrapped and dragged himself up on his way to power from the gutter, where he once functioned as the son of a blacksmith and his ruthless, self- seeking ambition is just what I need to keep me in the forefront of achievement. As long as he is useful to me I will keep him as first minister and vice-regent.'

'Yes,' I say smoothly. 'I do not like or trust him but see how useful he is to his king.'

'Oh he is trustworthy Jane, as I've told you before. He knows if he crosses me just once he returns to the gutter where he began. If I spare his life that is.'

We drink our wine and in the pause that follows, Henry smiles broadly.

'I tell you all this, little lamb,' he continues blithely, 'because it is important that you understand what is involved with the great scheme and plan I have for England and the English people. And an important part is keeping the people in this Island in line and knowing what they can do and what they can't. I am a great prince but a fair and just one and I will not allow a few rabble rousers at monasteries to defy me and disrupt my plans.'

'Yes My Lord,' I say. 'You have made it very clear.'

He bursts out laughing suddenly, a bright course sound that reverberates through the chamber. He tells me that he would not normally even mention such things to a mere woman but I am so special to him, so loved by him and trusted by him that he feels the need to give me such information.

'Those whores that lived in sin with me previously would not have been told a word, he adds.

'I'm honoured sir,' I say. 'Indeed.'

'And both, illegal as they were, were unable to produce a prince of the realm that lived.'

I nod, unable to make comment.

'Which is why, little white lamb,' he says, smiling broadly still, 'it is of paramount importance that you provide such an heir to the throne. You have the seed, the good, potent seed of God's representative on earth. The rest is up to you.'

So he does think he's capable of producing a son, I think to myself and say: 'I am confident husband that we will be blessed by Almighty God.'

'That is good,' he says. 'But let us to dinner go. There is roasted leg of mutton, roast swan, venison, chicken, onions and artichoke, lark, snipe, woodcock and a goodly selection of sweetmeats.'

TWENTY FOUR.

The last three weeks have seen Henry in a frenzy of activity. Following lectures to me on the safety and security of the country he seems to have gone to great lengths to initiate policies designed to strengthen our resources against foreign invasion. At first he seemed concerned with domestic matters such as the monasteries and the closing down of most and re-assigning of others in his own name and with his own, carefully chosen bishops, to control them. Now he has shifted his focus.

He must, he has told his ministers, have yet more man-o-war ships, fully equipped and with cannon, ready to sail and fight, if need be, before the end of this year. The task is impossible as many have pointed out to him but he continues to badger Cromwell and the Navy Lords to get things moving ever faster. He must be prepared, he says, for invasion at any time; the Bishop of Rome and his minions are ever threatening, by letter, by messenger, by any means and he finds it intolerable.

The sea ports and towns of the south of England must have more defences and those that are in place now must be strengthened. He wants more yeoman guards trained and ready to fight and use weapons. The armouries must be replenished with arms and kept up to date with the latest and most potent weaponry.

I often hear him shouting during councils that we are ill prepared for overseas invasion and he will even pour out his misgivings to me at times, particularly if Cromwell or any minister has frustrated him with urgings to be cautious or to consider the current state of the treasury.

'All they ever say to me Jane,' he complains, bitterly, 'is, "my Lord, consider the cost involved"'.

I tell him that I'm sure he knows best, he is a wise and vibrant leader and he must persuade those that are over cautious. They do not have the safety of the realm as their prime concern, as he does.

'Indeed, I sometimes think that I and I alone, protect and bolster this great country of ours,' he says, looking frustrated and ill done by.

'You will prevail,' I assure him. 'You will keep us safe from the foreign enemies as our noble, brave and fearless king.'

'Yes, you understand, white lamb,' he says, soothingly. 'You, light of my life, my one true love, you know what I have to endure.'

At nights, on these last temperate evenings of cool autumn weather, I have contrived with help from various accomplices, to have musicians play in the grounds below the king's bedchamber. Madrigals and rich ballads have floated up to our bedchamber and put Henry in goodly mood. Sometimes I order evening sweetmeats like preserved fruit, gingerbread and sugared almonds to be served with our sweet wine at nightfall. It all aids the mood of gentle, reflective love making and then, pleasant slumber with only the king's rasping snoring to add sound to the calm and ultimate silence.

He continues to berate the bishops and the clergy in general to promote the gospel and ensure that every church and chapel in the land has a copy of the new English language bible; something that Cromwell has been promoting actively and tenaciously on his behalf. When he is least calm and most in fear of foreign intrigue, I ask for music, beg him to play for me as his playing is sweet and tuneful and soothes me as much as it does him. It does take much persuasion for he finds it difficult to calm down after an intense council session where he has been blocked or halted in his progress. But then he will finally take up his flute or recorder, reluctantly, scowling at me and telling me that I ask too much of a magnanimous husband and, finally, settling down upon a cushion and playing sweet, melodic music, much of it composed by him. When his mood is less severe I suggest allowing Mary to join us in the privy chamber to sit with us and listen and this, when he agrees, much pleases him to receive our genuine and rapturous applause.

There are times when he brings in harp, fiddle, rebuc, sackbut and viola to join him in recital and the musicians all play with vigour and abandon and Henry, caught up in the spirit and the beauty of the moment, is at his most sublime, creative best.

There are other times when he relaxes by composing music, an occupation that takes much time and effort but which he finds most soothing and satisfying in the extreme. It is at these times when I sit with him, embroidery or general sewing on my lap, him working away with great concentration and me clicking away rhythmically for as long as it takes him to complete his compositions.

The worst of times are when he receives messengers or letters from Rome, Spain or France urging him to go back and renounce his new church and save his soul from damnation. These missives put him in foul humours which can and often do, last for days. But when he goes hunting, when his bad leg is not troubling him, a more and more infrequent occurrence, then he is happy and returns to me in fine fettle and cheery withal. A day of hawking can have the same effect and I also encourage a tennis bout or a forenoon in the skittle alley. All of his leisure pastimes consume him and brighten him and only the cockfights and bear baiting are alien and unbearable to me; I cannot stand to watch any of them and beg to be excused.

I am out riding with him, Henry on his black horse and I on the fine white foal. I have become fond of riding, at a fast clip that suits My lord and covering much ground in Surrey and occasionally Hertfordshire. We ride side by side for the most part and I keep up with him usually but when we get to a wide, uncultivated field, he will charge off at considerable speed as I wait under the shelter of a big oak.

Today is such a day. Henry has forgotten for the moment the problems and trials of state. We dine at leisure at the mansion of one of his baron friends and in the afternoon cover thirty miles in crisp, fresh late autumn weather. This is one of the very best days; Henry relaxed and not concerned for once about invasions, treason and treachery. I too am content and only wish I could keep him in this exuberant mood. As always though, I wait with trepidation to see what the morrow will bring!

TWENTY FIVE

OCTOBER 1536.

A rude awakening indeed; harsh voices, the sound of chains being drawn, iron doors opening and horse hooves without and all this at almost three of the clock on the third of October morning. We are at Windsor where I had hoped we would endure a peaceful few days in the castle at the onset of winter with huge fires banked up to keep out the bitter chill. It is not to be. Two squires have arrived in haste from Lincoln with ill tidings indeed.

Henry is never in the best of moods when roused early from his sleep but at this unseemly hour he is positively fuming. Hastily throwing on cloaks to cover our nightshirts we rush into the ante room where the visitors have been placed to find out what all the fuss is about. The two squires kneel before Henry looking abject indeed with dark, almost blackened faces from the long ride south and apprehension written all over their features.

'Get up on your feet,' Henry bellows coarsely. 'What in the name of heaven is going on?'

'I regret to report, Your Grace,' the first man says, nervously,' that we bring news of a major rebellion that is breaking out in Lincolnshire.'

'Speak up man,' Henry growls. 'Give me facts, details, not mumblings.'

Two further men are ushered in at this point; they have just escaped from Lincoln and have ridden hard at breakneck speed to report to the king. Henry gestures impatiently to the first man who looks even more nervous and confused than the others.

'It is spreading hurriedly, from Louth, from Horncastle, from Caister. There must be sixteen thousand men.'

'Details man, in God's name,' Henry shouts. 'Tell me exactly what is going on.'

'The commons are up sir,' the second man of the first arrivals says hurriedly. 'Beacons are blazing, bells ringing, priests running hither and thither; some of Cromwell's agents surrounded by an angry, seething mob as they attempted to seize the abbeys.'

'You mean they are stopping Cromwell's men carrying out their work?' Henry asks, red faced and livid of expression and, it seems to me, shaking but whether that be from anger or fear or both, I know not.

'Yes, Your Grace,' the first squire says, recovering slightly from his severe attack of nervousness in front of a furious king. 'They killed one man with staves and another was torn limb from limb.'

'You,' Henry screeches, seizing upon one man of the four. 'Tell me exactly what is going on?'

'They are all moving towards Lincoln,' the man replies. 'There must be over thirty thousand of them altogether. A shoemaker seemed to be at the head of the mob but there were members of the gentry among them sir. And they carried a banner with a chalice and a host and the five wounds of Christ.'

Henry fairly snorts and breathes noisily in his fury. Veins stand out on his neck and his face is changing from red to purple in his anger. He demands to know immediately, exactly what is the purpose of the rebellion and what this unholy mob wants.

'Well sir, it all started in St James Church in Louth after evensong-----'the man begins.

'Never mind where the fucking thing started,' Henry screams. 'Tell me what these creatures hope to gain.'

The man hands Henry a scrap of paper and he reads it swiftly, snorting occasionally or making little fierce noises as he reads. I look at Henry becoming redder and more out of control with every passing moment. Alarmed I ask him what the people are saying and he turns to look at me as though unaware, until that second, that I am here. He glares at me.

'What are they saying?' he roars. 'These vagabonds are asking for the abbeys to be restored to the monks, the ten articles of faith repealed along with the new land inheritance statute and heretic bishops to be deprived.'

He is shaking with rage. He sends messengers to fetch Norfolk, Richard Cromwell, my brother Edward, now Lord Beauchamp and the Duke of Suffolk. And, of course, Thomas Cromwell. He calls a council meeting and declares that he would rather sell all his plate than these rebels should not be put down. I attempt to comfort him but he pushes me away angrily.

'They are demanding to be allowed to continue worshipping as Catholics and they demand protection for the treasures of Lincolnshire churches. Who do these vagabonds think they are to demand like this? I will crush them, I will crush them all.'

'Will you not talk to Cromwell first?' I ask timidly but unable to stop myself. 'And the Duke of SuffolK?'

'The only thing I will say to Suffolk,' Henry shouts, 'is to mobilize his full army and send it to Lincoln to crush this disgraceful uprising.'

'But sir,' I say, tremulously because I realise I am taking a huge risk. 'If the people wish to pray as Catholics and want the monks restored to the abbeys, shouldn't it be considered?'

Henry, furious, dismisses the messengers abruptly and bids them wait in quarters until given further instructions. Alone at last he rounds on me.

'How dare you Jane?' he asks. 'How dare you question my state policy?'

I drop down to my knees, tears spurting uncontrolled from my eyes. 'Please Henry, consider restoring the abbeys. This may be a judgement for taking them.'

'Be silent woman,' he roars. 'How often have I told you not to meddle in my affairs? Get up.'

I stand up, shakily, trying to control my weeping and my sorrow.

'Remember what happened to the great whore and others that interfered in my business.'

It is a cruel blow and I am pained almost beyond endurance. I think for the first time that perhaps my love of Henry and his of me is not enough to guarantee my continued safety. The thought that I have kept down and refused to acknowledge, that I myself might end up in the tower and, from there, take the short walk to Tower Green, is now entering, unbidden and unwanted, into my consciousness. I take a linen handkerchief and attempt to dry my sodden eyes.

'The Duke of Suffolk and Norfolk are due here directly,' Henry growls, 'get yourself out of this chamber Jane and leave me to my council.'

I nod and walk out, realising that my tears are starting to flow again and also, more painfully aware that the king does not care; he can see my distress but does nothing to comfort me. His entire mind is focussed forcefully on this rebellion and how swiftly he can crush it. I reach the bed chamber and go in, leaving the door slightly ajar as I would wish to hear what goes on in the next several minutes.

Norfolk arrives first and I can hear through the slightly open door to our ante room the raised voices. He shouts at Norfolk that he will not tolerate this rebellion that he will grant the people nothing and he will have all the ringleaders arrested and hanged. The top people will be hanged, drawn and quartered or disembowelled and any women prominent in the rebellion will be burned at the stake.

'How should I proceed Norfolk?'

'Sir?'

'How do I begin to crush these imbeciles' man?'

'Send word sir, I suggest, accusing them of having no grace or naturalness about them. Point out how presumptuous it is of them, mere rude commons of one shire, to find fault with their prince, who they are bound by all laws to obey and serve, with both their lives, lands and goods.'

'Yes, good, that will be meet to send.'

'Write that they must disperse immediately or face the full force of the Duke of Suffolk's army which, you should point out, is already on the way to Lincoln.'

I hear the chains clanking once again and the creak of the iron doors, loud, raucous voices and realise that Suffolk, my brother, Cromwell's nephew Richard, Cromwell himself and many others are arriving for a hastily convened council and they will proceed to the appropriate chamber to arrange their war strategy. I can bear no more and I close the door of the bedchamber.

Henry will sleep no more this night. He will arrange to crush the rebels no matter what advice he receives from his council, of that I feel sure. And after the men have all dispersed to catch up with their own ruined night's sleep, he will pace and fret, curse and possibly even weep, shout oaths and obscenities and put himself in a frightful mood of ill temper for the day ahead.

I will return to my bed and lie in it, but I know that sleep of any kind will evade me through the early hours of this fearsome morning.

* * * *

It is over and I thank almighty God that it has only lasted a short number of days. With Henry's message to the people of Lincoln that they should lay down arms and return to their homes or face the might of Suffolk's army with another close behind, the result was, I suppose, inevitable. The people gave up the fight and were promised by Suffolk that some of their grievances would be looked into but Henry has been resolute throughout; he would crush the rebellion and extract severe punishment for all the ringleaders and prominent citizens that took part.

I have been treading very carefully with him since the rebellion started. He has little to do with me other than to share dinner and supper and, go through the motions of a loving session most evenings. I can find little desire or enthusiasm for intimacy with My lord and have lately found excuses to avoid lying with him at night. I have been 'unwell' and 'bleeding' and 'suffering belly pains' and consequently unable to perform my matrimonial duties! There is a chill, coldness in my manner towards him and I can't help it; he asks me constantly what is wrong and I reply 'nothing.' I cannot tell him for if I do I shall be accused of treason or supporting rebellion. Perhaps my feelings of revulsion will fade quickly now that the rebellion has been effectively and swiftly crushed. I can't say.

I walk swiftly long the corridor to Cromwell's office. It is a raw October morning and the ice still grips the small, latticed window panes. Cromwell stands by the window, looking down into the courtyard with hands behind his back. Clothed all in black and looking bulky of girth lately, he is a formidable, unpleasant sight. He turns to see me, bows his head in the smallest of gestures possible and stands looking at my face.

'Is it over, Lord Cromwell?' I ask imperiously. 'Are the Lincoln rebels all dispersed?'

'Not all Ma'am,' he answers soberly. 'But very few remain and those not enough to cause trouble.'

'I'm pleased to hear it,' I say. 'But what about the people who started the rebellion?'

He looks away from me and stares out of the window, looking down. I hear the sound of a horse's hooves on cobbles before he turns back to face me looking grave.

'They are being rounded up still,' he says quietly, looking away from me momentarily.

'And how many have been captured so far?'

'A goodly number.'

'And how many have died already?'

He sighs and answers that he really couldn't say. He directs operations for the king and by his orders but much of the routine work is carried out by agents, yeomen and others. Some, he can tell me, have already been executed. Others, like the man known as Captain Cobbler, the shoemaker and the vicar of Louth will be hanged at Tyburn.

'And the others,' I say grimly.

'There is a Louth Park Abbey monk, a lawyer and two or three others who are to be hanged, drawn and quartered,' he replies in a monotone.

I nod to him briefly and leave the chamber. There is much I should like to say about the severity of the sentences but it is not in Cromwell's power to alter or change any of them. It is the king's command that has initiated these sentences, arranged on the basis that he controls church, state and everything else; precisely the reasons for the uprising in the first place. I hate to think of people dying for their religious beliefs or from clinging to what they believe to be the one true church of God. But I can change nothing.

I go into the king's chamber where at least, my body shall be warm. I stand under the giant tapestry and feel the heat from the huge fire burning in front of me, flames leaping up from the massive pile of logs heaped on it. Henry strides in wearing green tunic and velvet hose and looking bright, cheerful and pleased with himself. He nods to me and praises my yellow gown which, in truth, I usually wear to please him.

'So Jane,' he says, loudly. 'Why the frown on so pretty a brow?'

'I'm sorry sir,' I say quietly. 'I was not aware that I wore a frown.'

'What is it?' he asks. 'You are not your usual contented self.'

I tell him gently that I dare not say what ails me for fear it will vex him sorely. He shakes his head and says nothing will vex him, he is in good humour, the rebellion is crushed and he can concentrate on the more fearsome problems of Europe. He invites me to sit upon his knee.

'No sir,' I say with a slight pout. 'It would not be seemly at this time of the day.'

Henry roars with laughter and invites me to sit next to him and he will have wine fetched that we may work up an appetite before dinner. I sit.

'So tell me, white lamb,' he says jocularly, 'what is it that you fear to tell me?'

'The sentencing of the rebels,' I begin, frowning again. 'Must the punishment be so severe My lord?'

He looks very fierce. I must understand, he says, that treason is a heinous crime that undermines our very stability and will always carry severe death penalties. If he treats these vagabonds lightly they will overthrow him tomorrow and chaos would ensue.

'But hanging, drawing and quartering their bodies and displaying the parts in public is abominable,' I say testily,' I cannot bear to think about it.'

'The punishments must fit the crimes Jane,' he says. 'I am a fair and just prince but cannot allow acts of treason and rebellion.'

'No, I realise sir, you are just. But merciful too. Could you not show some degree of mercy?'

'I cannot show weakness,' he says, brow corrugated. 'You are too soft and sensitive my lamb.'

'I know it sir,' I say, tears spurting from my eyes. 'I fear for those poor monks and friars who die for their misguided loyalty to an alien church.'

He signals to the servant, hovering in a corner of the room and bids him pour two goblets of wine. We take them and drink. He hands me a linen handkerchief and I dry my eyes. I look at him appealingly but am unable to fashion a smile on my face.

'What I will do,' he says, suddenly, 'is instruct Cromwell to select two of the least offensive monks from the Lincoln monasteries and commute their sentences to straight hanging.'

'Thank you,' I say softly. It is too little but I will not look a gift horse in the mouth.

'No drawing, no quartering, no disembowelling,' he says and I wince. 'A straight death for two of the lightest offenders. For you Jane because you are the shining light of my life.'

I nod and somehow I do manage to smile. We finish our drinks.

'Come walk with me Jane,' he says, mood buoyant. 'We will look in on Elizabeth and then go in to dinner. I have plans to re-open several closed monasteries and put bishops of the English church in charge. They will do good works for the commons people and generate incomes for the state that I will use and authorise their works wisely. This has been a difficult year of our reign so far but with luck and good management it will yet yield progress for the people and their lords and masters.'

TWENTY SIX.

It is not over. No sooner has the uprising in Lincoln been crushed and almost a hundred people executed than another, bigger, more horrific rebellion has started up in York. All over the northern counties of England, rebellious commons people have united in arms to demand restitution of the monasteries, to Catholic prayer and restoration of the original monks and nuns. They are also looking for a fresh parliament that will be fair and just to the people and they would want representation of parliament in the north, in York.

Henry is, again furious and although he manages to keep his temper and appear to be a clear headed negotiator in parliament, at home he is like a sore headed bear most of the time, only calming down to gentle behaviour at night, in the intimacy of our bedchamber. Even in the midst of a national disaster with upwards of thirty thousand men armed and ready to strike, he can find time and inclination to remind me of the urgency of producing a male heir to the throne! For me it is less straight on but I will grit my teeth and do my duty as I can find no real excuse not to.

Meanwhile the beacons are lit all over Lancashire, Yorkshire and Cumberland, bells ring out their sombre messages and the massed rebels march towards York. Henry has sent a letter to Charles Brandon, Duke of Suffolk instructing him to use all dexterity to get the rebels to Lincoln and cause all the boats on the Humber or means of passage into Yorkshire to be taken up. He also instructs Suffolk that if he detects any further uprising or any attempted new rebellion, 'you shall, with your forces run upon them with all dexterity, destroy, burn and kill, man, woman and child to the terrible example of all others.'

A letter to the Earl of Derby requests him to make ready his forces to crush the rebellion in the north but first, having heard of an insurrection attempted about the abbey in Salley, Lancashire, where the abbots and monks have been restored by the traitors, 'we now desire you immediately to repress it. To apprehend the captains and either have them immediately executed as traitors or sent up to us. You are to take the said abbots and monks forth by violence and have them hanged in their monk's apparel and ensure that no town or village begin to assemble.'

I usually manage to catch Henry at the point of composition or, at least, thinking over what the content shall be, of his various communications and he will always ask my opinion before sending even though, at most other times, he is at pains to inform me that I have no business interfering with affairs of state and I must always remember that I am a mere woman and not equipped to deal with such matters! Today I find him wrestling with the content of a letter to the Duke of Norfolk, poised with his army to strike at the rebels in York.

'Ah Jane,' he says, putting down his quill. 'Come in and sit with me a minute.'

'Who do you write to sir?' I ask. 'Is it about the rebellion?'

'I have no time to deal with anything else,' he booms, angrily. 'Of course it's about the rebellion. I write to Norfolk to tell him to crush the rebels swiftly and to show no mercy to the ringleaders.'

'Oh,' I say, sadly.

'Yes, you may well look at me like that my fine lady,' he says. 'Be assured though that if this rebellion isn't crushed and crushed swiftly, our way of life will be gone. Our very lives may well be gone. These monstrous people intend to rise up against their king and force him to change back to the old ways and the illegal church and give them a free parliament.'

'Which you cannot do,' I say, softly.

'Which I will not do Jane,' he says forcefully. 'I set a precedent here madam for myself and all future kings of this realm. As Head of state and church every act of parliament must be first approved by the sovereign.'

'Yes, I see that,' I tell him although I do not think it right.

He begins to chuckle suddenly, putting down his quill once more and positively shaking with laughter. When I ask him what is so amusing he tells me that word has got back to him that the rebels do not blame the king for the closing of the monasteries and having hundreds of destitute monks wandering the streets with no livelihood, they blame the first minister.

'Cromwell?'

'Aye, Cromwell,' he says, almost weeping with laughter. 'They think he and his agents and enforcers are to blame for the entire business.'

'How strange,' I say, frowning.

'Well, it serves the viper right,' Henry says, eyes twinkling. 'He is so efficient I should set him to organising and planning his own funeral next.'

Henry returns to his letter to Norfolk. He is frowning as he stares at the parchment in front of him. He mutters darkly about the rebels and their noble leaders, Lord Darcy and Robert Aske marching in front of an army of forty thousand men, with a banner of St. Cuthbert and the standard of the five wounds of Christ.

'How dare they use the name of Almighty God in vain,' he bellows suddenly, mood changing in the instant.

'Do this scum not realise that they oppose me, their king and God's representative on earth?'

'They are but simple commons sir,' I say, succinctly.

'No Jane, you err,' he tells me. 'There are lords and knights, barons and high born men among this rabble.'

He ignores me for a few minutes, thinking out loud, wondering if he should instruct Norfolk to go into battle with the rebels now and put up a hell of a fight or advise him to wait until Suffolk's army arrives. He even has a third army being formed at this very moment but wonders, talking to himself rather than me, how long it will take to get the two armies moving towards York. As he sits there, conducting a dialogue softly with himself, I look out of the window and see white flakes of snow drifting down. It is cold enough here in Windsor but in the north, notoriously frozen throughout the winter months, fighting a battle with staves, pikes and bows will be hell on earth. I feel a bitter sadness for all involved.

'The question is,' Henry says, looking to me now, 'can Norfolk hold out until the other armies arrive, given that reports of the rebel gatherings vary between thirty and even up to forty thousand men.'

'How many men has Norfolk got?' I ask, quite expecting to be told not to ask questions that do not concern me.

'Around eight thousand,' Henry replies, looking thoughtful.

'Then you can't ask him to fight sir, I say, alarmed. 'It will be carnage. A massacre of your own army.'

'I rather think I have no choice Jane,' he says, looking grim indeed.

'You could get Norfolk to open negotiations with the rebels,' I say softly.

'Talk to the scum, never,' he bawls irritably, face turning red as beetroot. 'I'd rather give away all my palaces and castles.'

You may have to, I'm thinking, or have them taken forcibly from you but I do not say that to him. Instead I say: 'it would delay matters, giving your armies time to group and reach York.'

Any delay, I'm thinking, will stop bloodshed and carnage in our northern cities. It is all I can think of to stop the slaughter, temporary maybe but better than nothing.

'I will not give an inch to this scum,' Henry says. Then he stops speaking suddenly and looks thoughtful. He rises and begins, in his usual manner, to start pacing round the chamber, arms behind his back, forehead corrugated and his face looking as though he is deep in thought and concentration considering his options.

'I need to think this matter through Jane,' he says, stopping in front of me. 'I will walk awhile in the grounds.'

'It is bitter cold outside Henry,' I remind him.

'I will cover myself appropriately,' he says, nods at me and walks out of the chamber.

I smile, a grim, bitter smile and put on my damask cloak and walk down to my privy chamber where my ladies are deep in conversation, animated, lively as the fresh winter morning, digesting, no doubt, the latest rumours and stories going the rounds of court.

I have brief words with Anne and Mary although their latest gossip is a bit out of date. The more bloodthirsty ladies talk about the fate of the many ringleaders, if they be so, who paid with their lives for the uprising in

Lincolnshire. Mary Norris tells me that there were a score, or more, who were hanged.

'They died a horrible death,' she says, giving me her shocked, pained look. 'Hanged, cut down alive, disembowelled, their entrails burned while they were still alive and, finally, had their heads cut off.'

'Merciful heaven Mary,' I say, stringently. 'You sound positively excited by the poor people's awful fate.'

'No indeed ma'am,' she replies, frowning fiercely. 'But isn't it just too horrible to contemplate?'

'Indeed it is,' I say severely. 'So let us not even think about it, leave alone discuss it.'

She pouts and resumes her embroidery, looking up at me when she thinks I am not looking her way. I shake my head and move away, have a brief few words with Margery and Jane, nod to the others and walk over to the window seat enclosure where Jane Boleyn is reading a book.

'Well, Lady Rochford,' I say, cheerfully. 'Are you settling in well withal?'

'I am ma'am indeed,' she says, giving me a crooked smile. 'It is as though I have never been away.'

'That is good,' I say, in friendly manner.

'I've become re-acquainted with two or three bright young men at court that I knew in Queen Anne's time. I know not whether you have met up with them, there are so many people at court these days.'

'Possibly not,' I say warily. 'Being close to the king in most matters relating to household I do not have much time for socializing.'

'I could arrange introductions for you,' she says, watching my face warily.

'That will not be necessary Jane,' I say crisply. 'I am busy enough with the king and the people I do know well already.'

'As you wish,' she says. 'I do hear through court gossip that the king may be in great danger of his life.'

She looks at me expectantly, trying to gauge the effect her words have had on me and, I feel sure, hoping to produce a look of shock and fear. I hold her gaze firmly and ask where on earth she heard such a thing.

'All reports and all intelligence reaching me,' she says imperiously, 'suggest a massive block of some fifty or sixty thousand armed men in the northern counties, swearing to overthrow the king and put him in the tower, pending execution.'

I smile. 'I think your intelligence is somewhat exaggerated Jane,' I tell her. 'Not to mention highly inaccurate.'

'My sources are usually impeccable,' she says, frowning.

'Half that number of men,' I say. 'Then you might be somewhere near the truth. Although I should caution you Lady Rochford, that speaking treason is considered by the king to be as bad as practising it. And you wouldn't like to lose your head, would you'

She gives me a withering look and returns to her book. Before I can settle with some embroidery of my own, a page enters and tells me that the king has requested my immediate presence in his privy chamber. I walk there swiftly and find him relaxed in a favourite velvet chair.

'Jane, come in please. I have thought this through and reached a decision.'

'Yes, My Lord?' I say, as he appears to dither.

'I will instruct Norfolk to hold off from battle but to appoint with the rebels,' he says truculently. 'It is my desire to know what is in their hearts and what they want. And it will give us time to put more armies in place.'

He looks as though he would like to hang all and every one of the rebellious army without trial or discussion but I merely smile and tell him I understand 'his' decision.

TWENTY SEVEN.

Henry is in council with his lords and ministers at Whitehall Palace and the atmosphere all through the buildings is tense. I can almost feel the fear and anxiety of everybody at court and that applies to courtiers of rank and not just the lowly servants. Henry bellows and shouts in council and his angry voice can be heard down corridors and even in chambers and the banqueting hall.

'I gave no permissions,' he shouts at Norfolk, 'to offer any pardons or any inducements to this scum,'

'No your Grace,' the voice of Norfolk is heard. 'My army and that of My lord of Shrewsbury numbered eleven thousand together. We were up against almost forty thousand rebels.'

'I don't care if there were only ten of you,' Henry bellows as I go into my privy chamber trying to ignore the raucous voices echoing all over the palace. Only Mary Norris along with Jane Arundell and Margery Horsman are present, sitting with their sewing but looking very sheepish and cowed.

'Where are the others?' I ask Margery, joining her in my favourite window corner where I see bright white snowflakes drifting slowly down outside.

'Staying in their bedchambers,' she says, smiling. 'Afraid almost, to come out for fear of meeting the king in a passageway.'

'Surely they are not that much a feared of him?' I ask surprised. 'He can be quite gentle on occasion,'

'Well, with respect ma'am,' Margery replies, 'you see that side of him but the rest of us rarely ever do.'

I shrug my shoulders and begin some embroidery. I want gold leaf motifs on white satin, a favourite gown I wear which pleases Henry much and I enjoy wearing. The gown is of exquisite quality satin and I must work my embroidery carefully, for fear of marking any part of it. A servant comes in and banks up the fire with large logs; the heat it throws out is intense indeed but localised rather in a large, high ceilinged chamber and fighting a losing battle with the icy draughts from the big windows.

Through the latticed window panes I note that the snowflakes are increasing in volume and stop what I am doing to rub my hands together. Margery and Jane look up and smile in my direction.

'It's a bleak winter indeed,' Jane says, emulating me by rubbing her hands together for warmth.

'The Thames completely frozen over this morn,' Margery adds.

'Is it already?' I ask. 'I have not been abroad this past two days.'

'Small ragged boys are running across it,' Margery continues. 'And it is raw indeed outside these chambers.'

I hear a distant rumble of raised voices and recognise Henry shouting angrily at somebody. I look up, frown and catch Jane's eye and she shrugs her shoulders and raises her eyebrows in a manner that suggests she finds the king's bad temper an amusing but irritating thing. I smile in return and continue embroidering unabated.

'The king collided with a servant yesterday,' Jane says warily. 'Then he grabbed him by the scruff of his neck and threw him against the wall.'

'Oh no,' I say bleakly. 'He rarely loses his temper as badly as that.'

'Well the lad had to have a head wound bandaged,' Margery says, looking harshly towards me.

'The king is under severe pressure at present,' I say apologetically. 'With this uprising in the north following on from the Lincoln one, he feels the strain. It makes him behave badly.'

The two of them stare at me blankly, looking as though they think I should have a solution or all round cure for his bad temper and terrible behaviour. 'I'm sure the king did not mean to hurt the boy,' I say, softly. The penetrating stares increase in intensity but neither of them speaks. I continue quietly, finishing off the section of embroidery I aim to complete this morning. I tell the women I am returning to the king's chamber to be ready to receive him and try some sweet words in his ear to calm him.

As I walk to the king's privy chamber I hear a muffled rumble of voices from the council room but they are subdued somewhat now; perhaps somebody within has advised keeping the volume down although I wager he will have attracted the king's annoyance before achieving his object.

Two sturdy yeomen of middle age stand on duty outside the king's chamber. Their sharp voices reduce to hurried whispers as they see me approach. I pass in to the ante chamber but pause therein before proceeding to look at a portrait of myself on the wall, painted by Holbein. I look rather hard and sharp of feature and reflect that although Holbein has a reputation for producing accurate likenesses of his subjects, he can be quite harsh, pointing up cruel expressions and emphasising unflattering features that do not show up in people's day to day appearance. He has, I feel, been somewhat cruel to me although the king expressed his satisfaction with the painting. I hear the two yeoman speaking now, not lowering their voices and unaware that I am in such close proximity.

'Keep distance from the king if you value your life Gregory,' I hear one say.

'Oh fie, his sharp tongue is more cutting than his wolf's teeth,' is the reply.

'I say avoid him, a sore headed bear has nothing on him this morn.'

'Be still man and do not be alarmed. The queen will sooth him with her sweet talk, warm caresses and soft wet cunt.'

They both laugh, a harsh, course sound indeed. I feel blood rush to my cheek to heat it temporarily and think to myself that I could have both men thrown into the tower, instantly. I will not do so. I will see that they both get night long duties for a week with no breaks. There is enough hatred and violence going on all over our land at present and we are more in need of tolerance and forgiveness. As I walk into the king's chamber to await him, as requested, I reflect that it is true anyway that I do try to sooth the king with sweet words and warm embraces but I do not wish to hear crude men making nasty references to our private relations. I will, I think, devise a stronger punishment for the two rogue yeomen.

Henry comes in, all of a flurry, looking heavy of body and mind, his tunic undone and some of his clothing looking ruffled and scrunched up. He is not in good humour, as I notice at a glance but I greet him warmly and despatch a servant for some of his favourite French wine.

'You look weary, My lord, I say sympathetically.

'I am surrounded by fools and malcontents in council, 'he complains, dropping heavily into his favourite chair. 'Norfolk has overreached himself, yet again.'

'What now?' I ask but fearful of the reply.

'The crass idiot has promised that northern scum that they will be pardoned for laying down their arms and they shall have a new parliament set up in York.'

I can only feel relief that serious bloodshed has been avoided, at least for the near future. I nod reassuringly, I hope and say that I'm sure it will all be resolved satisfactorily in the end.

'It will be resolved finally Jane,' he replies, 'when those vagabonds are all hanged and disembowelled.' The servant enters with our wine and Henry gabs his tankard greedily and takes a large draught. I shudder at the thought of many more hangings.

'I gave no authority for such negotiation,' Henry continues. 'They will not be pardoned. Every last one of them will be punished straightly.'

'Surely you could show a little mercy to some?' I say tentatively. 'You are, after all, a wise, merciful and magnanimous sovereign.'

'Too wise, too merciful and too magnanimous,' he says fiercely, his jaw shaking. 'Do not anger me further Jane, these scum must all die. It is treason, high treason and if left unpunished would set a precedent for future would be rebels.'

I do not respond but feel a weakness in my belly and a sadness at heart. Henry drinks his wine and calls for more to be poured into his empty tankard. He looks at me with a penetrating glare.

'The rebel leader, Robert Aske,' he says slowly. 'He's cousin to the Duke of Cumberland and, a third cousin to you Jane, I am informed.'

I blush scarlet. 'Yes, My lord,' I say quickly. 'A London lawyer from a northern family but I have not met him. And I certainly know nothing of his rebellious activities.'

'No, no, you are blameless white lamb,' he says gently. 'But I would wish to know more about him and find out what he hoped to gain.'

'Sir?'

'Norfolk can redeem himself to some extent by persuading the man to come to London to speak with me.'

'How so, my Lord?'

'Norfolk has persuaded all the rebels to lay down arms and return to their homes. The armies are broken up. I need to speak to this man and find out what he hoped to achieve.'

'And then sir, what then?' I ask, an icy sorrow piercing my heart.

'He will have a safe passage to return home afterwards.'

I look at Henry dumbfounded. He roars with laughter suddenly and smacks his thigh. He tells me that Norfolk has negotiated and made promises, all illegal in point of fact but it means that he, the king, can do nothing about it for the present time. That is why he was so angry in council but he has vented his displeasure at the Duke's actions and is no longer in ill humour. I say that I am relieved to hear it.

'My hands are tied at present,' he says, quite surprisingly cheerful. 'I can but enter into dialogue with Aske and then let him go back north.'

'I'm sure it is for the best Henry,' I say solicitously.

'We shall see, we shall see,' he says smiling. 'But for now it is too early for dinner and it is a long wait until nightfall. Come, little lamb and sit upon my lap that I may feel the warmth of your young body and kiss your pale white cheek. I must have the love of my life close to me.'

I raise an eyebrow and then rise, walk over and sit upon his ample lap.

* * * *

DECEMBER 1536.

We cover ourselves in several goodly layers of clothing; thick wools and furs and many items of undergarment. We go to Greenwich palace on this freezing cold, icy morning and it is the king's pleasure to ride over from White Hall, on horseback, over the frozen Thames. We could, of course, take horse and carriage which, I for one, would find more comfortable but the king is adamant.

'Are you sure my Lord,' I ask him. 'Is your bad leg not troubling you?'

'Do not fret Jane,' he says tetchily. 'I was practically born in the saddle. And riding horses since I was a mere youth.'

'The wind out there is bitter,' I say, reflectively, looking out of the casement at a few isolated snowflakes, drifting past the window rather than falling. Ice is everywhere, on the window frames, down on the cobbles below, clinging to pipes.

'And you, gentle Jane, love of my life,' he says. 'Are you equal to a fast trot on mostly solid ice?'

'I am equipped so to do My lord,' I say, more confidently than I feel.

We set out from White Hall palace with the whole entourage following on behind us. At least if there is a mishap we can transfer swiftly to a covered carriage. My horse snorts noisily as we set off, a cloud of white, icy breath flowing from his nostrils. As we trot onto the ice bound surface of the Thames I feel and hear the clunk of the hard surface under my horse's hooves. Henry bounds out, overtaking me, smiling broadly and obviously enjoying himself enormously. I follow him with the exhilarating but bitterly cold breeze biting into my face, the only area of my body uncovered. My eyes water momentarily and I have to fish out a silk kerchief from my heavily cloth covered arm.

As I wipe my eyes I find I can see clearly now; the sky is a bright whitish grey and we are trotting at a gentle but agreeable pace now. Henry promised he would not stray far from my horse's side and he keeps his word. It does seem strange to be in the middle of the wide River Thames, riding rather than sitting in our barge and with small, ragged boys on sleighs all around us. We increase speed slightly and the cold breeze begins to sting my face, it is so icy.

It seems a relatively short ride from White Hall to Greenwich palace with the river crossing easier than usual! We make good time and arrive feeling fresh, tingling indeed from the attentions of constant winter wind and the sort of all -round air that slaps rather than caresses. Henry summonses me to his privy chamber long before I am settled into my own or have time to see that my ladies are installed comfortably. I enter his rooms smiling but the smile dies on my face as I see his grim expression.

'What is it, My Lord?' I ask, fearfully. 'What troubles you?''

He hands me a letter. 'I'm so sorry my sweetheart,' he says sadly.

'What sir?' I ask, alarmed. 'What ails?'

The letter is from my mother. She tells me that my father died on the 21st December and it was peaceful finally, when the end came. My sadness is compounded further when I read certain portions of her letter. She says that he was afflicted, from time to time but not regularly, with a form of madness. There were disturbing interludes when he did not recognise her and his memory lapses were such that he could remember nothing of the recent past. Sometimes he was lucid and would talk to her and, as she reminds me, his faculties all seemed to be intact when I last visited, with Henry. On other, fairly frequent occasions in the last month, he would sit staring out into the distance and not speak for hours. She asked him often if he knew who she was and received no response whatsoever. Her letter ends with her saying he is at peace now and she is in reasonably good fettle and I must not fret. I begin to cry, letting my tears fall unheeded and unchecked.

'Am I to go to the funeral sir?' I ask but Henry shakes his head.

'I'm sorry lamb,' he says. 'It is not considered etiquette for the queen to attend family funerals.'

'Oh Henry, I am filled with sorrow withal,' I say. 'He was not, I think, a good man but he was my father and I believe he loved me as I loved him.'

He comforts me and I cling to his ample chest, wrapping my arms around him. I weep softly and quietly for a minute and then break free of the embrace and wipe my eyes dry.

'He was over sixty, a goodly age,' Henry says quietly. 'Now he may rest in peace.'

'Yes, you are right,' I say very quietly.

'I cannot bear to see you in distress,' he says. 'I should go to council now but I will tarry with you white lamb, if you desire it?'

'No, My Lord, please carry on with your duties,' I say. 'I will spend a quiet hour alone first and then join my ladies.'

He says that affairs of state are pressing but he will send a page to see that I want for nothing every half hour. I thank him and bid him go about his business now; I really feel that I would like a short time alone with my grief and my innermost thoughts.

'Well, if you are content,' he murmurs. 'I will cut short my meeting and leave Cromwell to wrap up. The Christmas season is upon us and you must rest up at your leisure my love. I have this man Aske visiting us during the Christmas season but otherwise we are free to pray and attend chapel, sing carols and give thanks to Almighty God.'

'Yes sir,' I say, forcing a smile. 'It will be a season of quiet and peace and goodwill. And my prayers will all be for the soul of my father.' He leaves me and I recline back, focussing my gaze on the brightly coloured, vivid pictures in the tapestry on the wall. I will begin to grieve quietly, at my leisure.

TWENTY EIGHT.

The priest conducts mass in the chapel. Henry sits with me and close by are Mary and Elizabeth with her nurse and beyond them the knights, esquires and general courtiers. The Christmas season is upon us and we all attempt to show good cheer and rejoice in prayers and carols sung, our allegiance to Almighty God.

We all hold lighted tapers and carols are sung. Mistletoe and ivy are everywhere, decorating fireplace surrounds, tables, portraits, anywhere they may be hung. Even in the chapel there is some to be seen. It is a time to be merry and full of love and kindness to each other and I must, in truth, bury my sorrow at the loss of my father and join in the spirit of the season.

Leaving the chapel we all go on our separate ways but Henry, smiling and of good cheer throughout this Christmas morning, has summoned myself, Mary and little Elizabeth to his chamber for the 'wassail.' We all settle down and Henry, in jovial mood calls for the steward who enters with a huge bowl and calls out 'wassail' three times.

I look at Henry who grins at me and takes the bowl. He drinks heartily and passes the bowl to me. It is a rich and spicy drink indeed; made up of hot ale, apples, spices and sugar. I take a little sip but even that tickles my throat with hot liquid and I cough suddenly and clear my throat. Henry roars with laughter.

'Drink up, my love, my sweetheart,' he says. 'Do not dally on Christ's day.'

'It is fearsome hot my Lord,' I protest but it only sets him laughing once again.

I pass the bowl to Mary who sips it as delicately as I although she manages to drink with no ill effect merely grimacing towards me at the end.

'And little Elizabeth,' Henry calls.

'Oh no, my Lord,' I protest. 'She is too young and it is passing hot enough to scald her delicate belly.'

He calls the nurse over and bids her pour a little into a chalice and cool it before letting the little mite take a drink. He then indicates that we must all drink again and he starts off then passes the bowl round. Finally, he takes the crust of bread at the bottom and consumes it, the duty of the head of the household.

Dinner is a festive time indeed. Minstrels in colourful costumes dance on the balcony and the musicians are in place in the banqueting hall to play throughout our dining. We have roasted turkey, a bird the king favours much at Christmas. There is also a large Boar's head, decorated with raisins and, the centrepiece, which I must confess I look on with alarm, the Christmas Pie, which is coffin shaped, huge and consists of a turkey, stuffed with a goose, stuffed with a chicken stuffed with a partridge and a pigeon. It is also decorated round the massive plate with hare, game birds and wild fowl.

Henry accepts a massive serving for himself, parts of the various fowls dripping with gravy and some partridge and pigeon to complete his feast.

The musicians begin to play carols and religious songs as the food is being served.

'Eat heartily Jane,' the king calls, spooning up a large mouthful of goose. 'And you Mary.'

'I can only take a small portion,' I say, watching carefully as my plate is being prepared.

'I too, can eat but little,' Mary says, pulling a face as she glances at me.

'Oh come along you wenches,' he says. 'It is Christmas season, be of goodly cheer.'

'I am of good cheer sir,' I say, smiling. 'And the pie is delicious.'

'Indeed it is,' Henry says, spooning turkey and chicken, mixed, into his mouth. 'But I bid you leave room for mynce pies. They have good mutton, saffron, vinegar, raisins and dates to tickle your palette,'

'I'll have to fast for a month after today's Christmas fayre,' I say.

'And I too,' echoes Mary.

The minstrels dance and play, the musicians play up a catchy tune for a festive day and we all eat heartily, too much for some of us. It is the Christmas season!

* * * *

Cromwell is announced and I bid him enter my privy chamber at Greenwich. He enters with his usual black attire and cap, no colourful Christmas clothes for this dark, sombre man. It is bitter chill without with frost and ice biting the small window panes but the gigantic Christmas log burns slowly in the fire; hot small logs underneath providing the fierce overall heat of the chamber and the monster sized piece of wood sizzling slowly. Cromwell gives a small, delicate bow.

'Master Robert Aske Majesty,' he says softly.

'Yes, please show him in my Lord Cromwell,' I say, equally quietly.

Master Aske enters and bows low before me. As he straightens up I see a tall man with fairish coloured hair and slight beard and a face of pleasing disposition, it seems to me.

'You are welcome to our palace sir,' I say, smiling.

'I thank you Your Majesty,' he says, smoothly. 'I am most grateful to receive your welcome.'

'Come, step in, move closer to the fire,' I say, smiling. 'You must be chilled indeed from riding.'

'It is a welcome sight withal,' he says, following me nearer to the radius of the fire's heat.

'And a wondrous great log,' he continues, admiringly. 'See how slowly it burns.'

'Yes,' I reply, looking at it and feeling the hot flush from the fire on my face. 'It is a green log and will, with luck, burn slowly through the twelve days of Christmas.'

I invite him to step even nearer to the hot fire, conscious of his chill state and desirous that, as our guest, he feels comfortable at all times in our chambers. I ask him if he will take a chalice of warmed red Christmas wine and spices and as he gratefully accepts, raise one arm to the servant and bid him bring it to us. I note that big white flakes of snow are falling slowly outside, their brightness and colour adding to the highly illuminated aspect of the big window.

'It looks so pretty without,' I say, smiling and indicating the big window. 'As long as one is safely enclosed in a warm chamber with a roaring fire.'

'Yes, Your Majesty, indeed it does,' he says contentedly.

'Our River Thames is fully frozen over this winter,' I say. 'It is a bitter season to be sure.'

We sit in comfortable chairs, myself first and then I invite him to follow. He sits down nervously, it seems to me and I would wish to put him at his ease. We have only just met for the first time but I find him a man of charm and breeding instantly, perhaps more by instinct as we are hardly acquainted yet, this distant third cousin who I have never previously encountered.

'You will, I hope, excuse the king,' I say. 'Affairs of state do not, lamentably, cease during the Christmas season and he is still in council meeting.'

'I'm honoured indeed,' he says. 'To be here at his invitation. And very honoured to meet you Your Majesty.'

Our refreshments are brought in and we take a chalice each. He waits politely for me to sip my wine and I do so, slowly, delicately, savouring the rich, spicy, warm and tangy wine. As he still seems nervous and slightly ill at ease I tell him that the king particularly and I, myself, are very pleased that the Pilgrimage of Grace, as it is being called, is over and the people all restored to their homes and occupations and, most importantly of all, there has been very little bloodshed.

'That is so much a goodly blessing to me,' he says. 'I am. I assure you madam, the king's most loyal servant and supporter. I only wanted to draw attention to the people's wish to pray in the Catholic faith they have followed all their lives and also draw notice of the suffering of the poor people, following a bad harvest this past two years and their loss of alms generally at the closing of so many small monasteries.'

'Yes, I can understand your concerns,' I say gently. 'I would however, caution you to tread carefully with the king if discussing the closure of monasteries.'

'Your Majesty advises wisely,' he says, cautiously. 'Although I was given to understand that he has agreed to a pardon for all the participants, is open to the idea of free speech and to give the north a say in the affairs of parliament.'

'Yes,' I say thoughtfully. 'You will though, I expect, have to accept that monastery closing will continue unabated.'

He looks at me, subdued. I see something in his eyes that suggests he is feeling uncomfortable and ask him to speak up, if there be anything that disturbs him. He clears his throat and is obviously ill at ease and, I think, a sensitive man unsure of how to proceed. I ask what ails him.

'It is just that I am much concerned Your Majesty,' he says, looking sheepish, 'for the fate of seven thousand poor priests in my company who are forced to wander the streets, destitute.'

'As many as that?' I ask, alarmed.

'Yes ma'am,' he replies. 'I mean no disrespect to the king, believe me and I know, forgive my impetuousness, that this is the result of Cromwell and his enforcers and, with great respect--' He hesitates.

'Yes, say it Master Aske.'

'Well, forgive me, we know ma'am that this is not the king's doing but that man Cromwell who advises his Majesty.'

I pause and glance at Master Aske. This man seems to me courteous and a true gentleman and honest and forthright as the day is long. I fear for him though that although Henry has given pardon to the rebels and promised that he will look into all their grievances that he may overstep the mark in conversation with the king and find himself labelled as a traitor. It is true though that he has given Aske a safe passage to come here and return home. That should, I feel, suffice.

'I would advise you to tread very carefully in discussions with the king,' I say, sombrely. 'Lord Cromwell is his chief minister and his most trusted advisor.'

'My sincere apologies Your Majesty,' he says, looking stricken. 'I have inadvertently given offence, the last thing I intended.'

'No offence Master Aske,' I say, sincerely and smile. 'I would just like to think that your meeting with Henry goes smoothly and you are not embarrassed.'

'Thank you ma'am,' he says, looking suddenly relieved. 'I am most grateful for your generous and kind counsel.'

I smile, then rise and walk over to the window. The snow is falling faster now and laying a thick white blanket on the cobbles and grass areas below. It swirls swiftly and I can imagine the icy wind outside that accompanies the snowfall. I invite Master Aske to partake of some more warming wine. I re-join him near the slowly smouldering, hot fire.

'My concerns are not for myself verily my lady,' he says soberly. 'I see myself as a poor but honest spokesman for millions of commons and even some gentry and nobility who would like to see fair representation of government in the north.'

'Yes, we understand your concerns,' I tell him.

We are summoned to the king's privy chamber and arrive to find an even fiercer heat being generated from an even bigger Christmas log. Henry is in his finery, ermine, satin and fur linings and he wears more jewels than I. He stands foursquare, feet apart, a big, imposing figure and I can imagine Master Aske's feeling of discomfort in his presence. But My Lord has a wide grin and opens welcoming arms.

'Be you truly welcome Master Aske,' he says, voice booming. 'It is my wish that here and before my council, you ask what you desire and I will grant it.'

'Your Majesty is most generous,' Aske says nervously, his voice low pitched and soft. 'I am but a poor servant of the commons of York and the northern counties.'

'So what would be your dearest wish? Henry asks, smiling broadly still. 'Speak up man.'

'Well, Your Majesty, forgive my presumption, but some representation in parliament for the people of the north and help for the poor with many monasteries closed.'

'Yes, 'Henry says, stroking his chin. 'I have a mind to open parliament at York and also to have the queen crowned there.'

Aske's face lights up and he is obviously surprised and delighted. I look at Henry and raise an eyebrow; he has mentioned nothing to me about my forthcoming coronation.

'Your Majesty is most generous and just,' Aske says softly. 'And, Your Grace, much as I hesitate to mention it, we do worry about the pernicious influence of Lord Cromwell and his dangerous scheme of closing down the monasteries.'

'Yes, now as to that,' Henry says, frowning, 'I say we must discuss it in detail in council. Doubtless though we can work out a solution that will please you and your people.'

Henry suggests going to council now as his ministers are still in chambers. Aske thanks me for my hospitality and bows low before leaving and I am much impressed with this lawyer from the North. I see a gentle, God fearing man of the old religion who I cannot think would agree to bloodshed unless all efforts at diplomacy had failed.

I walk over to the king's window and frown as I wonder what Henry is up to. A few weeks ago he was shouting fire and brimstone, cursing all rebels and threatening instant death to all. Now, it appears, he has given pardon to them all, is considering all their grievances and even suggested to Master Aske that he will consider a solution to the monastery changes.

I watch the snow flurries increasing without and listen to the crackles of the big, sulphurous fire and decide that Henry is playing some terrible game of bluff. I know him too well and know his true intentions and, with this in mind, I fear for the ultimate peace and safety of the gentle Master Robert Aske.

* * * *

We entertain Master Aske to supper on this fifth Christmas festive day. He eats heartily, partaking of the fresh boar's head glazed and decorated with holly withal. He drinks hot red wine, heavily spiced and sugared and appears somewhat under the influence of alcohol judging by the slurring of his speech. I do know that Henry has plied him with wine frequently earlier in the day and the poor man must be feeling the effects although too polite to refuse.

'Drink up Master Aske,' the king commands. 'It is the season of goodwill.'

'And much goodwill have I received from your Majesties,' he replies, contentedly sipping yet more warm wine.

'We have discussed the grievances of your people in council,' Henry continues. 'The poor crops that have hindered so many gentry and commons this past two years. The heavy taxation, as you described it at any event. The desire of many people to restore monks to the monasteries and restore certain church privileges. A chance for northern folks to have a say in the country's government. Have I covered everything we discussed?'

'You have, Your Grace, most adequately.'

'And I have satisfied you of our intentions to put certain reforms into action?'

'Yes, Majesty and I thank you for your generous, just judgements.'

'Good,' Henry says, looking over at me and raising one eyebrow. 'I would request a service from you Master Aske. I would wish you to write out in full the story of the Pilgrimage of Grace from its very beginnings with all relevant detail included, that I may study and better understand it all.'

'Of course, your Majesty, I would be pleased to do so.'

We take our leave of our guest, bidding him a good and peaceful night of sleep and he bows low and thanks Henry and then myself for our kindness toward him. He is due to leave in two days but the king makes it clear before we go that he is to have freedom of movement within the palace and he is to receive a small gift from the sovereign before he leaves.

We retire to my bedchamber where Henry has ordered warm wine and mynce pies to be consumed there. My bedchamber is warm with a good sized log fire burning and a dozen candles and some tapers to light up the gloom. Henry spreads himself in the biggest chair and bids me sit upon his knee. I do so and he becomes immediately amorous.

'It is not yet time to lie sir,' I say, grinning.

'No, but time for me to kiss and caress my true love, methinks,' he says, winking at me.

'Did all go well with your meeting with Master Aske today?' I ask softly.

'You need not concern yourself with him white lamb,' he says. 'Although I can say he will return to York a happy man.'

'That is good,' I say, 'he is a good man.

'You think so?'

'I do My lord, I do.

'Yes. Well I intend to give him a New Year gift of a jacket of crimson satin before he sets off home.

I nod and he immediately begins to nibble my ear and then plant kisses on my cheek. He remarks that my face is so pale that it looks like white porcelain of the best quality but he loves the colour and texture of my skin. He suggests I remove my clothing but I ask him to tarry awhile as I still feel slight chill from walking along the corridors from the banqueting hall.

'Give me a few minutes,' I say satirically. 'I wish only to please you.'

He begins to fondle me intimately and I feel his cold hand under my garments.

'So small,' he says, almost a murmur.

'I'm sorry they are not bigger sir,' I say, frowning at him.

'Oh no, you misunderstand lamb. I love small titties. Especially yours.'

'Do you indeed sir?' I ask, raising an eyebrow.

Henry says that the fifth day of Christmas is coming to an end and we should partake of a little more warm wine and eat a delicious mynce pie each. And then we must prepare and get to my bed to lie as he is feeling festive and of a mood most amorous.

TWENTY NINE

JANUARY 1537.

The last day of the Christmas season and a time for giving and receiving gifts. As always. A fanfare of trumpets sounds and this is the traditional signal for my servant to present the king with his Christmas gift from me. It all seems a strange, early practice, steeped in antiquity to me but is the tradition, that goes back hundreds of years so who am I to question it?

As I listen to the trumpets blare I know that my servant is now presenting the king with his gift. He is in his bedchamber still, another ancient tradition I learn to come to terms with and he will, at this precise moment, no doubt, be receiving a satin shirt with embroidered inserts, which I did fashion myself and a gold drinking cup. I do hope he likes my gifts.

My privy chamber servant approaches, curtsies, smiles and presents me with my gift from the king. It is a beautiful white satin cloak with gold beads sewn on and he has added fine pearls and rubies to the package. I accept it gratefully, pleased with this fine token of his love and his obvious wish to please me. Indeed the presents delight me. He knows what garments and what colours suit and pleasure me and if they are also the ones that he wishes most to see me wearing, what then?

The king arrives at my chamber and comes in smiling broadly. He thanks me for my presents which, he tells me, did delight him muchly. He goes over to the fire and rubs his hands together to warm them after walking down the cold and draughty corridor. I thank him for my presents and he leaves the immediate vicinity of the fire's hot radius to come over and embrace me.

'Well, white lamb,' he says, as we settle down together in my bedchamber. 'It has been an incident packed year to be sure but now is behind us.'

'Yes sir,' I say, sombrely, thinking back as images flash through my mind of the grim day that Queen Anne was executed, long hours spent almost alone in solitary gloom in the mansion once occupied by the late Sir Thomas More, the illness and death of the young Duke of Richmond and the terrible uprising of the commons and their leaders in the north and the threat they posed until calmed.

'The death of my poor young son,' Henry says sadly, his expression stricken. 'And the death of Katherine of Aragon.'

I gaze at him, trying to gauge his true mood. It is the first time he has mentioned the late queen by name in my presence. He will not though, I'll wager, ever mention the other late queen. He looks pensive now, staring towards the heat of the fire.

'But a new year Jane,' he says, snapping out of his melancholy mood. 'New beginnings, new opportunities. Shall we go to breakfast?'

'I am warm and comfortable here sir,' I say, looking up at him and shamelessly giving a pout. 'And the banqueting hall has many draughts.'

'Then here you must stay my white lamb,' he says contentedly. 'I'll have sent in some pies of dried fruit, mutton and spices. They are so suitable for Christmas Jane and, do you know, they contain a full thirteen ingredients representing Jesus Christ and his apostles.'

'How very pious of you sir,' I say, cheekily.

'Well, I am God's representative here on earth,' he says, blandly. 'And we will have hot spiced wine and mutton cake. And later today we will eat Twelfth Day Fruit cake, on this the last of our Christmas season celebrations.'

It has been a restful and pleasant Christmas season to be sure. The celebrations and excesses of food and wine consumption have been pleasant if indulgent. Meeting the charming Robert Aske was also an enjoyable interlude. And I have spent the past seven months in relatively leisurely fashion, always beside My Lord and master as he goes on Royal progresses or appears at public functions, trying always to soothe and calm his worst excesses of behaviour and mood, as is my duty, expressed by my motto, 'to serve and obey.' The New Year may bring many trials and tribulations to be sure but I must prepare myself to be ready for all eventualities. I do believe he saw me and chose me as his queen because he ached for warmth, love and tranquillity in his later years after the explosive excesses of the years with Anne and the frustrations of his earlier time with Katherine. I know not what the New Year will bring but whatever, I shall be prepared.

* * * *

I lie on my bed, waiting. It is not my most comfortable time. Sir William Butts, the king's physician has prodded my breasts, my belly and my lower extremities. He has announced that I have a brown discolouration around my nipples and a darkening of the flesh on my vagina. He has also identified a slight indentation line from my privy parts to my belly. He is currently swilling a chamber pot of my urine around and peering intently at it as he does so.

Henry looks on, full of impatience which I note in his expression and his moving of his feet agitatedly. But he says nothing. I lie still, as I have been bidden to do but it is my most humiliating experience and I long for a conclusion.

'Yes,' the physician says, gravely, still staring into the chamber pot as if mesmerised. 'The yellow colouring of the liquid would suggest a positive.'

'Which means?' Henry asks harshly but the physician ignores him.

'And you say it is more than seven weeks since you have had any bleeding?' he asks, addressing me.

'Yes,' I reply. 'Possibly eight.'

He turns to Henry. 'The light yellow colour, the discolouration of the nipples and the lack of bleeding,' he says slowly, ponderously, 'would indicate, Your Grace, that the queen is, indeed, with child.'

Henry's face beams. 'You can say, sir that she is certainly with child?'

They both ignore me but then, it is only my body and I am a mere woman!

'I would be fairly certain sir,' Sir William continues. 'I would recommend, Your Grace, the use of an amulet or small block of steel between her majesty's breasts, to ward off evil spirits.

'Yes, yes, of course. They will be procured.'

Henry shakes his physician's hand vigorously. It is the news he has been hoping to hear this past seven months he tells him. Today is a momentous day for him, for the queen and for the realm of England. I feel momentarily grateful that I have received a mention. The physician departs and Henry stands, watching him depart as if under a spell.

I rise from the bed and begin to complete my dressing. Henry turns, at last, appears to realise I am there with him and bids me sit down on the bed where he joins me.

'Well, Jane, this is a happy day,' he says. 'You are to bear me a son and heir.'

'Oh I do hope so,' I say. 'But the sex of the child is determined by Almighty God sir.'

'Yes but I have a good feeling about it,' he says, cheerily. 'I think it will be a boy, I am almost convinced of it.'

'Well let us verily hope and pray so,' I say in a hushed whisper.

It enters my mind, unbidden but also unstoppable, that I may well be carrying a daughter and if so I will be unpopular. I Will try my very best to think in positive terms like my lord and master. My mother bore eight children so we Seymour's are a hardy, fertile breed.

Henry can scarcely contain his delight and optimism as we go through to the throne room. We settle down and he tells me we will go shortly to his privy chamber and drink a chalice of the finest French wine the cellar can provide, in celebration. I smile contentedly, happy to be out of my degrading situation a few minutes ago and ready for anything. Henry says that first he must hear a report from my lord of Norfolk who is due immediately. Like Sir William, Lord Norfolk has a prominent nose and a somewhat straggly beard and this is the thought that runs through my mind, unbidden, as he enters and bows.

'Greetings Norfolk,' the king says heartily. 'You are first to know, your Queen is with child and a son and heir are on the way.'

'Congratulations Your Grace and indeed to you madam,' he says, lightly.

His face clouds over as soon as the words leave his lips. He wishes, he says, he had better news to report. Henry scowls at him.

'A new small rebellion has broken out in the East Riding of Yorkshire Your Grace,' Norfolk reports grimly. 'Led, we believe by one Sir Francis Bigot.'

'God's teeth,' Henry explodes. 'Then the rebels play right into our hands. They must be crushed with all speed and every leader and man captured and I will have them hung, drawn and quartered.'

'Only those few that rebel anew,' I say, panicking and throwing caution to the wind. 'Surely sir?'

'No Jane,' he hisses, causing me to flush. 'Every last member of this traitorous band of brigands and infidels that call themselves the Pilgrimage of Grace. They have betrayed me yet again and they will die, every last one. The men will hang and lose their entrails and their women will be burned at the stake.'

'This man Aske, who was lately here,' Norfolk says brusquely. 'He has offered to help defeat Bigot and supply men to join mine.'

'Then take advantage of the offer my Lord Norfolk,' Henry says bitterly, his anger showing in his rough speech and agitated demeanour. 'And why do you tarry here my Lord; assemble your biggest army with all speed, get marching, link up with Aske's men and get this battle won. I want this crushed swiftly once and for all. And I want all participants brought to swift, merciless justice.'

'Then I will take my leave,' Norfolk says and the king dismisses him with an irritable wave of his hand.

Norfolk bows and departs swiftly, unwilling to suffer any more indignity from the king's ire.

Henry rises abruptly and walks swiftly to his privy chamber. I follow feeling an intense pain in my intestine as I walk, fearful for the fate of all the rebels; traitors or not, I cannot bring myself to condemn them out of hand. I know their fate is sealed and their deaths now inevitable and the king's previous pardons will count for nought. I want to make one last appeal to Henry however, dangerous as my pleading will be.

In the privy chamber Henry calls for his best wine and turns to me, still agitated but says we will think no more on this matter, Norfolk will conquer a small uprising with his seven thousand men and he will follow up by sending on an army led by Suffolk as backup.

'Please Henry,' I say, going down on my knees. 'Robert Aske, he is an honourable man. You will spare him won't you?'

'No Jane, he is a traitor and will die with the rest.'

'But he has offered to fight for you sir, alongside my lord of Norfolk.'

'He will pay for his previous traitorous sins, once he has made good his promise to redeem himself.'

'Oh Your Grace, please show him mercy,' I say, and I cannot stop my tears from flowing down my cheeks.

'Get up Jane, 'he says irritably and I rise to my feet. 'We will drink in celebration of our good news. And we will speak no more about this matter.'

I drink with him but in silence. I cannot think about my good news now, bad tidings and forebodings have obliterated my previous joy. Henry watches me carefully and attempts to make conversation but I remain stony faced and silent; he could consign me to the tower now and I would not bat an eyelid or speak any pleading words to him. I dab my eyes with a fresh linen handkerchief. He announces that he will walk for a while and abruptly gets up and leaves the chamber. I sit holding my chalice firmly in my hands and do not move and scarcely breathe. I feel the warmth of the fire from a distance; it is a raw day outside.

Henry returns looking thoughtful but troubled. He calls for more wine and drinks in silence as I sit next to him staring gloomily ahead.

'I cannot abide having you in a state of distress,' he says, suddenly.

'Then show some mercy sir,' I say, tearfully.

'I cannot do that Jane,' he replies sombrely. 'Traitors must die if only as a warning to others who would rebel.'

I sniff noisily and remain stony faced.

'But because you are the love of my life,' he says quietly, 'I will make a small concession.'

'You will sir?' I ask, looking up, wide eyed but still tearful.

'When Aske is captured and brought to the tower,' he says softly still, 'I will have Cromwell question him thoroughly on all aspects of the uprising and ascertain his involvement in it, in fulsome detail.'

It is something. A small concession verily. But it is all I can hope for even if I have but little faith in the methods of questioning that Cromwell will employ. Or indeed the ultimate outcome of the interrogation.

'Thank you Henry.'

'It is for you Jane, little lamb and I would do it for nobody else who lives and breathes in this land.'

'And if he is innocent sir?'

'Well, let us not get ahead of ourselves. Time will reveal all.'

I try to smile but it must be a crooked expression that lights my features. He clinks his chalice against mine and we both drink. He tells me he has made this concession to prove that he is a just, merciful and compassionate sovereign.

'I drink,' he says, 'to the health and safe delivery of our baby son.'

'To the health and safe delivery of our baby,' I say and note his pained expression as I stare back, defiantly at him.

THIRTY

FEBRUARY 1537.

Sir Francis Bigot's army of new rebels put up a bloodthirsty fight and captured Scarborough Castle but once my lord the Duke of Norfolk, assisted by Master Aske and a contingent of his men began battle with him, he was soon defeated. He is now imprisoned in Carlisle Castle awaiting sentence but will surely die and die horribly. I do not think that the miniature uprising of rebels under Bigot did much harm in the fighting or caused many deaths but the damage he has done in undermining the pardons that Henry granted the other Pilgrimage of Grace rebels is inestimable. Many, most likely in their hundreds, will die as a result of this brigand's thoughtless warmongering.

Henry keeps me informed of everything that is happening, almost on a daily basis but only because I badger him to keep me in knowledge. He complains bitterly about me poking my nose into affairs of state and reminds me constantly that I may be queen but it is not my province, never was, never will be and I should be mindful that I am merely a woman! How could I possibly forget? He is though, very solicitous of my wellbeing and keeps reminding me that I am with child, carrying a future prince of the realm to rule the country and must not be vexed or upset by anybody. I have not been upset by anybody except him but I dare not say so.

I continue to brood over the fate of poor Robert Aske but on the one occasion I broached the subject he re-affirmed that the man will be questioned thoroughly and given opportunity to prove his innocence. I can ask no more, for the present at any rate.

Henry is quiet at supper on this night but eats heartily, as usual and shows much concern as to my welfare, how I am feeling and if I have any special requests. I tell him that I have a craving to eat quails but it is a delicacy that we seldom encounter here.

'I will order a large batch from France Jane,' he says, when we are comfortably settled in his privy chamber after supper. 'Anything else?'

'I could fancy roasted swan or perhaps turkey,' I say tentatively. They are both dishes that we have on occasion but comparatively rarely. 'Or lark.'

These foods do appeal to me at the moment but none are consumed with any frequency usually. It is my condition no doubt that makes me wish for a change of fayre.

'You shall have them all, as often as you wish,' he tells me jovially. 'Anything that my love wants, she shall have.'

'Thank you sir,' I say, smiling. 'And how went matters in council today?'

He frowns and then looks askance at me for some time before making answer. He tells me gruffly that I should not have to worry about such mundane matters; all that concerns him are my good health, comfort and keeping healthy for the baby.

'Yes sir,' I say, smiling, 'but it is very early days yet and I feel absolutely fine. How were things in council?'

He frowns again. 'My lord of Norfolk has crushed the Bigot rebellion and is now, under my instruction, requiring all magistrates, squires and gentlemen in various Yorkshire towns and cities to take the oath of allegiance anew and to renounce all previous oaths made during the late commotions They must revoke all statements made and beg their king for forgiveness. To keep and maintain all laws made in parliament since the beginning of the reign. They must promise never to attempt any new insurrection and to apprehend seditious persons and authors and tellers of new tales. They must always use themselves as true subjects of the king and his successors. They shall do no treason, murder or felony but discover it to the king. And swear to all, so help them God. Is that comprehensive enough for you Jane?'

'Yes, my Lord,' I say, surprised. I did not expect such intelligence to come my way. He is humouring me, due to my condition, no doubt.

'They are also required to assist commissioners in taking re-possession of monasteries within the act of suppression. Where monks and friars have been returned to the monasteries, they are to be removed, forcibly, executed and the true church bishops put back in control. Many small monasteries and abbeys are to be given over to landowners and farmers.'

'You will not, surely my Lord,' I say, horrified, 'execute all the monks and friars regardless?'

'Only those that have resisted the legal requirements for them to leave,' he tells me gruffly. 'And those that have illegally returned to monasteries they were removed from.'

That represents almost all in the Yorkshire region since this monumental attempt at rebellion but although I grieve for the monastery inhabitants, I know Henry will not be moved from his position. He continues, telling me that Norfolk has been instructed to reprimand Justices of the peace in the region for their lack of diligence. They should have reported the bad feeling that was boiling over.

'So, what of the promises to Master Aske?' I say, frowning. 'To look into the grievances of the people generally?'

'I have set it in motion,' he says, smiling at me. 'I have not neglected my promise Jane. Be assured. Norfolk is instructed to look into all complaints of people being subject to excessive fines. And Norfolk is to sit twice a week to hear cases of common justice. I am a fair and just prince, is it not so?'

I tell him that it is so. He is fully convinced that he is and would accept no alternative view under any circumstances. I have nothing whatsoever to gain by disagreement or arguing. The nature and volume of the punishments, the way the executions are carried out, disturb me muchly but I fear I can do nothing to halt them. I worry that it is affecting my feelings towards Henry; it has been a love match between us, verily but I find him cruel and unforgiving. Can love survive the horrors that go on daily in this kingdom? I know not but hope that it can as I am carrying a future prince or princess of the realm. My flesh and blood. The king's flesh and blood. The next in line to the throne by order of his parliament.

He notices me frowning with my private thoughts and looking much vexed. He bids me come and sit on his knee but I say I prefer to sit where I am.

'Everything that is done and being done is absolutely necessary,' he says starkly. 'There has been much looting and thieving going on both during and after the rebellion. It is being punished by execution of the felons by Norfolk.'

'So much death, so much suffering,' I say softly and sadly.

'Yes Jane,' he says, raising his voice. 'But the punishments will ensure a stable realm, now and for the future. Nothing like this must ever happen again.'

'No, no, I do see that,' I agree. 'And now I must go to my bed and lie.'

'Yes, yes,' he says solicitously. 'See that your ladies do make you warm and comfortable for a goodly night of sleep.'

I smile. He does not require me to lie with him further, not, at least, until our baby is born. Even in these early days he fears he could harm the unborn infant and, if I am honest, I am glad because I do not choose to lie with him at present. My mind and feelings are in turmoil at this juncture and relations with Henry of a privy nature would be of pain to me, physically and in my mind. I must clear my head and feelings.

Henry kisses my forehead and I smile again. Does he truly think that kissing my lips would somehow harm the unborn child? I know not; he is a complicated man indeed.

'Sleep well, my little white lamb,' he says. 'And Almighty God protect you and our child.'

'Goodnight sir,' I respond and head for my privy bedchamber.

*   *   *   *

MARCH 1537.

We sail slowly along the freshly thawed out River Thames, ice blocks and smaller slivers floating at strategic points along our route. We are bound for Hampton Court once again and the king is anxious that I see the newly built and extended banqueting hall where workmen have been busy this past eighteen months. He has another purpose in showing me certain chambers at the palace but will not divulge it: not just yet.

The lapping waters of the river are still icy and bitterly cold. We sit huddled up in swathes of fur and ermine, wrap after wrap to keep out the cold that is biting into our exposed faces. Every other extremity is well covered to minimise chills.

'Look yonder Jane,' the king calls out and I glance towards the still green banks and spy a large knot of commons people, staring at the royal barge. Did they expect or anticipate our progress down river I wonder, idly; there seems to be too many citizens huddled together or wandering freely on the banks to be unplanned.

Wave Jane, wave,' he commands, briskly. 'Always wave to the commons folk and keep them sweet.'

I wave happily, smiling and then rolling my hand round and round in the accepted manner of gesture. The citizens all wave back frantically and contentedly, judging by those facial expressions I can just make out in the distance. Others begin to appear as if from nowhere as we proceed and by the time we take the bend in the river that will shortly haul the palace of Hampton Court into view, my arm is stiff from waving.

As we alight I am consigned to a canopied seat to be carried into the building. I protest that I am feeling hearty and well capable of walking in but all to no avail.

'You must rest fully,' he commands gently. 'The baby grows apace in your belly and you must be kept in fine fettle.'

'Yes, my Lord,' I say, smiling, it is pointless to protest or argue.

He does allow me to walk the few brief steps along a wide corridor to the chapel. I stand at the entrance and look up to see, on either side of the big doors, a brightly coloured stone picture with Henry's initials and mine, intertwined and with love knots and flowers carved into the structure. It is a comely sight and I smile.

'To signify our love,' Henry says expansively. 'Our everlasting love and devotion Jane.'

'Thank you sir,' I say. 'It is quite delightful.'

'For you, little lamb,' he says. 'Only for you.'

I nod. If I am aware that previous stonework, here and elsewhere, once held in stone his initials with those of Queen Katherine and later, Queen Anne, I say nothing. This is of the moment and I am queen of England and all I survey!

We proceed slowly, to the newly furnished and decorated great banqueting hall and I am allowed to walk, assuring him that I feel right bonny and the stepping out will do me more good than harm. The hall is truly magnificent, the colours a riot of bright paint to dazzle the eyes. The beautifully carved out and crenulated wooden ceiling is also a sight to behold. Inside, Henry points out our initials, entwined again and the words 'Jane Regina,' in gold, under my coat of arms.

'Good food will taste but heartier, in such surroundings,' he says, gazing round the imposing banqueting hall.

'It will, my Lord,' I concur. 'It will truly.'

He will not, however, allow me to walk up to the privy chamber so servants are called forward and I go, with him, seated. In the chamber it is Henry, rather than myself, who seems more in need of a rest and he collapses into the large velvet chair.

'I am mindful,' Henry begins, when we are both seated, 'that you will need to go into confinement for a month prior to the birth of our boy.'

'Oh,' I say, disconcerted. 'I had not thought of that I confess.'

'I have it in mind that a chamber should be prepared, with colourful tapestries and here, in this palace, I suggest, would be an ideal location.'

'Well, yes indeed sir,' I say, thoughtfully. 'I shall be shut away for longer than I would care for but this is a comfortable venue.'

'That is settled then' he says, contented.

I rise and walk over to the fire which has been fully banked up and burns furiously. The heat comes out and warms my hands and extremities. Henry looks concerned. He wants to know if the fire is hot enough to keep me comfortable. I assure him that it is. Nevertheless he calls forth page and servants and instructs that he wants additional large logs applied so that the radius of its impact shall be increased. It is done.

'Come and sit down Jane' he calls impatiently. 'You are pregnant with child and must rest most of every day.'

'I am fully aware of my condition sir,' I say, smiling broadly. 'But do not require wrapping in soft wool.'

He is certainly most solicitous of my complete wellbeing but I must confess that I wish it were partly concern for me, personally, rather than an obsessive wish to obtain a male heir. He tells me that there are quails for dinner, he has managed to secure some. I thank him graciously, with a broad smile. He adds that roasted swan has also been procured although it is not the usual season for eating it. And he has ordered lark and woodcock as additional delicacies to tickle my pregnant palette! At dinner he presses me to eat sweetmeats but I am more sated than I would wish and can only pick, in desultory manner at the various crenulated castles of jelly and sugary almonds.

In his privy chamber he tells me that he wishes to command Master Holbein to paint a new portrait of me and wants to know if I can bear to stand for two or three short posing sessions. After that, once Holbein has made his sketches of me in full view, I may sit for the portrait at my leisure.

'Henry,' I say querulously. 'I am in good health at present and can move around normally for another month or more. I do not have to be coddled.'

'I'll be the judge,' he says crisply. 'I mean to take no risks.'

'Over protection can be as dangerous, if not more so,' I say, testily, 'as carelessness. At this early stage.'

He does not listen. He will not listen. 'I caution you to move slowly,' he says,' if you must move at all.'

'I shall be fine for a portrait,' I assure him. 'Although I do not look my best in my present condition. My complexion is somewhat pasty and I have eaten more than I should of late and look somewhat puffy of face.'

'Nonsense woman' he says testily.' You look as pretty as a picture and I shall charge Master Holbein to bring out the best of your features.'

'Poor man,' I say.

'You do yourself no credit Jane by false modesty,' he says. 'I know your worth and I see your beauty in front of me.'

I make a rather uncouth sound.

'I have it also in mind,' he says, looking thoughtful, but not at me, 'to commission a painting of myself, my father and mother along with you Jane and our son.'

I raise my eyebrows but do not speak.

He looks straight ahead as if concentrating hard.

'But that will have to wait a good five years until our boy is ready.'

THIRTY ONE.

My relations with his majesty, the king, are strained. Although I keep it in mind, always, to keep to my intention to 'obey and serve,' and cause no friction or put myself in jeopardy, I feel hurt and ignored and treated less than a queen consort should be treated. It has come to my attention, through circuitous routes again, that hundreds of men and women have been rounded up as ringleaders in the Pilgrimage of Grace and imprisoned in the tower or at York castle and many executed already.

Lord Darcy awaits trial and almost certain death. Robert Aske has been persuaded by my Lord of Norfolk to travel again to London to 'be thanked by the king,' only to be arrested on arrival and thrown into the tower of London. Henry refuses point blank to discuss his fate but reminds me that Cromwell will question him in great detail, as I was promised and has, over one hundred questions to put to him. How he will answer I know not but I fear they will be trick questions, devised by the slippery Cromwell, to implicate him one way or another.

The pardons promised to the people have been forgotten as has the promise of a free parliament and, it would seem, Henry's stated intention to open a parliament in York and also my coronation. None of this will he discuss with me but reminds me again that affairs of state are outside my province. The more so now that I must concentrate my thoughts and energies in keeping well in preparation for the forthcoming birth of our child.

I feel betrayed and ill-used and entertain a constantly growing feeling that Henry's cruelty and lust for traitor's blood outweighs their crimes. I remain silent with my misgivings knowing that to voice them would endanger my very being and that of my unborn child. How can I continue to love a man whose quest for blood and excessive power defies all reason?

We are at Whitehall and I sit, in solitary state by a goodly roaring fire, gazing, from time to time at the window where the weather without is bland, grey but dry with no rain this past three days. Henry sits across the room toying with papers of state that he glances at occasionally but not seeming to be fully engaged with this or any other task. I have not outwardly fallen out with him or disagreed with any statement of his but my replies to his questions are bleak and without warmth and our discussions die away with little to sustain regular conversation.

'I have summoned Cromwell to my privy chamber,' he says suddenly.

'Yes, my Lord,' I reply blandly, neither interested nor otherwise.

'He should be here directly.'

'I see,' I say and turn my attention back to the hot red flames and white ash of the fire. He tells me it would be fitting if I were to remain as some of the points for discussion may be of interest to me. I nod agreement but cannot manage to smile.

'And better still Jane,' he says quietly, 'if you were to join me here and we sit side by side.'

I rise, with a sigh, walk over to him and sit, maintaining silence. He looks at me vexed and frowns. He asks what ails me.

'Not a thing sir,' I say with quiet dignity. 'I am well.'

'You do not look well or contented my love,' he says, looking concerned.

'Do not concern yourself husband,' I say. 'I will be fine.'

'What is it Jane?' he asks. 'You know well I cannot abide seeing you upset or out of sorts. You are my true love, my queen of hearts.'

I am saved from making answer by the announcement of the arrival of Lord Cromwell, the baron as he is now styled although I think of this low born creature as the most unlikely in the kingdom to be elevated. Cromwell enters and bows. He is dressed, as usual in black and grey and has a face to match. Eyebrows drawn down over piercing brown eyes that look as cruel as I know their owner to be. He stands before us and Henry does not invite him to be seated.

'I have lately written to my lord, the Duke of Norfolk,' Henry begins. 'I have made it clear to him that I do not desire to travel more than sixty miles from London environs for the next several months.'

Cromwell nods perfunctorily, as though he has just been told the weather is inclement and he does not care one way or the other.

'It is in my mind,' Henry goes on, 'that the queen might take to her stomach such impressions as might engender no little danger or displeasure to the infant with which she is now pregnant, although God forbid that should occur.'

'I understand,' Cromwell says.

'She is now able to rest content with anything she desires which we think expedient to her yet considering she is but a woman, she may come across displeasing rumours by foolish or light persons that might be blown about in our absence that cause her upset or distress, physical or otherwise. For which reason I would not wish to be more than sixty miles from her during her pregnancy.'

'What do you wish of me then?' Cromwell asks, looking puzzled.

'You must ensure, Cromwell,' Henry says roughly,' that no state business or affairs of any wise are accepted or undertaken on my behalf. Norfolk is advised but you have control over all matters of state on my behalf.'

Cromwell assures him, obsequiously, that he will accept no travel plans or any state visits over that number of miles and will personally arrange all business of state or otherwise to be localised and comfortable to his majesty's requirements. A fine little speech of toadying indeed. I look askance at him.

'You may go,' Henry says, waving him away.

'There was, your Grace, one other matter,' Cromwell says in hushed tones.

'Yes?'

'You recall sir that I spoke to you of the offer of marriage to the Lady Elizabeth, the queen's sister, to my son, Master Gregory?'

'Yes, I think so,' Henry says, looking puzzled and unaware in reality.

'I understand the lady is of a mind to accept the proposal,' he says and looks directly at me. I fix him with a cold stare.

'I know nothing of her intention to accept,' I say, coldly. I have received a letter from my sister appraising me of the offer and saying that she is happy to go ahead but I will not give the viper Cromwell the satisfaction of thinking that I approve the match. The thought of a son of his, married to my little sister, Elizabeth, fills me with horror. But it is her decision to make. And Henry has said little to me about the matter.

'Is it your will that the marriage should go ahead?' Cromwell asks.

'I see no reason why not,' he replies and again dismisses Cromwell. Cromwell thanks him and then bows and leaves.

Henry rises and begins to stomp around the chamber. Then he stops abruptly and asks me if I have any objection to the match.

'I would have liked a little more discussion on the matter,' I say, peeved. 'You only mentioned it once in passing sir.'

'It is a small matter surely, 'Henry replies irritably. 'My first minister's son is desirous of marrying and has asked for your sister's hand. I see no objection if your sister has none.'

'Well, that's an end of it,' I say angrily, and walk over to the burgeoning fire and sit down close to it.

He sits in silence in his own corner for some time and then looks over to me and asks if I am going to sulk about it. I say that I will indulge in no such childish practice. It is just that it is my sister we are talking about and I would have thought he would have the courtesy to speak with me first before giving his blessing to the union, through Cromwell of all people.

He walks over to me, sits and takes hold of my hand. I see by his expression that he is quite vexed and a little angry and I wait for the outburst. It does not come.

'You are becoming quite feisty Jane,' he says. 'Do not presume to take advantage of me just because you are pregnant.'

'I would never do anything to vex or defy you sir,' I say softly. 'My motto is to obey and serve. Nothing has changed.'

'Then why do you look so harsh faced and out of sorts?' he asks, beginning to smile and caressing my hand gently.

'I'm alright,' I say. 'All is well, do not fret.'

'I don't think it is,' he replies. 'And you know I cannot bear to see you upset. Look here, I'm prepared to call Cromwell back and forbid the marriage for you. Because you know full well I will do anything to please you.'

'No, no, my Lord,' I say, shaking my head vigorously. 'It is my sister's wish. I would not want to stand in her way.'

He looks askance at me, the smile on his lips dying. He shakes his head and says he can make no sense of me. But my pregnancy proceeds and he will do anything to keep me well and in good humour until the child is born.

'And what then, my Lord,' I ask stringently. 'Am I to suffer later?'

He tells me not to be ridiculous, I will never suffer from his ministrations. His love for me will endure forever. I smile. He squeezes my hand again and asks if we can renew normal relations.

'Yes, of course we can' I say. 'But we cannot lie together.' I smile and widen my eyes as I gaze at him.

'No, no, we cannot lie together,' he agrees, eyes boring into mine interrogatively as though seeking the secrets of my being. 'Not until after our son is born.'

* * * *

Henry dictates to Wriothesley, his reasons for wishing to postpone his proposed visit to York until next year. He explains that his sore leg is festering badly and his physicians have advised him to rest it and not travel. Which is why he is resting now with his leg up in his antechamber and not in council. I sit at the back of the chamber quietly; Henry has expressed a wish for me to remain ever close to him now that I am quickening with child. I am content if not exactly happy to oblige.

I study the features of Wriothesley, clerk of the signet, as he writes the king's letter; he is a fine looking man, fair haired, tall, strong features including a long, straight nose. And very young, surely only my age or similar? I find myself wondering idly if Lady Rochford had ever really entertained notions of introducing him to me clandestinely and later tried to poison the king's mind with tales of our adultery. It is not so fanciful as it might seem; she was one of those that managed to get Queen Anne executed and implicated five men including her own husband. Why then, was Henry so gullible as to believe it all? Was he truly prepared to go to any lengths and sanction any number of executions just to be rid of an unwanted and troublesome wife?

'Make it known that I fully intend to travel to York next year,' Henry says imperiously. 'Once my leg is somewhat healed and her majesty the queen is delivered of her son there will be no further impediment to my travels abroad.'

'Yes your Grace, understood,' Wriothesley says, glancing surreptitiously over at me as he speaks.

'Write to Norfolk,' the king continues. 'Tell him that having been found guilty of high treason, the traitors

Darcy, Constable and Aske should be executed up there in York where their crimes were committed.'

'Yes your Grace,' Wriothesley mumbles.

'They should be dragged through York and hung, drawn and quartered in the square, on market day.'

I feel a sharp pain in my intestine as I hear these cruel words. It seems, as I predicted, that Cromwell's one hundred odd questions to Master Aske, only served to implicate him and find him guilty of high treason. I can do nothing to halt the progress and influence of this black snake. Henry continues to trust and encourage him as his first minister.

'I think that will suffice,' Henry says quietly and the clerk bows low to him and then to me and departs.

Henry rustles through some state papers for several minutes before rising, slowly, calling for wine from a boy hovering close by and walks over to join me. He sits, smiles and asks me if I feel comfortable.

'Yes sir, physically I do,' I tell him bleakly.

'But you look pained my sweetheart,' he says, pouring two goblets of the freshly delivered wine.

'In my heart,' I say, sadly, 'I bleed with pain for the fate of poor Robert Aske, one of the most true and honest men I ever met.'

'Have a caution Jane,' he says, brows set fiercely together. 'The man was straightly questioned in great detail, put to trial and found guilty at Westminster.'

'On the strength of Cromwell's questioning.'

'Cromwell found him guilty through a connection to the second and third uprisings,' Henry says, raising his voice. 'He is a traitor.'

'Can you not pardon him, my Lord,' I say, in pleading voice. 'Please?'

He raises the goblet to his lips and drinks deliberately, his expression harsh, his eyes glinting dangerously. I can see that he is very angry and trying hard not to explode. I must understand, he tells me, that he will do anything and everything in his power to make me comfortable and grant my wishes while I am in my present condition. But I must not, under any circumstances, question affairs of state or try to interfere with the punishments of traitors.

'Keep away from this matter,' he says in stark tones. 'And remember the fate of those before you that opposed me.'

I am chastised. And I feel the bitter hurt of knowing that his concern for my well-being is only for our unborn child. He leaves the chamber abruptly as he always does when vexed or wishes to think things over. I do not see him again until it is time for dinner and he tells me he has ordered quails for me, smiling expansively as if that admittedly welcome little delicacy will ease my pain and soothe my troubled soul.

THIRTY TWO

My privy chamber is livelier than usual with many of my ladies in attendance, sewing, embroidering or just sitting listening to the music. I have a motley crew of musicians to play today, some local to London, some from France and others from distant shores, far from this realm. It matters not where they come from, the music is unified as they play together wonderfully. The lute player has begun a performance of 'Pastime with Good Company,' the king's ballad, as it is known and composed by Henry some time back.

I nod my head and become quite bemused listening to the melodic strains of Henry's delightful tune; others have joined the lute player and I now hear harmony from sackbut, cornet and flute. It is a joyous sound and helps to soothe me in my recently troubled soul. The more I try to put recent events out of my mind, the more they surface, taunting and haunting me.

I rise and walk towards my favourite window alcove, nodding to Jane and Anne and Mary as I pass. Margery detains me, asks how I am feeling today and enquires how the quickening of the pregnancy is proceeding.

'I am well in myself Margery,' I say, a little sadly, for I am not feeling bright and full of joy. 'The warm weather helps of course and I am still craving for quail.'

'Merciful God in heaven,' she says, smiling. 'Any other unlikely desires?'

'No,' I say, 'but I got though twelve quails at supper yesterday.'

I proceed to my corner and pick up some sewing I am anxious to finish. It is a satin muffler which I am decorating myself. I gaze out of the latticed windows and note that the sun is shining brightly; this should lighten my mood and cheer me but it does not. I look down on the cobbles below and see Jane Boleyn in bright yellow summer gown looking as lively and contented as though she has just won a game of skittles against strong opposition. She is soon in my chamber and coming towards me.

'Lady Rochford,' I say, greeting her formally.

'You are well Jane?' she asks, 'I hope and pray.'

'Physically, I could not be better,' I say softly.

I Sit down in the alcove and invite her to join me. She sits, facing me, her brow suddenly knitted and her voice lowered. She asks me quietly if I am well informed on the executions of the northern rebels and I tell her I am. I take a deep breath; I do not particularly want this conversation but she will be aware of that.

'I have a friend, a commander in Norfolk's army,' she tells me. 'Lately returned to London to deal with family problems.'

'I nod, wondering what next from this wretched woman.

'He tells me it was horrible to witness, the deaths of those men.' she continues. 'And women, burnt at the stake.'

'Yes, truly vile and senseless,' I say, vehemently.

'Robert Aske,' she says tentatively, voice lowered yet further. 'Wasn't he the one that visited the king and you here at Christmas?'

'Yes,' I say very softly, feeling a little faint. 'A man I thought a fine, honest gentleman.'

'He was found guilty of high treason though,' she says in carefully modulated, mock horrified tones.

'Yes,' I hiss through gritted teeth, 'he was.'

I see her looking at me intently, trying to gauge how she can hurt me and how far she can go and get away with it. Her little eyes seem bright with spite as I hold her gaze. After a pause that seems an eternity, she speaks. 'My informant tells me he was dragged through the streets of York, hanged on a gibbet, cut down while still alive, revived, disembowelled, castrated and finally had his head cut off .'

I can stand hearing no more. I flush angrily and tell her to hold her tongue. She looks shocked, feigning innocence she protests that she merely wished to inform me as she thought I would wish to know. I shake my head vigorously.

'What was left of him was cut into four quarters,' she adds, spitefully. 'And decorated various streets.'

'Be silent Jane,' I shout, angrily. The other ladies look up, anxiously, shocked by my harsh tones. They all stare at us. The musicians stop playing.

'I'm sorry,' she says, looking concerned that she has indeed gone much too far.

'Leave this chamber,' I say with raised voice. She looks about to retort, thinks better of it, rises and leaves as quickly and in as dignified a state as she can manage.

I ask the musicians to pack up and leave. I apologise to the other ladies, explaining to them that I am feeling rather out of sorts, due, doubtless, to my condition and ask their pardon. I say that I would wish to be alone and they all troop out silently, along with the musicians. I am alone and I sink down into my seat and sigh heavily. I feel like weeping but control the urge. There is something I must do first. I summon Cromwell to my chamber.

He enters in his usual drab, black attire and cap and stands waiting for my direction. I indicate a seat and he sits, facing me.

'How many people have you sent to the gallows or the block?' I ask. 'In connection with the rebellions in Yorkshire and surrounds.'

'I would find it difficult to estimate accurately madam,' he replies, blandly, almost insolently.

'Try.'

He sighs deeply. 'It might run into hundreds.'

'Yes,' I say, grimly. 'Yes, it might well.'

'Am I being accused of something?' he asks, watching my face carefully.

'Oh, I'm well aware that you operate within the bounds of the law sir,' I say.

'Indeed.'

I take a deep breath. He sits motionless, almost without any expression on his face, watching me like a cat watching a mouse or bird it is about to attack.

'It is your methods and your interpretation of the law that I find difficult to comprehend.'

'I would be pleased to enlighten you on any points that are obscure,' he says and again I find his tone offensive and his manner obnoxious. I do not reply and he sits very still until, finally, he folds his hands in front of him in a familiar gesture. I take my time before slowly and deliberately mentioning the name of Robert Aske. I catch just a hint of apprehension in the eyes at the name but he recovers very quickly and the bland expression is back; the face immobile once more.

'You questioned Master Aske in great detail prior to his trial,' I say softly.

'I did.'

'I've seen a transcript of your question and answer session,' I say, coldly. 'And am much disturbed by its contents.'

This time he does react, looking surprised and then almost startled for an instant before composing his demeanour yet again into the familiar non- committal, bleak expression he wears constantly. I smile.

'You are surprised that I, as you think, a mere woman, should do so,' I say, still smiling grimly.

'A little Majesty, a little,' he says very slowly, a frown forming on his forehead before he controls it again and re-settles himself. I ask him to tell me his impression of Robert Aske, based on his memory of the questioning and bearing in mind that I have seen the transcript. He sighs deeply and composes himself into a state of injured innocence that sits badly on this master of rigid interrogation.

'He made no attempt to hide his involvement in the uprising,' he says, picking each of his words very carefully. 'He was straightforward in his answers, claiming that he joined and led the rebels to try and get justice, as he saw it, for the commons people who wished to continue in the Catholic faith. There were other forms of injustice he felt should be addressed but he insisted that once he had accepted the pardons and talked with the king he had no further involvement with the rebels and claimed that he was still and had always been, his Majesty's most loyal servant.'

'And why then, could you not accept that honest answer Lord Cromwell?'

'I did accept it, as far as it went,' he says, indignantly. 'But it did not go far enough.'

I feel my temper rising but make a monumental effort to control it. It is not in my nature to be unduly angry or aggressive but some things are beyond normal acceptance. I suggest that he outline exactly what he means by not far enough. Cromwell looks uncomfortable for the first time during my interview and actually shifts awkwardly on his stool. He answers roughly, almost angrily that he obtained statements from some of the prisoners that he believed implicated Aske in the latter uprising under Francis Bigod. I am gratified to see that I have made him uncomfortable at last by daring to question his motives and decide to keep up the pressure.

'But you know that to be untrue,' I say heatedly. 'You know full well that he joined up with my lord of Norfolk with his own army to assist in ending the rogue rebellion.'

'I could not be sure.'

'Oh, you could be sure enough; if you wished to be.'

'Other men said he was part of Bigod's army.'

'He wasn't and you knew full well he wasn't.'

'There were other factors,' he blurts out, defensively.

'Name them.'

'I found a letter signed by Aske and Darcy urging people to stay in their homes and not join the rebellion. I interpreted that as by implication telling them to stay at home and not join the king's forces and help to suppress the uprising and that, in my opinion, represented treason.'

'How,' I ask forcefully, 'on God's green earth could you possibly put that interpretation on it?'

'The king accepted my interpretation,' he says, heatedly, voice rising irritably.

I shake my head vigorously and glare at him intimidatingly. I 'm pleased to note that he looks uncomfortable under my gaze. I remain silent, still staring at him in horror and pause before speaking. I murmur in stark tones that he is despicable if he can take a man's life, an innocent, good honest man's life, horribly and savagely just to please his king and further his own career. He remains silent, looking shocked, the first time I have ever seen Cromwell in this state. It is little or no consolation to me.

The silence is finally broken as he says, 'I serve my king, rightly or wrongly, I serve my king.'

'Wrongly,' I say slowly but with much emphasis on the word. 'Does it never occur to you, Lord Cromwell, that your king is sometimes, perhaps, afflicted by something akin to temporary madness?'

His eyes glint suddenly and he appears to shake off his temporary malaise and become animated. I continue to glare at him notwithstanding.

'Such a thought, expressed verbally, is treason,' he says vigorously now. 'And by expressing it in words, you put yourself in mortal danger madam, with respect.'

'Do not threaten me sir,' I say angrily but in control, 'you cannot hurt me. I have something more powerful than even your hate and evil. I have the king's love.'

'You have the king's love,' he repeats insolently.

'I do. For all time, I believe.'

'But he no longer has yours.'

'You are,' I say, 'as I have heard you described before, a viper. As you live by the sword you will surely perish by it. Get out of my sight Lord Cromwell.'

He rises, says 'Your Majesty,' softly and leaves the chamber abruptly.

As he goes I feel able to let go the control I have exercised this last hour and begin to weep copiously. I shake all over for some time and feel a little giddy. When I calm down I start to realise the enormity of what I have done; nobody challenges Cromwell because it is known that he goes straight to the king to report it.

He will not approach Henry with regard to our recent conversation, of that I feel certain. He knows I spoke true words. Everybody at court is now aware that the king loves me and thinks of me as his first and only, true love.

I have though, just drifted out of my own normal manner of behaviour and challenged the mighty Cromwell. There is churning in my belly and again I feel quite lightheaded and shocked at my own aggressiveness. It is not like me. It is something that I do not regret however even if I only feel the very slightest sense of satisfaction in making that odious man uncomfortable. Verily, when it comes to analysis I only have room for one emotion at present and that is consuming me. Grief for the victims and, in particular the unfortunate Master Aske, haunt me to distraction.

* * * *

I move slowly along the wide corridors of Hampton Court Palace. I really have little choice for the bump in my belly grows larger and heavier by the day. Warm sunlight glints on the colourful stained glass window depicting a knight in shining armour, diffusing the light into the palace. I pause to look at the window but really my aim is to take a breath before proceeding.

I move out into the grounds and immediately feel the full warmth of the sun that is denied entry to the cold stone of the interior. I feel good physically, except for the extra load I am carrying. I walk slowly, down towards the river, waving away the attendants that follow me too closely and impede my progress. Sunlight dances on the surface of the water.

Henry suggests trips to Canterbury and Dover, if I feel up to travel. I do although I must admit to some misgivings concerning the pitted and cratered state of many of the roads and the rackety inclinations of our conveyances.

The king appears suddenly and I know not where he came from but, like me, he signals to attendants to keep their distance. He cannot really blame them; he issued instructions long ago to keep close to me to help swiftly if I should stumble and they are all alert and ready to jump to the aid of their king and queen.

'So Jane,' he says, jovially, 'you leave your ladies to walk alone.'

'I needed fresh air,' I say, sombrely. 'And peace and quiet and privacy.'

'I know the feeling,' he tells me. 'There is little indeed for you and I.'

Only when alone or, as alone as I can get in my situation, can I try to find peace and tranquillity. The events of the past few months have denied me that but I still need to walk alone occasionally and try to come to terms with my deep sorrows. Henry, I feel sure, knows nothing of my inner suffering and feels no remorse for past atrocities, thinking of them only as necessary acts of justice.

'I like to watch the fish jump,' I say, eyes on the sunlight glinting on the water and the occasional silver fish protruding.

He makes a guttural sound in his throat but offers no response. I see him watching me closely. He suggests I walk with him and we fall into a slow amble back to the gardens.

'Are you feeling bright and bonny Jane?' he asks.

'I am well sir,' I reply.

'No aches and pains ----below?'

'No more than usual sir,' I say, smiling in spite of my gloomy mood.

We walk in tandem and he offers me his arm, which I take. He tells me he has had a testing morning in council with much disagreement and ill -advised people vexing him. He had to take a break but, in truth, his main concern was to check on how I was feeling and keeping, in my present condition.

'The baby moves within me,' I say quietly. 'I feel the kicks.'

'That is good,' he says, a broad smile on his face. 'You know I have a very good feeling about this pregnancy Jane. I am confident it will be a boy this time and one that will live.'

'Let us hope and pray so,' I say, fervently wishing it to be true.

'Well, it is a goodly feeling to know you are well, contented and moving steadfastly towards the birth of our son,' he says briskly. 'I need some good cheer indeed. The council as a whole vexes me considerably. And Cromwell, in particular is in bad fettle. He seems distracted, grossly out of sorts. What can be the matter with the man?'

'I'm sure I don't know,' I tell him, frowning.

'Well, he's been useless for several days now. Something has put him out. I've just sent him home for he is worthless to me at present.'

'I wonder what ails him,' I say thoughtfully. 'Nothing trivial it is to be hoped.'

Henry chuckles, a loud, raucous sound. He says it is most unlike me to make such a statement. I am his little, docile white lamb, always meek and mild. Never bitter. I smile, a somewhat empty and vacuous smile. He knows I cannot stand Cromwell but I remind him again.

'And I remind you Jane,' he says, sharply. 'The man is useful to me in affairs of state, in facilitating the more obnoxious ways of ensuring no rebellion in the country succeeds and in a thousand and one other ways.'

'Could not another be trained to do the same things?' I wish to know, giving him my wide eyed look, may God forgive me.

'Yes, precious lamb,' he says, wearing a broad smile now. 'But it would take months of hard work and why go to that expense and trouble when I have the viper, who takes to dirty work like a duck to water?'

My expression is bleak and forbidding; I am aware of it but feel there is nothing I can do to hide my inner distress. We reach the palace and silent, invisible hands inside open the door. Henry frowns and asks why I look so sad suddenly.

'You should not ask sir,' I say gloomily. 'My answer might upset or annoy you. Or both.'

'Well, it has been a trying morning in council. I need no more upset so get away with you lamb. Go and join your ladies.'

I walk away slowly, ponderously, glad of the opportunity to move away from him without further explanation or justification. My ladies are all subdued and almost silent, stitching away for the most part or reading in quiet corners. Only Lady Rochford is unoccupied, standing in the alcove under the high latticed window where I normally gravitate to. A bright, elongated shaft of sunlight bursts into the chamber as I approach the alcove; I will not be diverted from my favourite spot by Jane Boleyn.

'Madam,' she says in sturdy, imperious tones and I stop in my tracks, facing her, eyebrow raised.

'A few days ago, I spoke out of turn,' she says, more softly now.

'You did Jane, indeed.'

'I should not have spoken as I did and I apologise,' she says, voice fading almost to a whisper with these words.

I nod and a very faint smile breaks out on my lips. I sit, just out of the range of the shaft of sunlight and with the briefest of gestures with my right hand, indicate that she may sit also. She does and composes her features into a serious expression.

'I should have realised that you formed a bond of friendship with the late Robert Aske and describing his demise graphically, was insensitive.'

'I don't think we need pursue the indiscretion any further,' I say, soberly.

'No,' she says and attempts a smile.

I watch her closely and soon realise she has more to say but perhaps is unsure how to proceed. I do not speak myself or give her any encouragement, other than the merest hint of the raising of one eyebrow.

'When we all left the other day,' she says hesitatingly, 'we all heard raised voices from this chamber.'

'Well, that Jane, was a private conversation.'

'Oh yes, understood,' she says, animatedly. 'It was just that the ladies, all of them, myself included, were so pleased that you managed to put a look of black thunder on

Cromwell's face. He stormed out of the palace that night looking like death.'

I look around the chamber and note that all my ladies are looking at us, some nodding, most smiling. I cannot resist smiling too. I remind Rochford gently that the man is first minister and it might be well to say no more upon the matter.

'Well, I don't know how you did it but I admire your spirit,' she says chirpily, more friendly in manner and appearance towards me than I have ever known before. 'You are simply not the quiet, self-effacing little creature everybody thinks you to be Jane.'

'Do not ever,' I say with mock severity, 'tell King Henry that.'

She smiles, I return the gesture and after a short pause I ask her to excuse me and leave me to my reflections. She rises and goes to join the others, sitting down next to Margery. I do not like her presumptuous manner of describing how others might see me but as I am in sufficient improved humour from her apology and words of intended comfort, I do not pursue the point.

As I begin my reflections however, gazing out past the black window lattices, at the green leaves of summer on the tall tree opposite, it occurs to me, as it should have done earlier, that Cromwell's severe irritation had nothing to do with remorse or regret for his actions I'll be bound but just for the fact that he was put in that position by a 'mere woman.'

It is silent in the chamber, no sounds from the ladies and none either from me. The baby kicks suddenly in my belly, a healthy movement and I smile and let out a long, deep sigh of satisfaction.

THIRTY THREE.

The lateness of the summer causes the hot sun to melt into mere warmth and the long days become shorter with darkness falling swiftly and unexpectedly. The progress to Canterbury proceeds slowly indeed, what with the crater lined, pitted roads and the fully laden waggons, filled with courtiers, attendants, servants and all the equipment of one sort and another that Henry feels obliged to travel with. We carry also a physician, an apothecary and minstrels to entertain him; he would not travel more than one mile from his palace without the former, fearing that if his health deteriorates on the road he must have instant goodly treatment to hand!

We take the road to Canterbury and Henry must visit the cathedral and inspect the recently desecrated edifice dedicated to Thomas A Beckett. He is much alarmed at the thought that precious stones and metals from the piece have been stolen. First though, we visit Christ Church Priory in Canterbury. This will be my last outing in public or under any circumstances before I commence my lying in, something which will keep me in a darkened chamber for a month just prior to the birth of our baby. I do not look forward to such dismal confinement for such a long term but I am powerless to prevent the custom of ages.

The roads are treacherous in many ways; avoiding the worst craters is one thing but swerving constantly to avoid colliding with shepherds and their flocks of various livestock is quite another. We are though, within a short ride of the priory now.

'Who greets us?' I ask Henry as we bump along. 'The good prior?'

'Thomas Goldwell,' he tells me. 'He is prior here and is, I believe a good man. He and all his monks signed up acknowledgement of the Royal Supremacy back in 1534.'

'Earlier than most,' I say, smiling.

'Yes,' he tells me. 'Ninety six monks in all.'

We reach St. Augustine Priory and are greeted by Thomas Goldwell, a man of advanced years in a brown habit and a care worn face. He takes us into an ante chamber near the main chapel, draped with tapestries of bright and glowing colours depicting religious themes and armoured knights. We are given cups of sweet white wine which is delicious to taste; it is the best vintage, we are assured, produced here by the monks.

'I would wish to see all the buildings of the monastery,' Henry says, 'and all your monks at work and play.'

'Yes, Your Grace,' he replies subserviently. 'I will accompany you personally.'

'Do not trouble yourself please,' Henry replies. 'I would wish to go alone, with just an attendant. You would please us if you looked after the queen here who, you will see, is with child.'

'Indeed, Your Majesty. Your wish is my command and may I add that all of our prayers here, day and night, are for the queen's safe delivery of a baby boy, an heir to the throne to continue your most gracious line.'

Henry thanks him and departs with an attendant. The prior fills my cup with more wine and says he hopes we had a safe and comfortable journey from London. I smile and thank him but point out that our roads from the capital leave much to be desired but we have arrived safely and in one piece. He smiles.

'It is a beautiful monastery,' I say, looking around the chamber.

'Thank you your majesty,' he replies sombrely. 'We have had our travails over the past few years but continue in God's work notwithstanding.'

He tells me that it is not easy acknowledging the king's supreme sovereignty over government and church and coming to terms with his own deep seated beliefs and love of God. He also says, looking at me warily first, that it is difficult to deny his belief in God's will, which he fervently believes to be interpreted by His Holiness, the Pope.

'But please be assured,' he tells me, looking most concerned and earnest, 'I intend no offence or disloyalty to the king.'

'That is understood Father Thomas,' I tell him and I smile.

'It is just that sometimes I feel I am putting my life and the monk's lives here in danger,' he says quietly, then looks up at my face and continues. 'Praying and continuing the Catholic rituals.'

I nod, implying my understanding of his situation but I do not reply. In truth I'm not sure how he stands in regard to his beliefs; Like Sir Thomas More he cannot give up his allegiance to the Roman church but unlike More he has taken the oath acknowledging Henry as head of the church in England. Surely the two positions are incompatible?

'I speak thus to you Madam,' he says gravely, 'because I am given to understand that you are not unsympathetic to our dilemma.'

'Where did you hear that?' I ask, still smiling.

'Oh we are not as cloistered and out of touch with what is going on in the world as some people think,' he tells me with a twinkle in his eye.

'My true beliefs Father Thomas,' I say quietly, 'I keep very much to myself.'

'I understand fully your Majesty,' he says quickly. 'Please forgive my indiscretion.'

I assure him that he has not offended me in any way and I'm glad to note the expression of relief on his wizened features. I like this old cleric and would be more open and frank with him if I did not think that I might put him and his monastery in danger by doing so. His honesty does him credit but I am reminded, painfully in my thoughts, that complete honesty did nothing to spare the life of poor Robert Aske and most of his men.

Henry returns and after more good wine we go to pray in the chapel and then to the refectory where a feast of monastery grown vegetables adds spice to the succulent and varied meats that the prior provides for us. I am surprise and delighted, as is the king although no quails are to be consumed by me on this day, alas!

Henry is in jovial mood throughout and keeps up this bonhomie as we ride out of the cathedral later and proceed towards Dover. He wishes to inspect the pier and it will be an enjoyable stop on our progression, my last before confinement.

We proceed at leisurely pace; Henry has instructed slow movement to keep me as comfortable and free of violent jolts as is possible. The pitted road does, however, cause me some discomfort despite the many soft cushions the king has provided for me. Enjoyable as it is, I shall be glad when this progression is over and I can return to the calm and quiet of Hampton Court Palace. Henry tells me he was impressed by our earlier visit to the Priory.

'He is an amusing and pleasant old fellow,' Henry says reflectively, as we bump merrily along. 'I do not think he is in any way disloyal.'

'Oh no,' I say. 'Not in any wise.'

'You agree with me Jane?'

'I do sir,' I say sincerely. 'I was much impressed.'

'Yes,' Henry muses softly. 'I'm mindful to give him a pension of a goodly amount, yearly.'

'That is good and generous of you My Lord,' I tell him, smiling.

The road is torturous but I feel content and at my leisure. The Prior is safe, I reflect, for the immediate future at any rate. Long may it continue?

* * * *

I sit quietly in the grounds of Hampton Court on a stone seat listening to the whispering of the leaves of the trees in the faint breeze. The nocturnal sounds of night time are so very different to the daytime birdsong and other murmurings. It is a very warm summer night and I love to sit in the calm of evening and listen to all around me as darkness encloses us in its shroud. I hear a distant bell pealing carried on the whispering wind. An owl hoots somewhere, quite close I would think judging by the clarity.

I carry a big load in front of me; my expanded belly is now full and heavy and would signify a healthy baby soon to make an appearance in this world of ours. I rest a lot, as indeed his Grace requires me to do and as I am happy to comply; I become weary withal if I seek too much exercise and general movement.

A shadowy figure approaches in the gloom; I can make out only the long dark cloak and three cornered headdress that indicates a female visitor. Anne comes into my line of vision at last, she is the one member of my batch of ladies-in-waiting that is always concerned for my welfare and follows me if I drift away from the pack.

I bid her a good evening and comment on the fresh warm air of a perfect summer night.

'Are you in good fettle ma'am,' she asks solicitously. 'We missed you in the chamber earlier.'

'I just required fresh air,' I say lightly. 'I will get precious little soon.'

'Ah, the lying in?'

'All four torturous weeks of it,' I say, frowning. 'I can scarcely countenance it.'

'But the reward at the end,' she says, leaving her sentence meaningfully unfinished.

'Yes,' I say and smile. 'That I am looking forward to.'

She looks around, catches a sound in the air and sighs then says she believes the lady Mary was looking for me. I assure her I am content and well and bid her to inform Mary of my whereabouts when she returns. She goes and I am shortly joined by Mary who sits next to me. I ask how she is faring.

'Oh, I am well enough in myself Jane,' she says, sighing. 'Loneliness plagues me somewhat, I must confess.'

I smile. 'Marriage would cure that ill,' I say lightly.

'Indeed, she responds, 'if I had a suitor.'

'I hear rumours that the king of Spain has suggested that he would wish to court you Mary; a Spanish prince,' I tell her enthusiastically.'

'Hmm,' she says,' father hinted as much but furnished me with no details.'

'Let me talk to Henry,' I say. 'And if he looks likely I'll gladly negotiate on your behalf.'

She leans over and kisses my cheek, saying that I am too good to her and she doesn't deserve such a loyal sister. I assure her that I will work tirelessly to help her find a suitor and promote her well- being and happiness in every possible way. It grows cooler and I rise to walk slowly back to the palace, holding my belly in both hands as I proceed. I tell Mary that I dread four weeks or more in an enclosed, dark chamber with no sight of the blue sky and the birdsong that I love and even the dark nights with all their unique sounds.

'You must visit me, I pray?' I say, nervously.

'Oh I will, be assured.'

'Frequently?' I ask, a frown expressing my insecurity.

'Of course,' she says, squeezing my hand. 'And I will bring you books to read and puzzles to solve.'

I am a little restored to comfort. As a creature of the countryside I cannot bear even the thought of not being out in the fresh air and not even viewing it for weeks on end. We walk even slower and she adjusts to my pace selflessly, moving in step with me.

'I have a present for you Jane,' she tells me as we reach the door and walk through together. I look to her to enlighten me.

'Quails, lots of them. I ordered them in from Florence expressly for you and they have been delivered.'

I laugh out loud, the sound echoing away on the wind as the door closes by page's hand behind us.

I embrace her and we kiss and I say that I ate so many last night at supper that even Henry was surprised at my appetite and made comment. 'So I need your new supply. It is though, very kind of you to think of me like this.'

I shall get through this confinement with her help. I've been told that Henry never visited his other wives in confinement but maybe he will treat me differently if I am really his one true love.

THIRTY FOUR.

SEPTEMBER 1537

It is not an image that comes readily to mind, verily! Henry Tudor, the caring, gentle, sensitive man, solicitous of every comfort for his wife and love! Me! Although it is happening to me at this very moment as he insists on walking with me, every step of the way, down to the grounds and out to parklands and their delightfully shaped hedges and bushes. I can only walk slowly and my baby grows ever bigger and more cumbersome to carry around although I do not mind; I treasure these last days of freedom knowing that I have not long to go before I am incarcerated into a dark chamber. Henry bids me tarry and asks if I would not be more comfortable closer to the palace but I tell him the walk will do me good and I desire it. His great concerns of recent days would sit more comfortably with me if I didn't know that his over-riding concern is for the safe delivery of our baby.

I walk on, listening to the bright bird song and taking more notice than usual of the cloud formations and the deep blue sky generally; my senses are more attuned this last several days.

'Will you rest awhile now Jane?' he asks, looking vexed and concerned.

We have walked some distance and I feel refreshed but a little tired. 'Yes, my Lord,' I say brightly and I smile at him. 'Indeed, I will.'

The attendants and servants are some way behind us but I am, as always, critically aware of their presence and wish, fervently but hopelessly that they would all fade into the shrubbery and never surface again. The penalty of being queen consort is that I am never, ever completely alone. I sit on the wide stone seating and Henry joins me.

'I will miss you sorely, white lamb,' Henry says, frowning. 'During your confinement.'

'Will you not visit me?' I ask, wide eyed. 'As I lie in?'

'I will be mostly out at Esher Palace,' he says gently. 'There is much refurbishment and building going on there which I have initiated and would wish to supervise.'

'Oh, but sir,' I ask, pouting shamelessly, 'surely a look in occasionally?'

'I will try,' he tells me, grinning. 'If I am at Hampton Court during those weeks.'

I do not pretend to understand this complete separation of men from their women during the pregnancy lie in. It seems so unnecessary to take it to such lengths. I accept that there must be no lying together during the final weeks, or indeed at any time during the nine months but that should not preclude occasional visits to the private chamber surely?

I have come to make my peace with Henry during the past weeks, unable in my innermost thoughts to forgive or understand his monstrous executions of the rebels in the north or his deep aggression; I know in my heart that I cannot change anything and my duty, as my motto commands, is to obey and serve. I know well that I have his love and that, I'm sure, will never change and as the days pass I feel more and more certain that my destiny will be fulfilled and I will provide an heir to the throne. If not this time then my next pregnancy.

I can come to terms with the lessening of my earlier, deep love for him and learn to live, in contentment, as wife and queen consort and, Almighty God willing, mother of the future king of England. What a prospect for a simple country girl!

'You must promise me Jane,' Henry says gravely. 'That you will lie in with a blank mind, rest easily and not exert yourself to any degree?'

'You have my word sir,' I say with a smile. 'Except that I cannot guarantee that my mind will remain blank throughout.'

'You are there,' he says sententiously, his expression hardening suddenly, 'to give birth to our son and heir. Nothing else need concern you.'

'Of course my Lord,' I say and I smile again. It is easier to just agree and let it go than argue or explain further.

The birds are singing, the sky is clear blue and faint sunshine occasionally floods field and hedgerow. A faint chill in the air reminds me that autumn is here and winter cold will shortly follow. All the seasons have their own delights for me and I am not dreading the harsh winter that is surely on the way. I look forward to walking, well wrapped, in the cold weather after my confinement is over and I can see the sky once more. And I shall be a mother; of a bonny boy or girl.

'I have a surprise for you,' Henry announces.

'Sir?'

'A present for you.'

He is being mysterious and smiling knowingly at me but telling me nothing. Back to the palace he says, if I wish to see what it is. So we walk back, retracing our steps slowly but steadily, with me occasionally applying both hands to my extended belly and his Grace holding my left arm. We walk through the myriad corridors of the palace, turning this way and that, noting the many attendants always in position along the route. Finally we enter a large, bare chamber, with no decoration or anything except one, very large bed. It is magnificent. It is a huge gilt bedstead with a soft mattress and covered with white and gold cloth. Satin and cloth of gold cushions are scattered on it.

'For me?' I ask, turning to smile at him as he nods.

'It is very comfortable,' he tells me, 'soft and luxurious but firm enough to support your frame. If you are to be here for four weeks and away from me, precious lamb, you are to be in the greatest warmth and comfort that can possibly be provided.'

I thank him heartily and plant a kiss on his left cheek. The room is huge, seeming more so because it is unfurnished, apart from the giant bed. I look around and note, sadly that sunlight is streaming through the big windows; they will not be like that for long.

'So this is where I am to be domiciled?' I ask, quietly.

'Yes, white lamb, you will be comfortable here,' he says gently. 'It will be fitted out in accordance to lying in regulations. All will be decorated fitfully for you.'

'Thank you sir,' I say dolefully, unable to conjure up any enthusiasm for my imprisonment.

'Cheer up Jane,' he admonishes me. 'Dinner will be very soon and quails are lined up. Hundreds of the things.'

We walk, arm in arm towards the banqueting hall. I tell him to pay me no mind, I am ready for my ordeal and will face it with fortitude. He tells me jocularly that he has another treat in store for me this afternoon. He has organised a cathedral choir, a large body of singers to perform sacred music with sackbuts and cornets to accompany.

Now that will certainly cheer me and put me in goodly humour for the rest of this day.

*   *   *   *

The chamber is transformed but not, I think, in a goodly way. I have come in alone as I would wish to get used to my surroundings at my own pace and with no idle chatter to distract. The bed is well fitted and I will at least be comfortable there and likely sleep well. A soft mattress, full of wool and straw is placed over the big gilt frame. Covers of silk and cloth of gold are all over it, along with cushions, various colours and in rich fabrics. Feather pillows, more than I will ever need, spread wildly.

There are cupboards and a large standing chest for my clothes. Stools, all covered in soft covers. The walls, every inch of them are a riot of bright colours; tapestries hang all over and any uncovered spot has a picture or a cloth hung over it. The windows are covered with dark, heavy cloths and only a chink of daylight, from one small corner of the window furthest from the bed, sheds shafts of brightness. Overall a dim, dark and cheerless chamber but fitted for my comfort; Henry has seen to that.

Most ladies of the nobility and aristocracy have only midwives, buxom women with knowledge to attend them during lying in. Henry has insisted though that I be seen regularly by his top physicians and it is Sir William that comes first to my chamber before anybody else. Sir William inspects my breasts for change, paying attention to swelling or discolouration of the nipples. He feels my swollen belly gently, running warm hands over the shiny surface as I lie back breathing noisily. He checks down below for discolouration around the vagina lips. Finally he swirls my chamber pot around and inspects the contents again, as he did when I first became pregnant and declares himself satisfied with all results.

You are in goodly shape your Grace,' he announces calmly. 'Pregnancy well advanced and ready, I'll be bound, to produce a healthy babe in three to four weeks.'

'Three weeks perhaps?' I ask, hopefully.

'Four, more likely madam,' he replies, handing the chamber pot to a hovering maid to empty. 'Three is a possibility however. You are big in the belly.'

'Thank you,' I say softly, raising my eyebrows.

'Do you still wear the silver tablet round your neck when fully dressed?' he asks. 'The one I recommended initially to ward off evil spirits.'

'I do,' I say, ruefully. 'The king insisted upon it.'

'That is meet,' he says, nodding his head contentedly.

He leaves me with an admonition to rest, not exert myself in any way, to keep calm and take heed of everything the midwife says. She almost collides with him, entering as he departs. She tells me she is Mistress Norwood from Hampton Wick and she comes highly recommended by Lady Lisle among others. I ask her name, which is Ellen and she departs. I pull down my nightshirt to cover myself completely again and settle down in the big bed; it is most soft, accommodating and comfortable in the extreme and I begin to feel a trifle cheered.

I am alone with my thoughts but a very short time as Anne, Jane, Margery and finally, Jane Boleyn arrive and set about tidying the room. They are all solicitous of my wellbeing and ask if there is any service they can do for me.

'Light some candles Anne, please,' I say.

'It is still daylight,' she protests.

'Maybe,' I say tetchily. 'But dark in here, you may have noticed? Please light them.'

Candles glow on chest and cupboard and over the fireplace, sending up a flickering, eerie light around the chamber but brightening it withal. Smoke creeps up from one or two and unfurls towards the ceiling. Lady Rochford pulls up a softly padded stool and indicates with a hand gesture that she would like permission to sit next to me by my bed. I nod.

'Well Jane,' she says, smiling, 'your time approaches rapidly.'

I nod agreeing. She has been much friendlier and no longer so provocative since the incident where she talked unwisely of Robert Aske's untimely death.

'And I do not need to ask if you would like to have a boy or a girl?'

I smile. 'We must all pray diligently,' I say. 'A girl would put us all in jeopardy.'

'Yes,' she says soberly, looking fraught. 'I recall when Anne gave birth to Elizabeth, Henry looked furious. I never saw a man more disappointed with his child.'

'Affairs of state and succession occupy all his waking thoughts.'

'And yet he loves you Jane, deeply and thoroughly and that gives you a tremendous advantage over the previous queens.'

'You have come to realise that, have you?' I ask, looking intently at her and surprised at the manner of her conversation.

'I have,' she says, softly. 'You only need to look at his face when he is with you. And you must make the most of that blessing.

'Don't worry,' I say, 'I fully intend to.'

'He could never consign you to the tower and the block,' she says, animatedly. 'For him, that would be almost like losing his own head.' She gives a little tinkling laugh which echoes oddly round the chamber. Then she assumes a very serious expression and asks me if I have considered carefully, who I will ask to be the baby's Godmother.

'I have given it thought,' I say, frowning. 'Although I've not reached a decision.'

'Well,' she says,' looking conspiratorial, 'I wonder if you feel it would be wise to choose somebody of importance who is, shall we say, not unsympathetic to the cause of restoring the catholic church back to prominence?'

'That is a dangerous thought,' I say warily.

She nods her head, agrees with me and goes on to assure me that she means no disrespect but only looks towards the future. The future of our countrymen and our country. I ask her to elaborate on her question.

'We cannot see what is ahead of us in the years to come,' she says softly, aware that other ears are in the chamber, some of them acute. 'But let me put this picture to you. Ten years from now, perhaps only five, who knows? Henry is dead. Your child is the new king of England and you are Dowager Queen. You have a godmother for the young king who is sympathetic to the cause.'

She sits upright and looks at me with one eyebrow raised. I tell her that I can see where she is going with this but perhaps it would be better if she goes no further.

'I've had my say Jane,' she says, smiling. 'I will say no more.'

She asks to be excused and I watch her depart from the chamber. I'm feeling somewhat weary and with nothing to do and nowhere I am allowed to go my only reasonable choice, I feel, is to have a short, midday sleep. I dismiss the ladies, bidding them return to my privy chamber and resume their needlework and usual occupations, as ever but without my presence. I send a servant girl out to the ante room, pulling her pallet behind her. She has been instructed to bed down next to my bed in case I am in need during the night but I tell her I will call her if needed. With solitude my only possible choice I prefer to rest awhile but alone; in this chamber completely alone.

The flickering candles provide a ghostly light in the curtained off chamber but the glow of the tapestries is dimly visible in the gloom. Tomorrow I will ask for a full complement of chamber candles, tapers and torches. Somewhere a church bell is tolling as I begin to feel very sleepy.

THIRTY FIVE.

Just under two weeks have I spent in this oppressive chamber but it feels like an eternity. I have never known the passage of time to move so sluggishly. Long, gloomy days with only conversation with my ladies to break the tedium are followed by longish nights; sometimes I slip off into deep, peaceful sleep and at others I lie awake thinking about the child in my belly, my future here at court, what will happen if the Spanish invade us and many other affairs I can do nothing about.

I worry about my coronation. Just before I entered this chamber to lie in, Henry indicated that it will be next spring at Westminster. As long as the plague is not rampant; he will depart from London instantly if plague is even forecast. I have not seen him since the day before I moved in here; I am feeling very neglected.

Mary is here to visit; she enters wearing a beautiful satin gown of blue with soft fur facings and covered in sparkling jewels. I am very envious. I feel drab and ugly as I lounge in my bed, unkempt as I have been forced to remain this past two weeks.

Mary settles down next to my bed and takes my hand. We kiss. I have sent the other ladies out as we two like to converse alone; it is one of my few pleasures.

'You are looking very well Jane,' she says with a smile.

'I feel quite well,' I say, puzzled. 'I've been lucky to sail along merrily through my pregnancy. So far at any rate.'

'So it will continue,' she says, ever the optimist.

I tell her, almost tearfully, that I am vexed withal. I have seen neither sight nor sound of my husband this past ten days. He has abandoned me I say, taken a mistress from the ladies around court or a pretty servant girl. I am bitter. I am convinced of his infidelity.

'No Jane, no, he would not do that to you,' she says animatedly. 'He spends almost all his time at Esher Palace, checking on building there. He is also at White Hall quite a bit for councils and always alone, always lonely.'

'You only see him occasionally yourself,' I say, pouting. 'What of all the other times?'

'I have an acquaintance at Esher who writes to me,' she replies. 'She says he is a lonesome, gloomy figure every night there, playing chess or close the board with courtiers and cursing angrily if he does not win.'

I smile. 'Yes, that's Henry,' I say.

'All is well,' she tells me, cheerfully.

'You have been a good friend to me Mary,' I tell her, squeezing her hand. 'I could not have wished for better.'

'Sister?' she asks, frowning suddenly.

'Oh yes, sister. My good sister.'

I tell her that when my baby is born the king will want him or her christened fairly quickly. Henry and I will not be expected to attend but I want everything to go off smoothly.

'I would like you to be Godmother to my child,' I say. 'Will you Mary?'

'Of course I will,' she says, gushingly. 'I would be upset if you asked anybody else.'

'That is settled then,' I say, contented. 'I know I can rely on you.'

'And we must have little Elizabeth at the ceremony,' she adds.

'Must we?'

'Oh, do you mind?'

I tell her, laughing that I am only joking with her; of course the Lady Elizabeth will be welcome and I intend to renew my efforts in the near future to persuade the king to restore both her and the child to their rightful titles of princesses of the realm. It is just that I thought she was none too enamoured of the little girl.

'Oh, she is a sweet child,' Mary says, looking thoughtful. 'And verily my sister! And in the last few weeks, here at court, I have found myself becoming better acquainted and, even, quite fond of the little mite.'

I smile and feel vaguely content although I begin to get feelings of pain intermittently, down in my pelvic region. It is only occasionally and in the past three days but when the pains come, as now, they are severe and disturbing. I wince suddenly and let out a little cry. Mary is immediately disturbed and asks what ails me.

'Oh, just minor pains that come and go,' I say. 'Do not fret.'

'You must have the midwife,' she says, more as a command than a suggestion.

'Oh no, do not trouble her Mary. It will recede.'

She will not listen to me and a summons for the midwife is sent out, stating that it is urgent. She arrives swiftly, curtsies and proceeds to prod and poke various bits of flesh until she hits the spot and I let out a cry.

'It is painful down there,' I admonish her.

'My deepest apologies your Grace,' she says. 'This potion will ease the pain and make you more comfortable.' She hands it to me gingerly and I take it. I drink it down and it tastes foul but the midwife assures me it will stop the pain and help to keep my baby safe and healthy until birth. She hands me a second potion which, she assures me, is mild to taste but is very good at keeping evil spirits away and ensuring a long and happy life for mother and baby.

'Here's to that,' I say, drinking. And again it tastes unpleasant but not as bad as the painkilling potion.

I tell them that I must rest and the woman departs hastily and then Mary bids me goodbye with sincere hope that I will recover swiftly and continue with my previous good health through pregnancy.

Alone again I will not summon my ladies back for a while. In the candle lit chamber, unnatural light floods the room as natural sunlight is kept blocked out. I long to go out and take a walk and breathe in fresh air but I cannot. I lie back, breath in deeply and expel air. I stare at the colourful tapestries but a sudden, stinging pain assaults my lower region and I cry out. I try to find a comfortable position in the bed but the pain, less intense now but still there, denies me.

I will not summon a midwife, to torture me further with potions or rough hands on my belly. I will lie here and rest, try to control the pain or learn somehow to live with it for a short time.

*　　*　　*　　*

I am feeling low and tearful. More than three weeks have passed and I have not seen Henry once; he has deserted me when I need him most. Likely he will not come until after our baby is born. The pain I experienced has faded but in its place I have a feeling of heavy, drowsiness and sickness; my head feels sore and my body is limp and unresponsive. Nausea assaults most of my waking hours.

I have regular checks by the midwife and Henry's physician calls at least once every week. He rubs my belly gently and says he can feel a healthy baby inside me and I must not fret. He gives me strange potions to drink and I do not know if they aid my health or not. The midwife bids me gently exercise my legs in bed to aid delivery when the time comes. It is, she says, very close now.

My ladies come and go; they sit with me and talk of babies and baby clothes and some are knitting little items for the mite to wear. When I feel heavy of body and nauseas, they leave me to ponder things in solitude. I ask about Henry every day but I am told he is here, at Hampton Court or he is at White Hall or Esher Palace or a hundred and one other places but I receive no visit.

Mary is my regular and most desired visitor after Henry. She tries to cheer me by saying he is very busy with affairs of state and building works at Esher and will be in to visit me very soon. I do not believe her.

Today I sit staring at the candles burning away merrily and lighting up kings and knights on the tapestries and wishing again I could walk out in the gardens. I feel numb with a dull, throbbing pain in my groin and a headache which throbs occasionally. I take a drink of Sir William's latest potion but I'm not sure if it is for relief of body pains or to ward off evil spirits; there are so many medicines and little pots that I am becoming confused.

And then the king himself marches in, unannounced, smiling and looking grand and fit in a bright yellow tunic with soft, luxurious hose and plenty of jewels on his chest.

'My little one,' he says expansively in a big voice, 'how do you fare?'

'A little better for seeing you sir,' I say quietly. 'At last.'

'Ah, affairs of state and church,' he booms. 'And in any event I wished to leave you in peace and quiet to ready yourself for the delivery.'

'I'm ready now sir,' I tell him with a trace of bitterness. 'And wish to goodness it was all over and done with.'

'Ah now, patience my little white lamb,' he says, leaning over and kissing my perspiration soaked forehead.

He sits next to me on my bed and takes my hand and gushes forth with a long list of things he has done, places he has been, people he has met---mostly young women it would seem---which pinches my belly with another sharp pain; a torrent of abuse against Cromwell and my lord of Norfolk and Suffolk and, finally, pausing for breath, he gets round to asking how I have been and how do I feel now.

'Not good my Lord, not good,' I tell him gloomily. 'I am sore below and in my head and I feel weak and tired most of the time.'

'You must be calm and quiet white lamb,' he says, looking worried and I suddenly feel a great pain and movement in my belly. I gasp and he grips my hand looking worried.

'Jane, what is it?' he asks gruffly.

'The baby comes,' I say, breathily. 'I feel it moving; it is coming now.'

'Quick, fetch the midwife,' he roars, jumping up from the bed. 'Call Sir William, get the wet nurse and ladies of the bedchamber.'

I grip the sides of my bed and feel the movement in my belly again and cry out. The midwife rushes in with her assistant, nurse and servant girls. Henry is ushered out swiftly and pandemonium breaks out in the chamber.

*   *   *   *

I lie back and try to breathe easily but the growing pain in my belly distracts me. On my right Jane Arundell mops my brow gently, as perspiration builds up constantly. On my left the midwife instructs me to breathe easily but deeply but not to push yet. 'Not just yet,' she says. At the end of the bed Margery Horsman and Mary Brandon keep watch and fold warm soft towels and soft satin wraps. The midwife, who I never seem to have got round to addressing by name, gets up frequently, goes to the end of the bed and checks what state I am in.

I feel the sharp contractions beginning to come more regularly now, much more frequently than in the past two hours. The midwife returns and sits next to me and tells me my cervix is fully open and dilation has taken place.

'Do I push down now?' I ask, anxiously.

'Not yet, Your Majesty, I will tell you exactly when.'

'The pain is fierce,' I say and wince as I feel another wave almost overwhelm me. I think that I am about to pass out but relief comes temporarily. Jane mops my perspiration soaked brow with her satin handkerchief. I begin to breathe more evenly, more comfortably but only for a brief spell as another wave of pain assaults my lower region.

The midwife tells me to push now and I do but the pain is intense. She bids me keep pushing but I cry out that I cannot.

'You must push now Majesty,' she intones nervously.

I summon what little strength I have left and breathe in. Then I attempt to push down hard but I am halted by pain. I try again, momentarily in agony.

I scream out suddenly, involuntarily, barely aware of what I am doing.

'Push again,' the midwife instructs.

'I can't,' I cry out, perspiration and tears running down my face together.

'You must,' she commands and then adds, nervously, 'your Majesty.'

'I can see baby's head, I can see the head,' Mary Brandon calls out excitedly and the midwife repeats her instruction to me to keep pushing. I push, gasp, wince with pain and cry out again; my belly feels as though I am straining hard in the privy and nothing is happening but, at last, I feel movement downwards, smooth, swift movement and I give one last agonising push and my baby is delivered into the waiting hands of my ladies and warm coverings for the little mite.

I hear the baby cry and listen to the midwife slap the child and I feel a warm glow of pleasure and satisfaction; my pain leaves me for the moment of joy. I smile expansively.

'You have a boy, a right bonny baby boy,' Mary cries out and I see smiling faces all round me. Suddenly I am aware that Henry is in the chamber and he takes the baby in his arms, smiling and with tears pouring down his face.

'A lovely big, beautiful boy,' Henry says, rocking the wee mite gently in his arms. He comes over to the bed and settles down on it, showing me my son. I take him in my arms although I barely have enough strength to hold him and Henry, sensing this, offers support from his own arm. The baby's little face is soft and white and pinched. He is lovely though!

'You did it Jane, you did it,' Henry says, running a kerchief over his flushed face.

'I did sir,' I murmur, short of breath again. 'And a goodly sized, healthy babe.'

'The heir to the throne that neither of those two whores could provide.'

'I am weary now,' I whisper, barely able to enunciate the words. 'The contractions seemed to have been going on for days.'

'Yes, you must sleep now,' he says quietly.

I close my eyes. I start to think about the long nine months of waiting and hoping, the praying for a boy and the pain in the last feverish days but I soon lose concentration. Henry is still talking animatedly but I am no longer listening; I am drifting off to welcome sleep.

THIRTY SIX.

Three short days seem hardly meet to allow me to make recovery but they have passed swiftly since my son was born and I am up, at last and dressed in fine gown and heavy robe and hopeful of venturing out into the gardens, if only for a few minutes, to see and breathe daylight once more; it has been sorely trying to lie in a darkened chamber for four endless weeks.

I have asked my lord to name our son Edward, he that was born on the twelfth day of October on the vigil of St. Edward's day. He is in agreement. Although I have had two days of rest and now begin a third I should like to continue in quiet peaceful seclusion throughout this day and night but it is my Lord's fervent wish that I accompany him to a celebration on conclusion of the christening. I must acquiesce.

All day yesterday and the previous day, guns have been firing, bonfires are lit in the streets and celebrations continue the length and breadth of the land. Te Deum has been sung in St. Paul's cathedral. Much goodly banqueting has taken place. Henry is in fine fettle, more cheerful and effervescent than I have seen him this past six months. He has even agreed, reluctantly, to let me step outside for a few brief moments and although he counselled strongly, even vehemently against it, he has given way and will even accompany me to ensure I suffer no ill effects after my confinement.

He comes to my chamber and offers his arm, which I take as I am very weak still and can only walk slowly and with aid. I am wrapped up heavily in warm garments and only a small portion of my face is open to the elements. He calls for a canopied seat to carry me down to the door and ignores my protests that I can walk with his help. At the door he steers me gently out into the gardens, on foot.

It is fresh, icy cold but dry out. The sky is clear, a greyish blue but no sign of rain or mist. I take my first tentative steps along the pathway and breathe in the fresh air I have been denied for so long.

'I am but twenty nine years of age,' I say, smiling. 'But today I feel about sixty.'

'You are not recovered yet,' he tells me, 'not by a wide margin and should be wrapped up warm inside the palace.'

'Give me but a few minutes,' I say, breathing deeply the fresh, invigorating Surrey air. 'Let me take in what I have missed so long.'

I walk a few more steps and Henry follows on, frowning at me as he walks. I look around me at tree and hedgerow, shrub and grass pastures, pathways and shapely sculptured bushes. I am acutely aware, once again, of the beauty all around me.

'And now we must return,' Henry says firmly. 'You have had your moment little lamb.'

'Indeed I have sir,' I tell him, contented, happy to comply.

In my chamber I hold little Edward close to my chest. His eyes are closed and he breathes easily, silently. I rock him to and fro. When Henry arrives he takes Edward in his arms and rocks him, as he chastises me for not returning to my bed. Mary will be here soon to take Edward to the Chapel Royal for the christening ceremony. The Godfathers will be my brother Edward, the Duke of Norfolk, who is Henry's choice of course, as is Brandon, Duke of Suffolk and Archbishop Cranmer. My little boy will be carried under a canopy by the Lady Marquis of

Exeter, Gertrude Blount, supported by the Duke of Suffolk to the Chapel Royal. Little Elizabeth is to carry the chrisom cloth, carefully supervised and watched over by her sister Mary no doubt. Tapers will be lit, candles too and Te Deum will be sung. It will be a lavish and abundant ceremony and Henry and I are not allowed to attend. I wish heartily that I could watch it all happen. So much for ancient tradition!

* * * *

Ironically, an event I would rather not attend, I have no choice but to be there! The ceremony following the christening is to be lavish indeed. As tradition again dictates, I am placed on an elaborate state pallet, embroidered on the back with the crown and arms of England wrought in gold thread. It has a coverture of white lawn and a counterpane of scarlet cloth lined with ermine. I have four cushions behind my head of crimson damask, with gold. And I am wrapped about my shoulders with a round mantle of crimson velvet, trimmed with ermine. To say I feel over dressed and over fussed over is putting it mildly.

Henry in gold tunic, lots of fur and an abundance of jewels is hardly less impressive. He smiles down on me as I lie, reclining on my pallet in all my splendour but feeling weary, lethargic and with pain down below that I must endure but dare not even think about at present. I could go off to sleep now, happily if unconsciousness came quickly and welcome if it could only release me from my duty.

'How do you fare, white lamb?' Henry asks, solicitously, sitting close to me.

'Sluggish sir and nauseous, in truth,' I tell him. 'But I will get through this ordeal if you stay by my side.'

'I will not move an inch from your pallet Jane,' he says, looking sincere. Bells are tolling in the streets all over London, their raucous peeling and metallic reverberations can be heard loudly here in the palace. No doubt they are ringing throughout the entire country, or soon will be.

A loud fanfare of cornets blasts out suddenly, to add to the sound and fury all around us. I grimace and Henry catches my expression and smiles in return.

'I'll need earplugs sir,' I say ruefully. 'Before this night is done.'

'Look cheerful and bonny sweetheart,' he says, lightly. 'You are Jane, Queen of the realm.'

We are carried along in raucous ceremony to the great hall; trumpets and cornets blaring, sackbuts offering growling harmony and cheering attendants and servants everywhere. My pain increases in proportion to the amount of noise and distraction I am feeling so I grit my teeth and keep my expression bland as possible.

In the hall there must be more than a hundred people. We are placed at the top of the hall, on a raised dais, under a canopy with the royal coat of arms. Wine is brought to us and I take a drink, with thirst to quench. Henry glances at me cautiously.

'Are you ready to receive folk, white lamb?' he asks, gently.

'As ready as I'll ever be, this night,' I tell him honestly.

There are so many of them. The Duke of Norfolk, Archbishop Cranmer, the Duke of Suffolk, their duchesses, Cromwell, now Lord Cromwell of course, Lord Montague, Thomas Boleyn, the Earl of Wiltshire and father of those unfortunate children of his, Anne and her brother, Lord Rochford. I spare a minute, thinking of him and what he must be suffering at this moment but then it is back to receiving congratulations, drinking to the health and long life of the new young prince. The Earl of Arundel comes forward and offers his good wishes and congratulations. Then the Lady Marquis and my brother, Edward, now the Viscount Beauchamp.

'Well sister,' he says with a big, broad smile, 'how does it feel to be lauded and loved and admired all over England.'

'Tiring,' I say, briefly and watch him retreat with puzzled expression. Henry laughs out loud as more and more people come forward to offer their best wishes and express their joy at the birth of a prince. The sound volume in the hall is ear splitting at times, except when the musicians play softly or stop playing altogether. During the quieter moments I overhear the Duke of Norfolk boasting of his conquests on the battlefield and, when he thinks he cannot be overheard, his conquests in the bedchamber! His loud, gruff voice is not suited to whispering.

'Thomas, Earl of Wiltshire,' I intone softly. 'Is he back in favour with you, your Grace?'

'He serves his purpose,' Henry responds. 'And it is hardly his blame if his daughter was a shameless and incestuous whore.'

I make no reply as none seems fitting and drink more wine and hope the time will pass quickly; I should be in my bed now, resting and not sitting here, regally, in fine garments, head spinning and feeling wretched.

'I feel that I should have a dance,' Henry says suddenly. 'Would you mind, little one?'

'No sir, please do,' I say quickly. 'Margery there is without a partner.'

He goes over to the line of dancers and joins in the jig, partnering Margery, my lady, who is looking nervous. I smile and then receive Jane, Lady Rochford, who I have not seen for three days. She expresses joy, warm wishes and long life for my little son, the future king of England.

'Well Jane,' I say ironically. 'I've missed your smiling face in my confinement chamber of late.'

'I'm sorry,' she says, wearing a brief frown. 'I find it difficult to face the birthing process or, even, to be in the same chamber as it goes on.'

'Well, we all have our little weaknesses Jane,' I tell her gently. 'And I'd hate to have been responsible for making you feel nauseous.'

'Oh no,' she responds, looking agitated. 'I mean no disrespect. It is my weakness and I can't overcome it.'

'I'm not offended,' I assure her, with a smile.

'And as to your choice of a godmother for your boy,' she continues conspiratorially, 'you have chosen very wisely.'

'Thank you,' I reply, smiling at her.

'The Lady Mary. Her time will come.'

'Perhaps,' I say distractedly, my attention on the pairs of dancers, trotting and moving their limbs flamboyantly.

She takes her leave and Henry returns looking puffed and somewhat exhausted. He is easily tired these days and not half the man he used to be. Only the very brave or foolhardy would tell him so though. He eases his considerable bulk onto his seat and glances at me.

'This celebration Jane,' he says gruffly. 'I think has gone on long enough.'

'Oh yes sir,' I say, relief in my voice I feel sure. 'And I am very tired now.'

It is not, however, over yet. He is distracted by late arriving well-wishers and the musicians are still making plenty of noise with their airs and jigs. When the last straggler has been seen and the final jig played we can, at last head back, with me reclining on my pallet, to my bedchamber. Henry leaves me with a kiss but it is disconcerting to hear the blast of cornets, loudly playing, as they did, following us all the way down.

They are silent at last and I lie in my big bed, head throbbing achingly, waiting for the rest and recovery that sleep will bring. The peal of church bells, however, near and distant, contrapuntally clanging and ringing incessantly, precludes sleep for a further period of the early morning.

THIRTY SEVEN.

I rise at seven in the morning, in some pain and distress and try to clear my head for the day ahead. My hoped for recovery from the previous evening's festivities has not materialised and has, it would seem, compounded a relapse of fearsome proportions. I feel giddy and have to return to my bed forthwith. I send for Margery, one of my most trusted ladies and she in turn, calls for the physician, Sir William.

I explain my symptoms and he examines me and says he fears that I may have contracted a fever and an internal infection. He gives me a potion to take and bids me rest, sleep and pray. He can do little to aid me or relieve my pain and suffering but he does not say as much. I take the potion and drink water. I send Anne to ask the king to come to my bedchamber but he is nowhere to be found and nobody, it seems, knows his present whereabouts. I send for Mary and she comes quickly and I see from her face that she is much concerned and distressed to see my current condition. She settles me in my bed and makes me as comfortable as possible, dispatches a servant to empty my chamber pot and clean it and wipes my brow with a soft, satin handkerchief.

'Oh, my forehead is burning sore,' I complain bitterly but I am dismayed to note the expression of alarm on Mary's face as she attends to me.

'You must rest easy and breathe deeply,' she counsels me. 'Do not speak if it pains you to do so.'

'What is happening to me?' I ask, in alarm, trying to settle back in the bed but in great discomfort and unable to stay calm.

‘It is a fever, doubtless,’ she says awkwardly. ‘Only to be expected after a difficult, painful and slow birth and you must rest easily and for a long time to facilitate recovery.’

‘I don’t think I’ll ever recover now,’ I say, agitated in the extreme.

‘Oh don’t say that, don’t,’ she cries out, tears spurting from her eyes, setting me off and we both weep uncontrollably. ‘After much rest and comforting you will be fine.’

I smile through my tears, wipe my face and tell her I don’t think I can recover now, I feel so weak and I am getting weaker by the minute. She asks me if I can eat and I shake my head negatively so she tells me I should drink sweet wine with warmed milk, which she sends for. I drink it as soon as it arrives and feel a little calmer and my throat is fresher.

As I become slightly calmer, the aches and pains begin to subside to some extent. I tell Mary that I am ready to rest now, to sleep again and she leaves me, promising to look in after three hours, to check that I am alright.

I sleep for a very short time but wake up in more pain than ever before. I feel the strength draining out of me and I find I am short of breath. I panic, thinking that my life is ending and call for the Bishop of Carlisle to be sent for immediately, to administer the Last Rites. Anne Bassett, Jane Arundell and Mary Brandon are all weeping as they receive my instructions but I bid them not to tarry but go about the errand immediately.

It is, mercifully, a false alarm. The bishop arrives, prepares to begin the Sacrament of Unction but I start to feel much better suddenly. I can move all my limbs fairly easily and my breathing is almost normal and even the sickly nausea seems to be in recession.

The bishop pauses, comes over to me and feels my forehead.

'You are recovering, majesty,' he says. 'It seems to me a miracle from God.'

'Perhaps just a temporary respite your Grace,' I say, cautiously. 'I am still very weak.'

'Yes, you must rest many hours,' he says. 'But my visit must end as its purpose is no longer valid. God save your Majesty.'

He leaves after blessing me and there is still much weeping from my ladies going on, this time from relief it would seem. I ask them all to be silent or I will not be able to sleep and I drift off after staring for a few minutes at the colourful tapestries, to the sound of whispered, urgent voices.

I wake up to see Henry sitting by my bed. I am lightheaded but able to sit up, gently, and lean my head back against the bolster. Henry grabs my hand and squeezes it gently. He tells me I have been asleep these many hours and he was very worried about me. I sigh noisily but make no reply as I am still recovering my full breathing agility.

'I should be at Esher, little lamb,' he says gently. 'But I cannot leave you while you are so unwell.'

I smile, finding breathing just a little easier although my head is throbbing again.

'Our son is created Duke of Cornwall,' he goes on. 'And he will be Prince of Wales, of course.'

'Yes,' I whisper. 'I produced a fine boy, did I not?'

He nods his head vigorously, agreeing but is suddenly caught in a fit of weeping; tears flood down his cheeks and he grips my hand tighter.

'What is it Henry?' I ask. 'Why so upset?'

'You are the true love of my life Jane,' he continues. 'You know that and you must know that I dread losing you. I want you with me for the rest of my days.'

'I'm still here,' I say, attempting a smile.

'Don't leave me Jane, don't go.'

'If it is God's will,' I say slowly and leave my sentence unfinished.

'I can't live without you, my little white lamb, I can't,' he says, although this seems to trigger a fresh bout of weeping.

'You will find a way, if you have to,' I tell him gently. 'We are at the mercy of God Almighty, all of us, always.'

But even sitting up and talking briefly has made me weary and I feel pain and nausea building up again. I kiss Henry on the cheek and he lifts my shoulders gently into a recumbent position so that I may sleep once more.

* * * *

It is now eight days since the christening and celebrations which left me feeling weak and ill. Recovery, as I foretold, seems impossible as I continue to grow weaker with every passing day, every passing hour. Henry has visited my bedchamber but is so fearful of illness and disease that he makes his excuses to depart after scarcely staying five minutes. He re-iterates his deep affection for me and repeats that he is a lost soul without me but in my present weakened state his visits are endurance tests for me, short though they may be.

I sleep, I awake, I sleep and awake again and every passing moment brings more pain, sickness, both physical and in my mind and my weakness increases to the point where I can barely lift my hand from the bed coverlet.

I call for warm, mulled wine, just about the only thing I can drink and I can manage precious little food. I am comforted by my ladies, from Jane Arundell to Lady Rochford, all with best wishes for the recovery we all try to believe in but undermined by their weeping and wailing. Only Mary, the Lady Mary, soon I pray to be restored to Princess, the title she was born with and deserves, gives me succour and comfort; not that she lacks tears for my suffering but she does have the good grace and consideration to hide her distress most of the time or excuse herself until she be recovered.

She comes into my bedchamber but I am only vaguely aware of her presence as I sink into a deep lethargy, half conscious, half drifting away into the unknown. Mary sits with me in silence for a while and then begins weeping softly.

'Don't weep Mary,' I say, trying to rally myself to full wakefulness.

'I can't help it,' she whispers.

'If the lord God is calling me, I'm ready to go,' I say, very softly as my voice is fading.

She shakes her head negatively but cannot stem the flow of tears.

'I've always tried to live a good life, not to hurt anybody, not to curse out anybody.' I pause, take a laboured breath. 'Except for Cromwell and he deserved it.'

Mary smiles through her tears.

'I don't fear death Mary, I can face my maker penitent but unashamed.'

I hear Mary snuffling but sight and sounds are fading now.

'The bishop will be here soon,' I whisper huskily. 'To administer Last Rites.'

She shakes her head and tries to control her noisy weeping.

'I've produced a prince, done my duty,' I say gently. 'I've fulfilled my destiny satisfactorily.'

'Oh you have,' she says vehemently,' you surely have Jane.'

When I manage to focus my eyes again I see Mary and hear her singing quietly.

Hail Mary, full of grace, the Lord is with thee.
Blessed art thou among women,
And blessed is the fruit of your womb, Jesus.
Holy Mary, mother of God, pray for us sinners
Now and in the hour of our death. Amen.

With one last effort I pull my hand up from the coverlet and take hold of Mary's. I try to press it but the pressure will be minimal as I feel the last of my strength drain away and I close my eyes to welcome sleep, deep sleep, rest and peace. Eternal rest, Eternal peace.

EPILOGUE

AFTERMATH.

The death of Queen Jane occurred in the early hours of 24th October 1537. Cause of death was a fever and an infection following childbirth, most likely puerperal fever. Jane Seymour was given a lavish state funeral, the first and as it turned out, the only wife of Henry VIII to get one. Mary Tudor was her friend; she was chief mourner, as Jane lay in state and the funeral, with twenty nine young women following the coffin, one for every year of her short life, ended at St. George's Chapel Windsor, where she lies to this day.

Henry married again, three more times after a period of mourning. One was annulled, to Anne of Cleves, one more was executed for adultery, Katherine Howard, and the last outlived him, Katherine Parr. After suffering migraine headaches, ulcers, paranoia, strokes, possible diabetes and almost certainly depression and mental illness, Henry died in January 1547 at the age of 56. His and Jane Seymour's son Edward V1 became king.

King for just six years, Edward died of tuberculosis in 1553. Thirteen days later his half-sister Mary Tudor became queen. Sadly she proved to be her father's daughter in the worst possible way but changing the religious oppression, executing people at a moment's notice if they were Protestants and earning herself the nickname 'Bloody Mary.' She briefly restored Roman Catholicism into England but died, aged 42 in 1558, possibly from ovarian cysts or uterine cancer.

Mary's half-sister Elizabeth became queen and reigned from 1558 to 1603 the longest period of all the

Tudor monarchs. She died aged 69 in March 1603. She was the most loved of all the Tudor rulers and fondly remembered. She restored England to the reformed Protestant religion, once again. She never married.

Jane Boleyn, Lady Rochford was convicted of aiding and encouraging Queen Jane Howard in adulterous behaviour with Thomas Culpeper, a courtier. She and the queen were executed on Tower Green in 1542.

Thomas Cromwell did, eventually, fall foul of the man he subserviently served, flattered and worked so tirelessly for and was put to death, being executed on Tower Green in July 1540 aged, approximately, 54.

Henry claimed all his life that Jane Seymour was his one and only true love and instructed that on his own death he should be buried with her. They lie side by side in St. George's Chapel Windsor, together through eternity.

Lightning Source UK Ltd.
Milton Keynes UK
UKOW06f0603080116

266034UK00001B/1/P

9 781909 484276